AN EX KNOT

A Different World War

(PART VII)

HUGH LUPUS

APS Books
APS Books is a subsidiary of the APS Publications imprint

www.andrewsparke.com

First published worldwide by APS Books in 2021

A catalogue record for this book is available from the British Library

ISBN 978-1-78996-293-2

AN EXTRA KNOT PART VII

To Ryan…welcome to the family

SAY GOODBYE

The woman stood absolutely still in front of his desk flanked by two children of perhaps ten years of age and an older woman with grey hair cut short. None of the group bore any family resemblance to each other but that was no unusual sight in the Asturian Republic after long years of war and what he was seeing was a family made from the wreckage of others.

All wore clothes that were practical rather than decorative for the Twin Republics had no time for frippery when there was a war to be fought and a land to be rebuilt but despite that the woman had embroidered three thin red stripes on her sleeve, with each stripe indicating a confirmed enemy kill, while each child was adorned with similar, though smaller stripes.

Only the older woman who performed the office of grandmother was undecorated, but he knew she bore her own scars, submerged and hidden in the well of her soul.

He looked back at them, seeing warriors who were desperately trying to wash away the tears of war and return to the familiar, to rebuild a new normal that could only ever pay homage to the old.

The old thoughts, the old arguments rose unbidden in his mind. 'What have we done?' He wondered. 'We turned children and women into killers, we burnt our land rather than give it to the enemy, we bled and bled and made sacrifices, so many sacrifices.'

He glanced at the photograph of a lost wife and child and gave them the old excuse. 'We had no choice, my loves; we had no choice.' But the images gave no reply; his wife's smile was both shy and eternal while his daughter's grin was engraved and silent.

So many sacrifices.

He broke his eyes away from an image that was burnt into his eyes and gazed once more at the woman, clearing his throat as he did so.

'Your husband, Sergeant Yves Massu, who failed to return from his mission…is alive.'

The woman staggered a little and then with a warrior's effort pulled herself erect again.

'Alive?'

'Alive,' he confirmed. 'He was seen by one of our agents in Genoa, last week in the company of a woman, three children and another man. Alas our agent was not able to make contact but it seems that your husband, for whatever reason, has decided to take personal charge of his mission. This may be just as well as his original contact on the French border was discovered to be a traitor and would surely have betrayed him. Of course, there is still danger and…'

'Yves will return.' The words were spoken flatly and in a tone that would brook no dissent by the young girl who had been adopted by Massu. 'He always returns.'

'Our father is a clever man,' agreed the girl's brother, 'and he will return.'

He looked at them and at the two woman who were nodding in agreement and knew that their faith was based not on knowledge, for they knew that when War and Death walked hand in hand then ill luck often gamboled in their wake, but on hope; hope that a new found father and husband would return, and a new life would be built around him. Not to have faith would be to return to an old life as single atoms, lost in a harsh world.

Not to have faith would mean tears and renewed effort when the storeroom of effort was near empty.

So, hope, have faith and believe. Hope and refuse to face the truth that every bullet has a billet and that a father's chair may remain empty forever.

There could be no arguing against such faith, so he returned their nods and added a smile. 'Sergeant Massu is one of my best men, and I am sure he will return. In the meantime, you will of course remain on the regiment's dependents list and will continue to draw rations. This will be our last meeting as I am taking the first battalion on manoeuvres tomorrow, but should further word arrive it will be communicated to you without delay.'

This last statement was a half lie and everyone one in the room knew it. The first battalion was going to be part of an Allied army in the final battle against the Nazis, but all kept knowing smiles from their faces and thanked him for the news and left the room.

He was alone now, alone with his thoughts and eyes that could not leave the photograph of a loving wife and a mischievous scamp of a daughter. She had cut the hair of her doll, he remembered. His wife was horrified but he had just swept the girl up in his arms and told her that the doll was just as beautiful as ever and wiped away her tears. In the photograph she was still clutching the doll and was half turned, grinning with joy. She would always grin; she would never change, but it was time to face facts, time to say goodbye. He forced unwilling hands to open a desk draw and pull out a black ribbon, his tears splashing with silent agony as he tied the ribbon around the photograph.

They were lost, and lived only in memory and his only hope now was that kind hands had found them and that they had been buried with charity and together.

It was time to say goodbye. The newly adorned image was placed back in the drawer and he took a last look around the office before stepping out into the courtyard where the First Battalion stood ready.

It was time to say goodbye.

She had always been there, eternal and unchanging. Night or day, white cloud or bright blue sky, she had always been there. Sagarmāthā, the great mountain head that lifts into the sky had been part of his life always, and it had made him tough for Sagarmāthā was a harsh mother and sparing with her favours but the man who came to the village was not impressed with his toughness. He had looked at him with scorn and laughing eyes

'You will never do',' he had said. 'A boy like you should stay with his Mamma, lest harm befall him.'

Dark anger had suffused him, and he had puffed out his chest 'Anything you can do, I can do!'

The laughing eyes laughed again.

'Oh ho! We have a live one here! Tell me little one, do you really think that you can equal me?'

He had thrown away caution and allowed pride to speak for him. 'I do.'

The eyes lost their laughter and turned black. 'Then say goodbye.'

And with that the man turned and left, not walking but running down the road that led away from the village that lived in the shadow of the mountain that the foreigners called *Everest*.

There was time only for hurried farewells for the man was now a dot in the distance and he too began to run, pulling in cold, thin air in lungfuls that were never enough.

And still the man ran, turning only to see that he was still followed and no matter how often he turned the distance between them never changed.

Mile after mile he had run with vision narrowed to a small, black edged slit, but pride urged him on for he could hear the man's laughter borne faintly on the wind. 'Is that the best you can do, little one? Will you let an old man beat you?'

He hated the man in that moment and forced weeping legs to move again and again, so that one mile merged into another, with every hour killing the one that came before, until dark came and swallowed the running man.

And still he ran, blind eyes urging blind feet, pride and hate joined in an unholy alliance until he darkly ran into an outstretched hand that threw his heaving chest onto the ground where it lacked the strength to rise.

'You will do, little one, you will do.'

The voice of the recruiting Sergeant lacked any laughter now and pulled him up to stand on unsteady feet.

And that was how Minraj Tamang joined a Gurkha rifle regiment.

Andrew McFarlane hated the street, hated its offal-tainted cobblestones, hated its sunless light, its blank faced windows. He hated its perennial poverty, its constant drunken men and its perpetual downtrodden women that every week tried to make a penny do the work of a shilling and every week failed.

And he was tired, tired of an aching belly, tired of ragged clothes, and a despairing mother that could see no way out of a Glasgow tenement.

Tired and filled full of hate he had said goodbye to wretched streets and walked up to the man with the bright red sash and the silver topped cane and scrawled a name on the proffered paper, seeing a future where he too rode the world in resplendent uniform.

The reality was different...very different. The Scots Guards looked at him not as a valuable addition but merely as the King's latest bad bargain who must be treated with hard kicks and harder scorn.

But he had endured. The alternative was a return to rags and poverty and that could never be for he had said his last goodbyes to foul gutters and meals that never filled.

And he rose, rose with grim eyes and hard scrambling fingers. The goal was ever the red sash and the silver topped cane, but war intervened, and a sandy desert beckoned. A hard land for hard men, bitter cold by night, bitter hot by day, but the Scots Guards showed that they were the masters and more than the masters of the battlefield.

Lunge, twist, withdraw.

Lunge, twist, withdraw.

The mantra was ever the same, for where the bullet and the shell failed to convince, the dull shining bayonet had the last word and the sand received blood and vomit in unequal measures.

And still he rose with a hard soul hardened yet more by war's hot breath and now he was due the sash and the silver topped cane. Poverty was long distant but still a spur to a hard man who had vowed that a goodbye was final and eternal, and that pity was for fools and weaklings.

A hard man was Colour Sergeant McFarlane, hard of boot, harder still of voice. A man to be feared and a man to be obeyed.

But a man to be followed...

Grandfather was wise and if wisdom was not enough then the burning hulk of a brother tank was more than enough to impart wisdom...and caution.

The town had seemed empty, showing its pre-war glory with a forlorn pride that begged the viewer to overlook shabby hotels and sparse filled shops that were built when Napoleon had last reigned in spendour.

But Grandfather was not deceived and had moved slowly along the single street that led away from a beach littered with bodies and the blasted remains of bunkers.Slowly, for he hated street fighting where every building crowded in with suspicious eyes and his caution rose as the street grew ever wider and the buildings grew larger.

They were almost at the square now, though still scant kilometres from the sea, and he fancied he could still smell the sea air, though this was an illusion as the rank perfumes from the burning tank had overpowered any airy gifts that Father Neptune could bestow.

Still, despite what fancies his nose might tell him, there was no fault with his eyes and a burning tank was sufficient warning. His tank came to a halt, rocking a little on its suspension as it did so. There was something in the square that killed tanks and it was no part of his duty to find out what that something was. That was the duty of the infantry that followed and surrounded them in a marriage which benefited both.

He gently raised the cover of his vision slit a little more and saw two infantrymen run forward in small spurts that took advantage of every doorway, with their companions splattering the far side of the street with rifle fire that pockmarked walls and shattered glass.

Gradually the two men reached the area where the street ended and the square began, though their arrival was not welcomed, and a storm of bullets and mortar fire greeted them. They took their baptism coolly enough, and made sure that all that could be seen was seen.

He closed the vison slit once more, for experience had shown that a bullet fired through the narrow slot could cause more death than one.

The tank returned to the semi gloom that had become so familiar to him and he waited for instructions. He did not have long to wait; the crew heard a scrambling noise on the outside of the tank and then the muffled sounds of the tank telephone being unlatched.

A strange accent entered the tank and grandfather shook his head trying to decipher the words. Like all Basques, he had learnt Spanish as well as his native tongue and later he had learnt the strange polyglot language made up of Basque, Spanish, English and a host of others that the Spanish wars had birthed, but these words though they seemed English, were an English that had suffered a drastic mutation and he asked the man on the outside of the tank to repeat himself several times. Eventually the man's meaning became clear and he nodded in agreement for the idea was sensible and just what he would have suggested himself.

The street was dangerous for both simple soldiers and drivers of tanks. Buildings that appeared empty could be filled with the sniper, the machine gun or worse yet with explosives awaiting only an incautious foot to bring about death.

Therefore, the street would be removed, house by house, shop by shop until only rubble, flame and broken timber remained.

He had no qualms of conscience doing this; the Basques had destroyed their own homes as a path to victory and so had little enough problems destroying the homes of others.

He called up a second tank which acquired its own human target director and together they began to track turrets upon targets.

An old game this, played in Spanish towns while strangling a German army soon to be humbled. First a round of armour-piercing low aimed to make a breach. Then if mercy spoke loud, a round or two of high explosive sent through the same hole as the first, the better to bring the house down around the ears of its defenders. But if mercy spoke not at all or was drowned out by thoughts of Nazis marching over the graves of Basques, then a single round of white phosphorus burnt both lungs and eyes and gave painful wounds that lasted a lifetime where they did not kill outright.

He grinned at the thought and at old memories. A Nazi covered in white smoke and coughing up bloody lungs while staring with blind red eyes was a sight worth seeing, but he would put such pleasures aside for now.

He turned and looked into the eyes of a loved grandson who merely nodded and smiled while loading the yellow tipped shell whose colour betrayed it as one designed to break armour.

His tank rocked back upon its haunches and a second or so later he felt but did not hear the second tank launch its own package of destruction, and so the work of demolition began.

Alas for cunningly crafted stone, alas for a building that had been the last word in beauty. The shell blasted apart stone from stone, turning some to dust while only the most fortunate survived to live on as rubble.

Incoherent words of approval came from the telephone and allowed a round of high explosive to follow through the gateway made by the first.

Shouted instructions saw motors turn a long barrel onto a new target and a second wall went from faded glory into new made wreckage.

On and on with power mixed with caution, rolling thunder blasting open shops that once sold the very latest fashions or expensive trinkets of silver or gold.

On and on. The porticos of hotels that once saw high bought mistresses addressed with a smile and raised eyebrow gone, brought down in crashing ruin while an evil tide of rolling steel and cautious flesh crept down the street leaving only dust and burning behind them.

Grandfather never sees the long tube that points out of an upstairs window, never sees the commanding arm that points nor hears the order which produces a torrent of bullets that causes the long tube to fall to the ground and a blood seeping figure to follow it.

He has no need to see or hear or even think of these things for that was the job of the infantry and soon the point was moot indeed as two shells remove both window and the walls that surrounded it.

On and on with a grisly trail to mark their passing and the square with the burning tank before them.

A shell sent from an enemy gun roars past them, but this is a signal not of defiance but of desperation, for in the square was a constrained killer. The mangled voice had seen the square and what the enemy had made of it. A stately building built to serve overpriced coffee and over-sugared cakes to tourists had been transformed into a fortress with a concrete-lipped slot out of which poked the brazen mouth of a heavy gun, which no matter how far it was slewed round could not reach the Basque tanks. While from the opposite buildings sat mortars and machine guns well entrenched behind sand bags, and both mortars and guns dared the world to approach.

A mortar coughs high up into the air and a screaming shell splatters burst steel onto the sloped front of Grandfather's tank, but there is no fear inside though this is a livid sign that the battle is not over.

And now a conference of war with the mangled voice, for the buildings which once stood as guardians to the square were no more, and further rounds ensured that tumbled brick trembled anew for in war there was sometimes a time for caution and grandfather had lived a long life by knowing exactly when, and when not to show apprehension.

Besides the attack on the square would be an infantry affair now and even the mangled voice agreed that this was so. The buildings that tank shells had wrought into ruin made ideal jumping off points for men who could now be sure that behind them nothing lived that could hurt them.

The inside of the tank was silent now and blind in its twilight. None could see the rushing figures, and the sharp music of bullets was no more than the sound of gentle rain on a dry roof, but Grandfather did not care.

Lorena, his Lorena had laughed, laughed with power and spite. A daughter's laugh had been filled with joy and dispelled ill-humour with grace but this Lorena laughed out not kindness, nor yet mercy, but only harsh disfavour.

And that was exactly as it should be.

Colour Sergeant Andrew McFarlane was an educated man.

Self-educated of course; graduates of Glasgow slum schools who left on their thirteenth birthday had little in the way of formal education, but had an education nonetheless.

Andrew McFarlane, had degrees in Army life and bending men to his will. Lately he had done graduate work in killing and passed with high honours. He had educated ears and educated eyes that could distinguish the difference between the stutter of the MG34 and the rip of the MG42 and see just where the best path to an enemy's death lay.

There were others less educated and he was looking at one poor student who lay at his feet and gave the man a last epitaph. 'Ye glasik wee bampot. Did I not tell ye t' keep yeer bunnet doon?'

There was no reply from the lieutenant; men who had exposed themselves to machine gun fire often had difficulty replying, especially when dead, and McFarlane really did not expect an answer.

The lieutenant had taken too seriously the intelligence that the beach was defended by third rate troops and had not understood that rifles, machine guns and mortars could be deadly no matter who fired them.

It was not a mistake McFarlane was about to repeat; he had achieved a coveted rank and would not allow death to snatch it from his hands.

A burst of machine gun fire threw sand over his face; an MG34, he noted with professional ears; an MG34 which was standing in his way and would therefore need to be eliminated.

A tank or two would be nice, but a glance behind him showed that their arrival would be long minutes hence, which left only older and more direct methods.

An old task then, much practiced in deserts that either baked or froze and he rolled to his side and turned to face a man disfigured by a livid white scar that ran from cheek to chin.

No war wound this, but a memento of the vicious gang wars that had pulsed through Glasgow for the past twenty years.

Corporal 'Razors' Frazer thought he was a hard man when a judge had given him the choice of three years or enlistment, but five minutes at the end of McFarlane's fists and boots had proved to him that hard or not, he had met a harder and he met the Colour Sergeant's gaze with perfect calm.

'We need t' be flittin, Razors. Time I'm thinkin' t' be using that wee contraption of yours.'

There was no reply from the scar faced man as he unpacked a canvas bag and began to slot together long tubes packed with high explosive which he pushed before him, being very careful not to expose himself to the bullets which flew all around him.

Not trusting temperamental electricity, he lit a long cord and gave the Bangalore torpedo a last shove forward and rolled away.

Long yards of tube shredded into cutting shards which slashed at rows of barbed wire, carving them into impotent fronds hanging limply from tumbled stands, and long before the last of the blasted sand had resettled earthwards a large group of angry Scots had arisen and disposed of the MG34 and ensured that it and its rifle pits would cause no further harm.

He began to look around for further targets when a slightly out of breath Major MacMurray ran up with eyes that searched for a missing lieutenant but found only McFarlane's thumb which pointed backwards.

'Yer man's deid.'

MacMurray wasted no more time asking questions but instead pulled out a torn map and spoke briskly. 'I need men to advance up the main drag of the town while the rest of the battalion advance up these side roads. The Basques will provide armour support. Rendezvous point is this church here. Any questions?'

McFarlane shook his head and ran with his men to where three tanks stood waiting with wet sand still shining on dull painted sides. Each bore the insignia of a charging red bull which the Basque tank regiments had long ago adopted as a battle sign and as he watched one tank, slightly smaller than the rest ran forward on churning treads and was soon lost to view.

The other two were more cautious and with a loud revving of engines and clouds of black smoke began to slowly rip up carefully laid cobblestones.

I dinnae lik' this. Whaur ur a' th' white flags?'

The voice of the soldier was puzzled. The inhabitants of the small town must surely have seen the overwhelming force that had arrived on their doorsteps and the sensible thing to do would be to hang bed sheets out of windows to show peaceful intent, but every window was firmly shut and not a single person had come out to meet them.

McFarlane was puzzled also, but he was not about to allow that puzzlement to show; nor would he allow doubt to creep into his command and his reply was harsh.

'Hush yer greetin!' Noo git in behind that lest tank. Razors. Tak' three men an' gang ahead 'n' cover th' left haun side, watch th' windaes!

He was about to give further orders when there was a loud bang, and a column of smoke began to rise from where the street widened out into a public square.

Very naturally the two tanks stopped their cautious movement and stood waiting with idling engines. It was not the job of tanks to investigate such things. That task was given to infantry as McFarlane knew very well.

'Razors, tae me, th' rest o' ye, covering fire, even numbers richt, odd numbers left, watch fur snipers.'

He began to run forward in quick bursts, diving into doorways with Razors only yards behind until they reached the very edge of the square and risked a look around the cut blocks of an ornate hotel.

The small tank which had hurried forward now lay on its side with flames and greasy smoke rising from it, the dead body of its driver hanging limply from its open hatch.

McFarlane was not interested in dead Basques or light tanks which were of no further use. What he was interested in was why the tank was burning and how the tank driver had died.

He risked a further look and was rewarded with a burst of machine gun fire which chewed into the side of the hotel and showered him with dust and stone chips.

'Fuck! Ah cannae see fur a' th' smoke! Gimme covering fire.'

He ran forward towards the tank, sheltering behind its bulk while Razors emptied an entire clip into the smoke.

From this new vantage point he was able to see the killer of tanks and men. The golden sign which proclaimed the building as the *Café Royal* still hung drunkenly from rusting brackets, but the building held no helpful waiters and had long since served its last coffee. Instead it now sported a slit out of which thrust the mouth of a tank-killing gun, while its upper windows no longer held sparkling glass but dull sandbags propping up the barrels of machine guns.

The café had a near twin facing it, but this bastion was equipped with mortars that lay behind sand-bagged walls.

He had been spotted now and he saw the gun begin to slew round and once more target the tank which was his cue to sprint back to the comparative shelter of the hotel with the shrapnel of an ill aimed mortar to give speed to his legs. The gun fired again, but the angle was too extreme to follow his fleeing body.

There was only one course of action to take now and he knew exactly how to carry it out.

BINMEN

No tank commander worth his rank would unbutton his vehicle in the middle of a battle and in earlier days this understandable reluctance had led to difficulties between tanker and foot soldier but practical minds had come up with a solution and steel boxes holding a telephone had been welded to the back of every tank. Alas the boxes had been attached next to the tank's exhaust which both deafened and choked McFarlane as he attempted to make his ideas understood to the commander of the tank.

McFarlane had never fought in Spain, his war so far had been spent in North Africa where he had picked up a little German, less Italian and a few Arabic insults. But Spanish and the strange amalgam of languages which had become common currency amongst the soldiers of the Spanish campaign was a mystery to him and he struggled to make his words understood.

At last the words he needed came through the telephone. 'Si, si. Je understand bon, edificos morte, my tank kill, oui? I tell, ami, you wait for bang.'

McFarlane muttered his thanks and turned to his men.

'Richt lads we're aff tae bring th' steret doon 'til we git tae th' square 'n' then we've git a bawherr fightin' tae dae. Keep yer een open, eh.'

There was little need for more words and little time, for the first tank rolled forward a little and then slewed a turret round until it pointed at the portico of an ornate building with firmly shut doors.

The shell cared very little for doors shut or otherwise. It turned wood into splinters and exploded into an expanding ball of superheated flame that knocked down walls and blew out windows. Nothing could have survived that blow, but a second round of high explosive was given as insurance and the building collapsed, wearing a broken roof as a cap of defeat.

The second tank performed a similar duty, and slowly, leaving flames and smoke behind them the two tanks and Colour Sergeant McFarlane's men advanced.

A door burst open and men tumble out to be greeted by shots that ripped and tore.

Their intentions remained unknown, perhaps surrender, perhaps a last defiance…it mattered not. McFarlane's men played a hard game, asked few questions, and dead men gave no answers.

The long tube of an anti-tank weapon points from an upstairs window and McFarlane shouts a warning causing a dozen rifles to speak with aimed voices and the tube clatters to the ground and a blood dripping arm dangles from the window.

And then both arm and window vanish as a tank shell demolishes the house, revealing a smouldering staircase and tattered wallpaper fluttering in surrender.

The hotel, behind which McFarlane and Razors had sheltered received particularly sharp attention and the Colour Sergeant nodded his approval as the end of the street was reduced to rubble.

The two tanks had ensured that his men had good jumping off points which not only gave shelter but outflanked the enemy in the square.

And so, it turned out to be. The company Bren and half his rifles made sure that the mortar pit and its defenders had nothing else on their minds other than survival, while McFarlane's group crept up to the side of the café and thrust grenades into the concrete lined slot and then ran before the upstairs defenders could react.

The blasts roared out of the slot in a vomit of dust and smoke that brought a brief grin to McFarlane's face, but there was still more to do.

A barred door was kicked in to a chorus of pleas in a language which was neither German or French and a desperate white cloth was franticly waved by an arm which led frightened men down wooden stairs.

Kicks and unkind prods from bayonets sent the prisoners out to meet the survivors from the mortar crews who had decided that Scottish rifle fire was a thing to be avoided if at all possible.

'Ah cannae ken a fookin' word thay say. The're nae Germans.'

Razor's face was creased in puzzlement and he gripped the nearest captive by his collar and pulled him close to a mutilated face and bellowed out a question. 'Are ye a fookin' kraut?'

A babble of noise fell from white lips and Razors gave an expression of disgust and pushed the man back down.

'Ukrayina? Noo whaur th' fook is that?

Razors frustration was interrupted by the arrival of the two Basque tanks who sent cautious guns on a tour of the now captured square before opening steel lids and allowing cramped bodies onto the cobbled stones of the square.

Fook me! Tis auld men 'n' wee jimmies!

The words confirmed what every man could see; the tank crews were made of grey-haired old men and young boys. Of men in their prime there was not a single one.

The oldest of the old men picked out McFarlane and walked up to him and upon seeing the rank insignia on his arm grinned a welcome. 'Eskerrik! Bienvenue! A good kill!' He pointed to his sergeant's chevrons that were topped with a gold embroidered tree. 'I sergente grande, you sergente grande, together will kill beucoup bastardos.'

McFarlane could not help laughing at this strange Irish stew of languages, but between laughs introduced his own men and was in turn introduced to the Basques who threw out hardened hands and broad smiles.

'My…' There was hesitation in the old man's voice as he placed his hand on the ill-shorn head of a young boy of perhaps twelve years of age. 'My petit son.'

Seeing the confusion on McFarlane's face there was an explosion of words amongst the Basques until one came up with a better word. 'Grandson.'

Fook me,' Razors muttered, 'Tis a folk outing, whit's neist, th' auld folks yule pairtie?' But despite his disbelief he followed McFarlane in shaking the boy's hand. 'A'm chuffed tae mak' yer aquaintence, Jimmy.'

There was laughter from the Basques at this new nickname for the boy, which ended as the old man saw the prisoners and gave out a long ululating cry which sent shivers down McFarlane's spine and caused every Basque to pull out long knives and advance on the captives with the obvious intention of slaughtering them.

The Colour Sergeant ran between them, waving his arms and without thinking spoke in what he hoped were words that make sense.

'Stop! Prisonaro, no kill, prisonaro surrendero!

The old man and his group stopped, though McFarlane noted they still held their knives in a very professional manner.

'Why? Nazi tres bad, Kill mucho Basques. Basques kill Nazi.'

The old man's face was white with anger and McFarlane finally realised just why the tanks were filled with old men and boys. The Basques had very little left to send and every man and boy here must have lost family and friends.

He thought quickly, not wishing to see prisoners butchered, but also not wishing to cause a breech between new allies. He turned to his corporal and pointed to the now terrified prisoners. 'Razors, gang up 'n' skelp that bastard again, quaistion him solid, tak wee Jimmy wit, ye.'

Razors grinned and held out an inviting hand to the boy and then proceeded to punch and kick his victim while asking questions in an incomprehensible Glasgow dialect until he held up a drooping man who mumbled wrong answers out of broken teeth.

'See, prisonaro, interegato, all prisonaro interegato. Interegato…. Understand? Later, officer interegato…understand?'

The old man had hesitated while watching the beating, but looked unconvinced until a sly smile came to his face.

'OK no kill Nazi. Bastardos go on tank, no kill bastardos.'

It was a strange bargain, but every prisoner was made to clamber on board the tanks except four men who were made to walk in front of them with the waving arms of the tanks machine guns a mute reminder that the price of running would be very high indeed.

McFarlane received an airy wave from the old man and then the lid of his tank clanged shut and the strange procession made its way out of the square with McFarlane and his men bringing up the rear, sheltering in blue exhaust fumes while every captured eye looked outwards and upwards, for the eyes had guessed the old man's purpose.

Any further attacks would have to travel through captured bodies and mines set to catch the unwary would kill their feet and not the following feet of McFarlane and his men.

McFarlane was a hard man, who had seen and done many terrible things in his life and he was torn between admiration for the idea and an appalled rejection of this disregard for the rules of war. But the old man had seemed not to care and perhaps his decision was a wise one for the road was invitingly empty of resistance and temptingly quiet, and bade even the most cautious to travel its long, curving length to the wide plaza and the church which sat at its centre.

Pious hands in ages past had placed mighty stones in ordered array so that the church anchored compass point roads in such a manner that all, no matter where bound, could stop and share in the comforts of faith. Newer ages had swallowed its fields in brick and tile, but still it stood, firmly seated where north met south and the east held a western hand. But now ancient transepts had been transformed by hands far less pious and a place dedicated to peace had been transformed into a stone fortress complete with moat dry and wide, while behind the moat the plaza had been sown with iron teeth, the better to trap the tank, and barbed wire, the better to trap the man.

It was obvious to McFarlane that the café and its like had been mere inconveniences along the way and this bastion was where the enemy had decided to halt any invasion.

He walked back to the waiting tanks and their reluctant passengers, sweeping them off into a group and guarding them with pointed bayonets that he hoped would protect them from the uncertain mercies of the Basques and consulted with his allies.

The old man, after his own reconnoitre had returned with a simple shake of his head and an even simpler word. 'No.'

There was nothing more to be said and McFarlane thoroughly approved of the decision. Two tanks and a platoon of infantry were far too weak a force to try conclusions with an area that had transformed itself into a very reasonable imitation of a fortress and he was content enough to wait for the battles he could hear in neighbouring streets to conclude and further orders to arrive.

At his suggestion one tank pointed back along the route already taken while the other faced along the curving road to where any sally from the plaza must come. Sentry duty was shared amongst the two groups and now there was nothing more to do than wait.

The old man, however, had very definite ideas on how a few moments of peace should be spent to best advantage and grinned at McFarlane while uttering one of his favourite words. The Colour Sergeant knew that tanks had many virtues, but in his opinion one virtue in particular outshone every other. Every tank ever made could produce hot water on demand, and hot water meant only one thing; tea.

The old man produced a much-battered steel kettle, and a trouser pocket gave up an envelope containing precious leaves, while a small spigot on the back of the tank was turned until water ran hot, clear and steaming onto the sun warmed ground. Only then was the old man satisfied and after carefully inspecting the contents of the envelope stirred the leaves into a kettle filled with scalding water…and waited.

McFarlane could not see what standards the old man used to judge the exact moment the tea was ready, but whatever they were, they were very good ones as the liquid poured out into his waiting cup was both delicious and refreshing.

It was a strange thing indeed to drink tea and smoke cigarettes in the middle of a battle, but a hard life and a hard journey up the ranks had taught him to take what little comforts life offered him without question before they were stripped from him by malicious fate. So, he stood in the shade of a tank and tried to converse with the Basques using simple words filtered by an accent formed by poverty and dank streets.

His decision to take hold of fleeting comforts proved exactly right, for as the last dregs of tea stared back at him a shout from a sentry brought his head up to see an odd-looking individual walking towards them as if this was no more than a Sunday jaunt and the grim-faced soldier pointing a loaded rifle no more than an escort of honour. The man wore a tattered sheepskin coat and had a rifle slung over his shoulders, but McFarlane had seen all manner of dress in this war and the sight did not raise any alarm. The man was obviously a scout of some sort and perhaps the herald of reinforcements or even the carrier of new orders. Either way he was about to offer the man some tea when he noticed that every single Basque had risen and was standing absolutely still as if one and all had been stricken by some dread disease.

The man continued his gentle sauntering until he drew close enough to stir vague memories in McFarlane's mind. He had seen the man before, but the memories were faint. Perhaps it was just before that last battle outside Tobruk? Or was it in the happy days after the surrender of the Axis forces in Africa? A photograph? A newspaper article? He did not know, but wherever he had seen the man it would not explain the strange effect he was having on his allies and he was about to question the old man when the stranger's face broke into a smile of recognition and he almost ran over to the Basque Sergeant with open arms and a cry of pleasure.

The Basques uttered that strange war cry again and then clustered around with shouts of joy, and much to McFarlane's disgust, tears, until the man was able to untangle himself with an embarrassed grin.

'I apologise, Sergeant, but these men are old comrades of mine and they seem to be pleased to see me.'

The words were in English, with a veneer of Spanish cadences and were spoken by a man McFarlane could now see was in his middle twenties, but one who held himself with the assurance of someone much older.

The young boy had meanwhile run up to Razors and was uttering the same exited cry over and over. 'Jorge, euskaldunen askatzailea!'

'Ah dinnae ken, Jimmy, slow th' fook doon,' but the boy was beyond calming and kept repeating the sounds until a gentle word from the sheepskin coat halted them.

'The words are in Basque, Corporal and say that I am Jorge, the liberator of the Basques. In truth the boy is wrong, for the Basques liberated themselves and I am no more than a peasant.

'Fook!' The words escaped Razors lips before his mind could act and he turned a bright pink. 'Sorry sur,' Ah didnae ken ye!'

The man shrugged and grinned. 'I have said much worse. Now, Sergeant is that tea I see?'

Over a second pouring McFarlane and the old man explained how they had got here so quickly and just what dangers lay around the corner.

Jorge chuckled at the description of the shelling of every building and the Basques use of captured flesh as shields against further attack.

'Old tricks, Sergeant, old tricks much practiced by both sides in Spain.' A look of pain erased the chuckle and Jorge's voice took on a somber tone. 'Had you been facing Basques they would have shot their own people and then killed the tanks.

McFarlane shot an appalled look at the old man who gave a brief confirming nod.

'That is why the Basques tried to kill your prisoners. There is much hate in their hearts and few left to carry that hate, but you were quite right to hold your position and once the rest of the side streets have been cleared then I will introduce you to my friend who has his own ideas about how such things are to be done.'

They did not have long to wait as gradually the rest of the battalion wore down the residual resistance in the town placing three out of the four roads in their hands and only the path pointing north blocked by the church turned bastion.

Jorge's group was now joined by a still out of breath MacMurray and a tall Basque Colonel of tanks, and together with an escort in the shape of the old man and Razors they poked cautious heads around the gentle curve of the street until they could see for themselves that the plaza was exactly as described.

A volley of rifle shots and high arching mortar fire greeted them, and their journey back was far swifter and far less dignified than their approach had been and Razors comment, 'Fookin' bastids,' seemed to sum up the situation with the minimum of words, although Jorge seemed not at all distressed and turned to the Basque Colonel, who smiled and sent an aide running back down the street as if ten thousand devils were at his heels.

McFarlane and his men waited while whatever message was delivered, and tried, as enlisted men in the presence of officers have ever done, to make themselves inconspicuous and it was fortunate indeed that their powers of invisibility were not tested for too long for every eye was now turned back down the road to where a dolorous clanking and screeching was heard coming ever closer.

'Mair armour, wur aff tae blast oor wey thro.' Razors had long since learnt the trick that every stage magician covets and spoke without moving his lips. 'Tis a guid idea, that steid is tae pure tough fur mah liking.'

McFarlane was about to reply using a similar trick when the source of the mournful sounds hove into view and drove any thoughts of answering from his mind. A small tracked scout car led a procession of some of the strangest vehicles he had ever seen. There was a tank not dissimilar to the ones used by the Basques but this one had suffered a most grievous injury, for where a long gun thrust out in pride from the tanks of the Basques, this tank sported a poor barrel much reduced in length, though a laughing fate had widened it beyond parody. Two further tanks carried great bundles of bound sticks before them and so high were the bundles that men sat precariously on top of them, guiding a driver made blind by a surfeit of wood. The fourth vehicle though could barely be called a tank at all, for it carried no barrel not even the poor stub of the first. Instead it bore two outthrust steel arms holding a device which looked for all the world like an iron bedstead, though no bedstead McFarlane had ever seen had come equipped with such cruel hooks and wickedly pointed daggers. What purpose such strange beasts could have was beyond his comprehension, but it was obvious that the man who had just left the scout car knew, for he shouted orders to every tank commander and then strode with surprisingly fast feet past his gathered group and began a brief discussion with the sheepskin-coated man.

McFarlane recognised the man, though they had never met - Colour Sergeants, for all their exalted rank rarely mixed with generals and Percy Hobart was undoubtably a general.

'Hobart good general.' He spoke the words to the old man who grinned and nodded.

'Tres mucho good general. Kill mucho Nazi.'

This was obviously the yardstick by which the old man judged his companions and McFarlane was about to reply when a wheezing Major MacMurray and the long-legged Basque colonel ran up and gave orders which saw him and his men clinging to the sides of the old man's tanks tasked with escorting the tank with the sadly deformed barrel.

Tanks for all their many attributes are not silent and the enemy emplacements were ready for them and their greeting was a warm one which grew warmer still as the trio of tanks turned the corner to face into the plaza.

McFarlane scrambled down the side of the tank; his place was not here. Besides tanks made large and inviting targets and it was in everyone's interest that he put some distance between him and the vehicles which seemed determined to roll right up to the edge of the ditch.

'Pick yer hings tae aim fur! single shots ainlie! Huv a go fur th' guns foremaist!'

His words were unnecessary, his men were well trained and knew that their task was to protect the tanks and therefore the anti-tank guns must be given as much discomfort as possible.

He hefted a long familiar rifle to his shoulder and ignoring the sounds of battle sighted on the loader of an eighty-eight millimetre gun which took pride of place in the centre of the plaza surrounded by sand bags piled up just a little too low.

'Amateurs he muttered as he squeezed his trigger and the man fell with sprawled limbs.

He heard a soundless shout and saw a pointing hand turned in his direction and faces white with fear pointing and firing wavering rifles towards him but none of the bullets were engraved with a Scottish name and the pointing hand received a copper-jacketed bullet for its pains.

The Basque tanks were firing now with guns depressed for the range was but short, a danger made plain when one tank grew sparks and smoke from a round fired by a team of men franticly trying to reload a smaller gun with fingers rendered clumsy with fear. Alas for them, though the tank was wounded its machine gun was unharmed and, aided by Razor's Bren and several rifles, it tore flesh apart and ensured that any further action from the enemy guncrew was extremely unlikely.

By now the strange tank, aided by the last Basque had reached the edge of the moat. It lifted up its shortened barrel and then much to McFarlane's amazement the world ended.

Or so it seemed, though as he later realised the world was unharmed except for that part of it occupied by the plaza. He watched as first a small column of smoke reached to the sky and then a mighty circular blast wave swept the plaza like an iron broom. The eighty -eight was powerless before its anger, toppling over like discarded toy, even its wide spread legs not enough to withstand its power, and men found that air compressed beyond madness was as hard as tempered steel and vomited lungs out of mouths ill used to such fare. The barbed wire coped only a little better, but its ordered ranks were thrown into tangled disarray. The blast wave rocked the tanks and continued on, and was, much to McFarlane's relief positively jovial as it threw debris and smoke at him before surrendering the last of its power in a retort that echoed from buildings that now held not a single sliver of glass.

He pointed a questioning rifle forward, but all the rifle could see was a wasteland; parts of guns, parts of men, and, in the centre, a great smoking hole with blacked edges where whatever weapon the strange tank had used, had impacted. His muttered "Fook me!" seemed wholly inadequate to the task of describing what he could see, but one thing he was sure of was that only a fool would try and withstand such power.

The occupants of the church were obviously of the same mind for one of its great wooden doors opened up slightly, and a hand waving a white cloth was seen, the hand soon followed by its owner behind whom the great door slammed shut with a dull boom.

McFarlane cried out, 'Haud yer fire! Tis a wee lassie!'

He hoped his words could be heard over the roar of tank engines, but he could not be sure, so he ran to the edge of the moat and shouted what he hoped were encouraging words. 'Ower 'ere, lassie. Dinnae be feart!'

The young girl did not acknowledge his words, but looking neither to the right nor to the left, skirted the still smoking hole and then scrambled first down and then up the sides of the moat and into the strong arms of the Colour Sergeant.

Only then did she burst into tears.

McFarlane was a hard man, who had learnt that pity was just another word for weakness. His vocabulary was exactly what could be expected from such a man and held little in the way of soft endearments but the girl's tears not only soaked his battle dress but drove a warm stake into a heart unused to emotion. He patted the head of the little girl and tried to put unaccustomed softness into his words. 'Thare, thare lassie, hush yer greetin', tis aff tae be a'richt.'

The only reply was more crying, and he knelt down and pointed to his chest.

'They ca' me Andy, whit's yer name?

The tears stopped for a moment and McFarlane was introduced to Marie Christine. He tried to rework a parade ground voice into something a very frightened young girl could understand. 'Weel, Marie ah aff tae mak' sure yer safe, now lassie tak ma hand, thare's a gud gurl.'

A small hand was grasped in his, but as it did so he saw the church door open again and a second figure emerge followed by an outthrust hand holding a pistol.

McFarlane knew exactly what was going to happen and clutched Marie's face into his chest. 'Shut yer een, lassie.'

The pistol barked twice, and the emerging figure crumpled and fell, spilling a wave of blood down the wide steps that led up to the church doors.

The door boomed shut once more and Marie resumed her crying, for though her eyes had been blinded, young ears had told the tale readily enough.

He picked up the girl and left Razors with strict instructions to watch the church with keen eyes and then with the two remaining tanks and the crew of the third retreated back to safety.

'Fuck Nazi Bastardos.'

The old man made his views very clear. Whether his words were due to the loss of his second tank or were a more general view was not clear, but he repeated himself in case there could be any doubt as to his opinion.

McFarlane could only agree, angered by what he had seen. His desert war was nothing like this, a cruel war to be sure, with blood, pain and death, but once his blood had cooled and the battle was over a man with his hands up was no longer an enemy; an inconvenience undoubtedly, a man that had to be clothed, watered, fed and guarded, but no longer an enemy and absolutely not a thing to be bargained with.

This war was different, and he was not at all certain that he approved of it.

Marie had refused to leave his side, so he was there with her when she was gently questioned by Jorge and Hobart. There was a reason why the streets were empty, for at the first sight of an invading force the townsfolk had been herded into the church and promised that any attempt to break into the church would result in their deaths.

The second figure thrust out of the doorway had been that of the Mayor and his murder was a sign of intent.

Marie had been very brave, giving not only numbers of the hostages but also of captors and using her child's hands she drew a passable sketch of the interior of the church. Then she had looked into the stone faces of Jorge and Hobart and had begun to wail once more. The church had to be taken, there was no choice. It stood on the only good road north and already the beach and the small port was filling up with men and equipment. Both Jorge and Hobart cared little for the port, its carrying capacity was far too small to cause any concern, but the beach beside it was perfect for a large mobile harbour - a harbour ready for assembly. The church must be reduced, and Marie could see the future of her captive family written in the hard faces of both men and no soft words could ease the tears.

McFarlane took her to a waiting ambulance where a kindly medic gave her a draught to give much needed sleep and promised to look after her. His repeating the tale to the old man and his companions had birthed the comment that Nazis were indeed all bastards and looking into those old eyes McFarlane saw not an ounce of pity. He remembered the Asturian general's words about the Basque attitude to killing; if they would kill their own kith and kin to shed Nazi blood how much worse would they give strangers? He knew that If the order came to fire on the church and reduce it to rubble they would do so without a second thought, relishing only the chance to kill a hated enemy.

He pulled air through a gloomy cigarette and looked over to where the officers huddled over a temporary table and was once again glad that he had achieved only a coveted rank and no more, because try as he might he could think of no other solution to the problem of the church.

He saw Major MacMurray being questioned by General Hobart and allowed himself a small grin. The General had a well-deserved reputation for chewing junior officers into small lumps if they failed him and MacMurray could be seen squirming as he was interrogated. McFarlane bore the Major no ill will. As far as officers went he was competent and fair and that was as much as he had come to expect from any man who held the King's commission, but at this point in time he was glad that his ambition had kept him within the bounds of a humble King's warrant and his grin grew by another small degree.

The conversation ended and McFarlane swiftly lost any trace of the grin as MacMurray ran up and demanded his presence at the general's table and for all his toughness he felt a splinter of fear enter his mind, though he was careful not to show it as he stood to attention before the two generals.

Any general could break a Colour Sergeant for any reason or even no reason at all, but he knew of no reason and Hobart did not have that reputation; humourless certainly, driven and very clever, but not malicious. The Asturian was an unknown quantity, but he had seemed friendly enough, so he damped down the splinter and fixed his eyes on a spot exactly twelve inches above the men's heads and waited for fate to strike.

Hobart barked a question. 'Major MacMurray tells me that you are a capable man, what do you say about that?'

McFarlane still kept his eyes on the invisible spot and certainly did not turn and face MacMurray, but he could almost hear the man sweating, for if it was true that any general could break any Sergeant then Hobart had just placed the Major's career in his hands; a denial now would shatter any hope MacMurray held of further promotion. But the man, for all he was an officer had always been fair, so he addressed the air that lived above Hobart's head. 'Ah think th' major is a braw judge o' character, sur.'

Hobart's lips thinned at this attempt at humour, but his companion threw back his head in laughter. 'Very good, Sergeant and I hope that you are right.'

Jorge looked over at Hobart and to McFarlane's amazement received a warm confirming smile which he took and gifted to the Colour Sergeant.

'We have a problem, Sergeant. The church stands in our way and must be removed. Now I can destroy it with tanks, I can call in shelling or air strikes from the ships at sea, but all those solutions are destructive, and it is not our intention to have our first day on French soil marked by the shedding of innocent blood. But there may be a way to take the church without too many deaths. Jorge's smile faded a little and his voice asked a question. 'If you and your men can get into the church, can you kill those holding the townsfolk while sparing as many French lives as possible?' There was no smile on the Asturian's face now, the good-humored man who had earlier shared tea had entirely vanished, and his eyes had taken on the same pitiless look as the old man. 'Before you answer, Sergeant you should know that if you fail, if you are captured or killed, then the church and everyone inside it dies. I will have no choice. Make no mistake about that, sergeant; one way or another, before another hour passes this army will move north.'

Despite the sunshine McFarlane shivered, for there was winter in Jorge's face, a hard, frost-covered winter and it was a fearful thing to question such a face, but he was a hard man and hard men did not achieve any coveted rank by being cowards nor fools and the thought of fighting his way through iron bound church doors did not appeal and it would be as well if everyone knew it.

'Ye'll nae git us thro' they kirk doors, harder than th' de'il's hert they're.'

The sentence hung there for a moment until Hobart turned slightly, the sunlight glinting off the thick lenses of his glasses. 'I quite agree, sergeant, and you need not concern yourself with the doors, but the question still stands. Once you and your men are in the church are you capable of disposing of the enemy while at the same time saving as many captives as possible?'

McFarlane thought about his men, for they were his men; lieutenants came and went, but the core remained the same. They had seen much, done more and done it together.

There really was only one answer he could give.

'Aye.'

'Lik' fleas oan a starving dug,' had been Razor's wry comment as they clambered up steel sides and made themselves as comfortable as possible.

McFarlane's men were clustered on the sides of the tank that stood with engine rumbling waiting for orders that only their commanders could hear.

And a strange procession they made; the old man's tank would lead, followed by the two strange tanks clasping great bundles of bound sticks to their hard bosoms and bringing up the rear was McFarlane and the tank that held up the iron bedstead on long outthrust arms, though he noticed that the bedstead now came equipped with two wood and steel pillows that trailed long wires back into the cocooned interior of the tank.

General Hobart had smiled the smile of the proud father when he told the secret of the bedstead and McFarlane could only hope that it had been thoroughly tested, because if he was uncertain about Hobart's child then he was very certain that its failure would have severe consequences for a man who had said goodbye to Glasgow slums, but now there was no choice. The convoy lurched forward with roaring engines and long plumes of blue fumes and one by one vanished into the red swirling smoke that banks of friendly mortars had spread over the ruined plaza.

The old man led the branch-bearing tanks up to the very edge of the moat and the bound branches were unceremoniously dumped into the moat, filling it and allowing the two tanks passage onto the ruined plaza. As they did so McFarlane's throat grew dry, for the discarding of the bundles revealed the tanks true nature, and he saw that they were not mere humble carriers of wood, but copies of the wide mouthed beast that had destroyed the plaza.

They had rolled forward and now lay panting blue fumes with paws outstretched and brazen tongues uplifted. What he was seeing was Jorge's insurance policy. Should he fail, should he die, then the brazen tongues would speak, and the church would be removed from the face of the Earth.

He swallowed trying to dampen a dry throat, but it was too late now, for they too now rolled over a wooden bundle, past the crouching beasts, and swung round to face the flank of the church.

Skilled hands in ages past had piled its stones with many a cunning joint, and the hands had then rested, content enough that their children would revere the living god within its walls. But the wall had met a new child now and this child was a child of destruction. The tank rolled up to the wall and whining hydraulics pushed the bedstead up against the stones. McFarlane and his men hastily clambered down the sides of the tank and withdrew a safe distance, for they had been warned of the tank's power and had not the protection of armour plate.

At that moment the gun barrel of the old man's tank vomited smoke and flame. The Basques loved their tanks; tanks killed the enemy in large numbers; tanks were a visible sign that they had survived and were unconquerable. They loved each shell; the armour-piercing, the high explosive and the phosphorus, but most of all they loved cannister shells. They made their own in a camouflaged factory hidden in a mountain fold and it was a happy tank commander who ordered the steel cannisters loaded, for a thousand steel balls could sweep many many men to their deaths.

It was not men who were the target today but ancient wood and stone, and the steel balls hammered against the front of the church like angry fists demanding admittance. Wood flew, stone chipped and the body

28

of the mayor was transformed into pink gruel but the balls made a terrible noise which turned every eye inside the church towards the clamour and thus they never saw the side of the church explode.

The two shaped charges had been made as small as possible and packed into steel and wood boxes and the tank had held them at extreme length. They exploded, blasting cut stone into rough pebbles, rocking the tank backwards and warping the steel frame of the bedstead into scrap.

The pious hands had built better than they knew as the wall did not collapse but the smoking hole was more than enough to allow entry to McFarlane and his men.

'Steel', he had told them. 'Use the bayonet where possible.' For bullets once fired had no conscience and a church filled with both the innocent and the guilty was no place for a fire fight.

It may have been the shock of the explosion, or it may have been the war cry that thundered from McFarlane's throat, but his first victim offered no resistance, taking a long bayonet to the stomach without a cry, only a grimace of pain, while Razors reverted back to Glasgow streets by planting a hobnailed boot firmly in the groin of his opponent and then slashing a shrieking throat with a honed blade.

His men were pushing civilians to the floor in their eagerness to kill and he saw one of his men drop to one knee and target his rifle on a fleeing uniform. He was about to shout a warning but then saw what the man saw; a woman frozen with shock, about to be taken as a shield and this could not be.

The shot passed cleanly through the would-be hostage taker and carried on, blowing a gilt laden statue of the Virgin Mary into shards.

There was no time to admire such accuracy for there was still work to do, and his men hunted through a jumbled waltz of figures that danced to a tune made of shouts and screams.

A shot is fired, and a woman screams, but a bayonet discovers a new home in a ribcage and more hot blood is added to a holy floor. A Scottish rifleman disdains sharp pointed knife in favour of the blunt wood of a stock and nine pounds of rifle propelled by hard muscle splinters an enemy forehead, driving bone shards into a brain that registers pain far too late. An enemy sees only implacable foes and makes a dash for freedom, running with flailing arms and wailing mouth towards a ruined wall, but an outstretched foot trips him and then places a hard-soled boot on his throat. The phrase '' Shift 'n' yur'e deid.'' Was probably not understood, but terrified eyes stared up at the black mouth of a downward pointing rifle and this was a powerful inducement to stay still and learn.

And then it was over, scant minutes, each one an eternity, divide the blasting of the wall from the last victory and McFarlane was left only with the familiar.

His breath rasped with sharp agony through punished lungs, his ears hearing the shrieks of the wounded and the silence of the dead, while his eyes lifted a red veil and saw the blood and the faces of those shocked to still live. All this was familiar to him, old friends who never really left but always followed within summoning distance.

He heard Razors walk up and turned to see the Corporal holding a rifle that held a still dripping bayonet. 'Two prisoners, three civilian deid, some wounded, anaw Private Taggert.' Razors put his hand up to his shoulder indicating where the wound was, and grinned, the white scar on his face pulling his face into un-natural areas. 'He'll bide oan a while.' He looked around the church seeing all that McFarlane saw and shaking his head in regret. 'Pity aboot th' casualties, bit whit's a man tae dae?

'Aye, Razors, a pity, but tis best dane this wey ah think, now best we be flittin' afore thay think we ur a' deid.'

The great doors were opened, and McFarlane led the civilians down the pockmarked steps and into the sunshine with Razors and the two prisoners bringing up the rear.

The lid of the old man's tank opened up and a grey head appeared with a congratulatory wave though the old eyes gazed at the prisoners with hate-born hunger.

A steel bridge was being thrown across the ditch and McFarlane's band was given the honour of being the first to cross to a waiting Major MacMurray who received his report and then hurried on for he had Generals who demanded answers and would not wait.

There was nothing to do now, but breath in fresh air, feel the sunshine on his face and wipe away grit-fouled sweat.

He pulled out his canteen to take a long swallow of warm water and as he did so, he saw a woman in a torn dress gazing with increasing anxiety into the distance and calling out, obviously searching for a lost friend or relative. She turned and recognising McFarlane as one of her rescuers ran up and blasted him with a stream of high-speed French of which he understood not a single word.

He was about to turn away, the concerns of French civilians certainly not the concerns of Scottish Colour Sergeants, when the words were repeated once more but slower so that he caught something.

'Marie Christine?' He placed his hand flat at hip height indicating length, 'A wee bairn?'

A vigorous nodding of the head and a fresh outpouring of tears signaled that he had guessed correctly.

Andrew McFarlane was a hard man who had dragged himself out of the slums and the struggle had left little time to grow delicate feelings, but Marie Christine had been brave, far braver than any ordinary girl and such bravery deserved reward. He did not speak further but gripped the woman's wrist and dragged her past marching men, squealing tanks and towed guns to where he had left the girl.

The medic was in the midst of setting a broken bone but greeted McFarlane with a nod and the information that the girl was still sleeping, but on seeing the girl the woman broke out into more wailing much to the exasperation of the Colour Sergeant who realised that the woman thought the girl to be dead.

'Fur Gud's sake wumun, the bairn is ainlie sleeping!'

It may have been the woman's cries, or it may have been McFarlane's anger, but Marie instantly woke and threw her arms around the woman adding her child's tears to the tears of the woman's and once more a stream of high-speed French passed between them expressing joy at their reunion.

Marie saw him then and stretched out a shy hand, but McFarlane turned away because his eyes had started watering, obviously because a large amount of grit had entered them; it had to be that and only that, because hard men from Glasgow slums who had made Colour Sergeant did not cry.

He dashed the tears from his eyes, forced a stern look onto his face and turned back to face Marie, pulling out a bar of American chocolate from his satchel as he did so. 'This is fur bein' a brave lassie.' And with that he was gone, telling himself that he had done more than his duty and that a soldier in battle could not afford pity or any emotion at all.

A small voice within him spoke fearfully that this was not the case, but a harsh upbringing squashed that voice with fearsome power and it was heard no more. Besides, he had stopped to look at the first of the tanks with the truncated barrels, that had, with one shot destroyed a plaza and curiosity was an emotion which still survived.

The tank was Basque for it bore the sign of the charging bull on its flanks and a wiry man with a sunburnt face was busy painting a white ring on its barrel. It seemed only polite to thank the man for his efforts, so he called out, and pointing to himself tried to imitate the strange alphabet of the old man. 'I soldier, mucho thanko for bang.'

The words were un-natural in his mouth and he felt a little embarrassed speaking them, but to his surprise the man laughed and reached out a friendly hand.

'No need for that lingo, chum. Charlie Higgins is the name; tank-driving is the game.

McFarlane was confused. 'But yon tank's Basque!'

Charlie laughed again. 'So it is, chum, so it is, and I'm a sort of Basque. Left the Big Smoke back in '37, joined up to fight the Fascists. Course when they heard I was a lorry driver back in Blighty they gave me a tank.' A wry grin crossed his face. 'And rotten tanks they were, not much more than a roller skate with a bit 'o boiler plate bolted on, but I survived. Hooked up with a Basque woman and never looked back.'

'So, you'll gang back tae yer guidwife whin this is over?'

A particularly bleak look crossed the man's face only to be replaced by a thin, hard won smile.

'No chum, she's gone. Near a year back it would be. We were fighting together, and then poof! She'd gone, not enough left for a decent burial.' He shook his head, trying to clear painful memories. 'At least it were quick, there one moment, gone the next.'

The smile returned just a little, 'But maybe you want to see my little poppets?'

He looked up and spoke to his loader who passed him up a large, yellow painted metal tube with four tiny vanes at one end and a huge pointed spike at the other.

'Here she is, chum, the wonder of the age. The twelve-inch general purpose petard mortar round, suitable for all occasions, price no object, birthdays and weddings a specialty!

'Known to those in the trade as the Mark One Dustbin, hence we wot fires them is known as *Binmen* and a sorry lot we are, as we need to get close on account of the range of the aforesaid twelve-inch mortar round is bleedin' poor, and hence we need half the bleedin' army around us, lest we get our delicate arses shot off! Mind you, once we let rip its *Goodnight nurse,*' and *Who turned off the lights?*'

'So, I saw,' agreed McFarlane, you'll be comin' wi' us then?'

'Have no fear, Jock, where you go, Charlie Higgins won't be far behind and he's got more than one trick up his sleeve, you can be sure of that!'

McFarlane gave his thanks once more and continued his walk back to the ruined plaza. The battalion was forming up now the way was clear, and every compass pointed north.

He did not know what dangers lay in front of him, but he knew two things with absolute certainty; firstly he was a hard man and secondly, he was a Colour Sergeant.

And those were no bad things to be.

'Not even a real Scot,' said McFarlane gloomily, looking up at the evening sky that was filling with dark clouds. 'Oh, aye born in Scotland right enough, but went to school in England. Grandfather is High Sherriff of Lanarkshire, father is a Chief Constable, and his uncle is a fookin' Kings Counsel.'

'Fookin' rozzers' commented Razors, now equally gloomily. 'You're sure?

'Had it fae Wee Henry his-sel, th' papers wur oan th' major's table.'

Wee Henry was the Major's Batman and therefore a most reliable source of information.

'Henry said that thay wur a' thare, personal letters o' recommendation 'n' service record. Th' laddie is barely twenty!'

A murmur of discontent ran round the men. Since the death of their last lieutenant, they had been led, and successfully led, by the Colour Sergeant but though Army bureaucracy moves slowly it does move and had finally produced a newly minted officer to replace the one that had failed to make it off the landing beach.

'Some biscuit arsed, rozzer's son, still hangin' on his mother's tit,' was the consensus from McFarlane's men who had seen lieutenant's come and go, and had every expectation that they would see this one come, and they would see this one go…permanently.

PLATOON

Major MacMurray rather suspected that his tent had first seen service in the latter years of Queen Victoria's South African wars and he half expected a bloody assegai to poke yet another hole in its sides at any moment, but he considered himself lucky, for in this campaign tents were a luxury. Indeed everything apart from the absolute necessities were considered a luxury, because this little army was supplied through a single temporary port that thrust out its arm into the hopefully gentle waters of the Mediterranean. He had heard that the Free French had captured Marseilles so perhaps the supply situation would improve, but in the meantime, he considered himself lucky to have his own tent, complete with cot, desk and the single chair that he was sitting on looking up a very young Lieutenant with the brightest red hair he had ever seen.

MacMurray was feeling every one of his forty-nine years, and a tinge of envy coloured his words as he lifted up a slim folder and glanced through its contents. 'At ease, Lieutenant and welcome to the battalion.'

'Thank you, sir.'

'If you don't mind Lieutenant, I'd like to ask you a question.'

'Please do, sir.'

A look of confused exasperation crossed MacMurray's face.

'Why, Lieutenant? I mean why here, why now? You left university mid-way through your year, and I've a letter here from your tutors telling me that you could be Advocate General for Scotland one day if you return to your studies. Your family is well off and well connected, you could have got a deferment, could have sat out the war in comfort, so why didn't you?'

Bright black eyes stared back at him and he could see the thoughts marshaling themselves in the boy's head.

'The law, sir, that's why. My family are lawyers, policemen, judges; always have been, probably always will be. One way or another they serve the law, and the law exists to preserve order, protect the innocent and punish the guilty. I've always been told it's a moral duty to confront evil and strike it down. There's none so guilty as the Nazis, sir, and there's never been any doubt in my mind that they are evil. I can't fight the Nazis from a lecture hall, sir. It's not no more complicated than that.'

MacMurray was impressed, he had expected some sort of adolescent desire for death or glory, but the Lieutenant had obviously considered long and hard before donning a uniform and hadn't taken the easy way out by taking a staff job mile's behind the lines.

Which made his decision all the easier.

'I'm short of officers, and I have a platoon which is presently commanded by a Colour Sergeant. You will take over command of that platoon.' He held up his hand, forestalling any comment that the lieutenant might make. 'Do not thank me. The platoon is my problem child; every man of it comes from the slums of Glasgow and more than a few of them are criminals, sent here in all probability by members of your family. That said they fight hard and I always feel more comfortable knowing that they are in the lead. Colour Sergeant McFarlane is a former boy soldier who rules them with some success. He's a hard man himself, who comes from the same slums. They are desert veterans who have served together since the summer of '41 and you will be merely the latest of a long line of officers to command them. Some died and some broke, but the platoon has remained largely unchanged, so I do you no favour giving you this command. You'll find them bivouacked four fields over next to three Basque Shermans. Go and introduce yourself and I'll send up orders tomorrow at first light.

'Any questions? Then good luck.'

The field was not too hard to find even though the day had come to a premature end and dark clouds had lowered so that it seemed as if only a little more effort would bring them down to touch the ground. The three tanks were mere blobs of darkness surrounded by the shadows of men and he was about to advance towards them when he felt the cold barrel of a rifle pushed into his back and heard a harsh demand for the password hissed in his ear. He hadn't seen the sentry, but the sentry had undoubtably seen him and was taking no chances.

He replied in a calm voice, the pressure on his back vanished and the harsh voice bade him walk on. He turned to thank the voice but there was no one to greet. The sentry had vanished.

He grinned, a lesson learnt that he was about to command no mere squad of amateurs, and so he was unsurprised to find a group of men standing utterly still waiting for him.

'You'd be Mr. Donaldson?'

His questioner was a tall man with an air about him that would tell even the most insensitive that any man who crossed him would have a short and uncomfortable future.

'And you'd be Colour Sergeant McFarlane?'

'Yes sir.'

There was no friendly grin from McFarlane nor was there a salute. This was a formal handing over of power and salutes tended to draw the unwelcome attention of snipers.

'Then perhaps you'd better introduce me to the men.'

Now and only now was there a brief grin from McFarlane. 'You've awready met oor sentry, Private Taggert, bit this is Corporal Frazer 'n' this is…' McFarlane introduced each man in turn with Donaldson committing each name to memory, seeing faces that no man would wish to see when alone on a dark night and then realising that he was alone on a dark night.

Another group of men appeared, and a mug of warm tea was thrust into his hand.

'Mr. Donaldson, this is Senior Sergeant Mikel Erentxtun of the Fourteenth Tank Regiment of the Basque Republic 'n' this is his grandson, wee Jimmy.'

More introductions were made while Donaldson sipped at some of the best tea he had ever tasted. He made approving comments about the flavour and the old man nodded, his face beaming in pleasure at the compliment.

'My Lorena, she make the tea, tres bon.'

Donaldson looked around for a female, for he knew the Basques, out of grim necessity did not distinguish between men and women, but he could not see a female in the shapes which surrounded him.

There was a burst of laughter from the Basques and even McFarlane ventured a small smile.

'Lorena is the name of Sergeant Erentxtun's tank,' he explained, 'Lorena was wee Jimmy's mother.'

'My Lorena, she kill Nazi bastardo's, you wait. Mucho bangs, mucho morte.'

The smile had left the old man's face and he took Donaldson's now empty cup, handed it to his grandson and then tapped a grubby finger against a wristwatch.

'Journada is finis, sleep.'

It was as broad a hint as Donaldson had ever received and he bade goodnight to the Basques.

'They hate the Germans,' explained McFarlane as the first of the rain began to pour down in large drops, '…hate taking prisoners as well. I'd watch out for that if I was you, sir.'

Donaldson nodded and asked about sentry duty, but as he expected the Colour Sergeant had long since set up a structure which allowed both sleep and duty and he saw no reason to change what obviously worked.

'Looks like it will be a bad night, sir, I'll get one of the lads to dig you a foxhole.'

Donaldson looked up at the sky where the final strands of purple day fled before night tinted clouds and then looked at the face of the Colour Sergeant. The last of the evening light gave no clue as to what the man was thinking, nor did his tone give away his opinions, but there was a trial somewhere in the words and he knew all about trials.

'No need, Colour Sergeant. Let the men have their sleep; I'll dig my own.'

'Very good, sir. Good night sir.'

The ground was surprisingly soft, and his entrenching tool made short work of it, the exercise keeping him warm despite the chill night air and the cold rain that was now a continuous downpour, and soon with the aid of a ground sheet he was asleep.

It was full dark when he awoke with the realisation that he was very wet. It was still raining heavily, and his foxhole had filled with water.

He had always thought that cursing was a sign of weakness, that a mind devoted to logic and justice had no need for such things, but despite that the words sprang up unbidden and it took an effort of will to resist saying them and an effort of will to drag his dripping body out the foxhole and lie down on the wet grass wrapped in a wet ground sheet.

Sleep did not easily return but it did return, and he woke in the early pink of a wet dawn to find both the Colour Sergeant and the Corporal standing over him, their faces numb with the effort of hiding wide grins.

'Good morning sir, how did you sleep?'

If last night's words were a trial then this morning's words were a challenge. The men were expecting a long hymn of curse-filled complaints and he was determined not to give them what they expected, so he fixed a bright smile on his face while standing up and squeezing water out of his battledress.

'Good morning, Colour Sergeant, Corporal. Why I slept very well, in fact I slept like a fish.'

As he expected looks of puzzlement crossed both men's faces.

'Like a fish, sir?'

'Why yes Colour Sergeant, like a fish. I believe that fish sleep very well under water.'

He added emphasis to his words squeezing yet more water out of his battle dress while looking straight at both men. Now it was his turn to challenge, his turn to say *I am a man, I will not complain, and I will lead.* The only question was would the two NCO's accept or oppose him?

For a long moment there was only silence between the three men and then a slow smile spread across McFarlane's face. 'Very funny, sir. It was a little damp last night, wasn't it?'

He turned to the corporal and Donaldson saw for the first time the disfiguring scar that marked the man's face. It gave the man a look of sardonic evil and that look was another challenge to overcome.

'Assemble the men, Corporal. Let me have a look at them in daylight.'

There was a brief moment of hesitation and then a cough from the Colour Sergeant which might have been a mere clearing of throat, but then again might well have been something else entirely different.

The corporal stiffened to attention. 'Officer on parade sir?'

'Officer on parade, corporal, just this once. I won't make a habit of it.'

'Verra gud, sir.'

The corporal vanished, but his voice was soon heard marshalling the platoon into order while McFarlane gifted the new lieutenant a slight nod of acceptance.

And that was how Mr. Donaldson took over his platoon.

BETTER TO DIE

A man could make a good living from land such as this; there were low hills for goats, pastureland for cattle and flat fields for grain. Yes, a man could grow fat here, buy himself a wife and raise strong sons who would help in the fields.

Of course, there was the question of ownership, which was presently disputed and the small matter of cash, for such land would command a high price and Minraj Tamang was a poor man and, what was worse, a poor man far from home.

But like every Gurkha he was an optimist with a smile never far from the surface of his face and despite lying in a hastily scratched woodland home he was content enough and the dreams he had were not enough to keep his eyes off the enemy. A rather surprised enemy who had been resting contentedly enough in this valley until the arrival of Minraj and his companions, who, it must be admitted were just as surprised to find the valley occupied. A short, confused firefight had ensued with an enemy which seemed to consist of two oversized companies pouring a good deal of fire upon the Gurkhas who very sensibly retreated back the way they had come, ceding possession of a section of road, a small stream-fed orchard, a farmhouse and the fields which surrounded it.

And there the matter stood. The enemy seemed content to hold the valley while the Gurkhas held the slopes of a wooded hill under fire from a more numerous enemy with superior firepower and no desire to move.

The English lieutenant who commanded them was no fool and he would not risk his men without cause. He had made contact with an enemy who held a superior military capability and took the only rational action. Minraj had no complaints about the lieutenant; the man was young that was true, but he had the courage of a lion and that was no bad thing for he despised cowardice as did every Nepalese. Theirs was a simple creed that death was not to be feared and it was better to die facing the enemy than live as coward.

Which is why his companion, a stocky man from the hills who had gained much honour as a champion wrestler complained. 'Why do we run so? To run is shameful. It is better to die than run. The enemy sees only our arses and laughs.'

Minraj kept his own council, concentrating on the woodland path still littered with last winter's leaf fall that lay before him and the fields below, lush with this summer's grass. There would be time enough to talk when the battle was over, and besides what profit would there be in a death that caused the enemy no harm? They had been tasked with scouting, with finding the enemy, well they had found him and now was a time for patience.

He added a precautionary edge to the short, curved blade that every Nepalese soldier carried and waited for orders from the young English lieutenant who spoke Minraj's own language with hardly an accent and rarely gave orders, but only suggested that things should be done.

The orders were not long in coming; Minraj and the wrestler were to hold while reinforcements were sent up and then they were to aid in the taking of the farmhouse and the road upon which it stood.

He smiled at the orders, the distance was no great obstacle, being nearly all downhill and his skill as runner well known.

The earthworks which revealed defensive positions he entirely discounted, the men who sat in them were already corpses that had yet to taste death.

He took another look at the farmhouse, noting the expensive glass that decorated every window and the costly red tiles that adorned the roof.

Yes, it would cost much to buy such a property and yet the dowery for a wife would be much less than normal, for what family would not vie to be allied to a man who could afford luxuries such as glass and tile? Yet there was much to be changed on such a farm; the roof was pitched at far too shallow an angle and would surely collapse when winter snows rested on it and there was no shrine in the courtyard to keep away evil spirits and honour the dead.

Yet the land was good and dreams were free.

A chorus of low greetings from behind him broke his visions of a Gurkha farm in France, for the reinforcements had arrived and the time for battle had come with them. As one man they rose and exchanged delighted grins, for what use was a life unless to fight?

'Ayo Gorkhali!'

'The Gurkhas are upon you!'

Only once was the war cry uttered. No more was needed for there was an enemy before them and what need was there for war cries when blood was already stirred and blades longed for cutting?

Minraj, the wrestler and the Lieutenant ran forward under a sheltering hail of rifle fire and blossoming mortar rounds. They disdained the smoke rounds that would have hid them as unmanly. Better they said for them to see the enemy and for the enemy to see them, the more to fear. And if death came to a Gurkha then it would be in plain view of his comrades and the tale of an honourable passing would be taken back to his village and his name mentioned in pride.

So, in plain view they charged down the hill, lungs bred to thin mountain air sucking in the warm breezes of a French valley.

They ran as others ran, hard, fast, never in a straight line, with eyes not on trusted brothers, but on the enemy, who had his own ideas about how this battle would be fought and how this battle would be won and for every Gurkha rifle there was an enemy rifle and for every mortar an enemy twin and the valley was soon filled with the chattering of guns and the harsh blasts of mortars, but still the Gurkhas ran through lush summer grass.

Fewer than started reached the chattering stream but the three companions reached its banks and dived into its warm waters. The enemy had seen them and though bullets passed over them the high, arching fingers of mortars sought them out and it was obvious that a wet stream was no safe harbour.

A white painted wooden fence stood before the orchard and beyond the orchard lay the farmhouse, but the orchard was busy both with swarming bees and swarming men who knew that half hidden in the stream lay a massed enemy. They were sure that they would prevail, for they had machine guns and rifle pits, a farmhouse built of age hardened stones and their oppostion were few in number and small of stature.

The men from Nepal had different thoughts. They had not travelled across oceans to lie resting while an enemy threw insults at them. A flurry of grenades flew from the stream bed and once more the war cry announced that the Gurkhas sought only war as they scrabbled up the stream bank towards the foe.

The wrestler disdained to climb over the fence but used a powerful body to crash through it, and fling himself onto the nearest enemy. An arm knotted with muscle wrapped itself round a throat and squeezed until vertebrae split while a second arm wrenched a reaching rifle from hands far weaker.

'Ayo Gorkhali!' The wrestler's shout was filled with the joy of a master craftsman delighting in his work, but Minraj had no time to compliment him as his place was with the others who ran through the orchard.

Somehow the lieutenant had managed to get ahead of him and was sheltering behind the trunk of an apple tree. He ran to a nearby tree, flinging himself to the ground and firing off five rounds at a machine gun which was proving particularly troublesome.

Not a single shot hit, but the sudden attack caused the machine gun crew to slew their gun around to face this new danger giving the lieutenant the chance to run forward.

'Ayo Gorkhali!'

Minraj had no memory of uttering the challenge but ran with others to cover his lieutenant's charge.

The orchard was full of running men now, running men and flying bullets that thudded into tree trunks or tore into men.

Smoke and the cries of anger and fear rose up to a smiling sky as he stopped and fired another clip at a group who were coming to the aid of their comrades. The men fell, killed by his bullets or others, he did not know.

'Not seeing my arse now, are they!'

The wrestler had re-joined him, bleeding from a scalp wound, but grinning in triumph. He heard the words through battle-stifled ears and grinned back pointing towards where the lieutenant was emptying a pistol at the machine gun crew. The man had enough courage to lead Gurkhas and so there was only one path to follow. Forward.

'Ayo Gorkhali!'

They ran on, with the lieutenant giving covering fire from a blood-covered and captured machine gun.

A long trench, dug through tree roots is next and its occupants rise and attempt to stem the flood of Gurkhas. The wrestler, eyes dimmed by blood flowing from his wound, takes a bayonet to the chest and crying out drops his rifle, but draws his kukri and slices open the throat of his killer, his last act. Another Gurkha passes from war into peace but the wave of Nepalese crashes into the defenders.

There are no shots fired now - to the delight of the Gurkhas this is close quarter fighting. Each one of their blades had been sharpened so that edges were thin beyond measurement and they had held such weapons from boyhood, practicing in farm and field until the tool was an extension of their arms and, just as Minraj had foretold, the enemy were no more than walking corpses. The heavy blades rose and fell like scythes through ripe wheat; the very design of the blades aiding in the slaughter, first slicing into flesh and then cutting deep into bone with little effort.

Minraj slid past the thrusting bayonet of a man with corporal's stripes and slammed the sharp edge of his Kukri flat into the man's shoulder drawing it down to the elbow, his efforts at sharpening allowing the blade to part flesh until it hit bone which splintered beyond any surgeon's skill to repair. The man howled in agony and clamped an unwounded hand over his shoulder in a futile attempt to staunch spurting blood but Minraj ignored him; the man was effectively dead and so no longer a concern.

His next opponent held a long knife and believing its length gave him an advantage, he stabbed forward in a fluid movement which indicated much practice. The blade cut through Minraj's twisting body, cutting through his tunic and drawing a long bloody line along the side of his rib cage. He felt no pain only a sharp wetness which served only to enrage him still further, but now it was time to show that where a long blade had failed a short blade would not.

Simple geometry and even simpler mechanics gave him the advantage; it would take time for the longer blade to be withdrawn back to a position where it could strike again, but Minraj's Kukri was already pointed forward. He lunged, stamping his left foot forward as he had been taught, the point of his knife crashing through his opponent's chest, the weight of the blade dragging his arm down so that an edge, microns thin, hewed a passage from heart down to gut.

'Marchu talai!'

'I will kill you!'

He had withdrawn his kukri and was already swinging the knife in a long arc which would surely sweep the enemy's head from his shoulders, but his threat was uttered to a man rendered deaf by approaching mortality. Red blood and blue tinted gut spilled from him and he toppled back into the trench, leaving Minraj now wincing from pain but without further enemies. Or at least nearby enemies; the orchard may have been cleared but the farmhouse still remained in enemy hands. Already a bloody lieutenant was ordering men forward, just as other officers were ordering their own men.

To follow the lieutenant was easy, for the man ran forward under a covering spray of bullets which much to Minraj's dismay did much damage to a building which he coveted. But war has little regard for the rights of property and Minraj ran with the lieutenant to reach the front wall of the farmhouse.

A hand reaches out of an upstairs window and drops a grenade onto the lieutenant's group where it explodes with a steel-scented blast; two die and others are wounded, but the danger is seen now and the window reduced to splinters of wood by angry Gurkha rifles. The hand is seen no more.

The men from Nepal also have grenades and these are thrown in succession through the windows which flank a shut and barred door. The windows are blown out in a gale of glass and dust, the door creaks in agony as stout hinges fail and the Gurkhas burst through firing into the room.

There is no resistance to their shots; a kitchen is filled only with broken pottery and smashed pans, while a living room holds nothing more than splintered furniture and the broken bodies of men. There is only silence and swirls of smoke that drift in the summer breeze.

As if by a miracle two photographs remain hanging untouched on the living room wall and Minraj stares at the stern faces of a man and woman long dead. Obviously, they are the ancestors of the now vanished farmer and he tells himself that perhaps one day his face will adorn the wall or a similar wall. It is a good thought, this dream of Minraj Tamang, farmer, husband and father of many strong sons, but alert ears hear the ceiling above him creak softly and the Gurkhas stiffen even as a machine pistol is fired down into them.

The bullets are fired blindly, for centuries old beams and cut planks lie between the shooter and the targets, but quality of aim is overrated sometimes and some shots strike home.

Minraj is the first to move to the stairs to combat this new menace.

It is then he sees the thrown grenade. It tumbles down from one wooden step to the other, falling slowly it seems, taking its own time to descend.

In silence it speaks, for the noise of his comrades firing upwards disguises its intent. But still it falls, bouncing down from step to step until, wooden handle pointing upwards, it comes to rest at his feet.

Time, already slow, stops and then flashes forward as if ashamed of its lethargy. Minraj stoops to pick up the grenade, intending to hurl it through the broken window. He does not intend to die, few men do, but the slow tumble down the stairs has wasted vital seconds and though the grenade has left Minraj's hand and started its journey it explodes scant inches from his body.

There is no pain. From a moment of dawning relief that he has removed a danger to the moment when non-existence claimed him is a time invisibly thin. There is no pain, no pangs of grief or regret, but Minraj's body takes the full force of the blast and in doing so saves his comrades, who stare first in shock and then in anger.

Terrible is their revenge when they burst up the ruined stairs. Pleas for mercy are ignored. This is no time for pity, but to teach the lesson that to fight the Gurkha is to embrace only death.

Later when the battle is over, there will be time for hurried ceremony and dry-eyed grief, but for now there is but a single thought.

Ayo Gorkhali.

A man could make a good living from land such as this; there were low hills for goats, pastureland for cattle and flat fields for grain.

And a cemetery.

A small cemetery, proudly kept and neatly, without so much as a blade of grass out of place.

And in that cemetery lies Minraj Tamang.

For this land is his.

His.

IN THE DARK

They were scouts and saboteurs, killers in the dark.

Many nations had seen their birth, many nations had raised them, but now all fought beneath a single flag. All had taken the same vow.

Kill the enemy, kill without mercy, without ruth, without pause.

In Spain they were a nightmare legend, feared and dreaded by sentries and generals alike. Like poison tipped thorns they struck and then vanished, leaving only horror behind. Sometimes a single man, sometimes a building, a car, a train or a bridge. But always the target was studied, always there was a plan and always there was death.

Tonight, in the dark they had gathered, in soft dark garments matched with hard dark faces.

Tonight, in the dark there were whispered voices, thin grins and careful gestures…and tonight, in the dark the killing begins.

They were the Second Guards Regiment of the Asturian Republic.

And they were in France.

It was a hot night without a breath of wind to thin air thick with warmth and so the door was left open the better to give comfort to a body overheated by a thick uniform and the heat from a hundred glowing tubes that could pluck voices from the air and turn the invisible into sound. But tonight, the radio was silent, the telephones were mute, and the bright brass of the telegraph refused to chatter.

Night radio duty was undoubtably boring and sitting on a chair was surprisingly hard on the body.

He stood up and stretched, ripping the headphones from ears pink with effort, turning towards the door and gasping in shock, for the doorframe held not empty air but a figure dressed in deadly black.

The figure gestures with a curiously thick-barreled pistol and he presses a spine cold with sweat against the warm wooden wall of the building.

And still the figure remains silent but spares a glance at the radio and the bank of telephones and then turns back towards him without expression.

The curious pistol sighs almost without sound and he feels a blow to his chest as a small calibre bullet hits him in the chest. He slumps and stares without comprehension at the blood that stains his tunic and so never feels the coldness of a pistol pressed up against his left eye or the second shot that blows out the back of his head.

Neils Erikson was a long way from his native Copenhagen, a long way from a lost family, but he had found a new home and a new family that had honoured him with the first kill of the night.

He gave his victim no more thought but sat in a newly vacated chair and waited for orders.

There was more killing to come, but for now his part had been played.

The sentries had some excuse; two hours lost sleep had little reward out here in an obscure village. Two hours of pacing staring into the blackness knowing that sleep once disturbed would be hard to recapture in this hot sticky night. So, they had some excuse for not seeing black shapes that saw them all too well, some excuse for not hearing black cloth rustle as the figures leapt on them and some excuse for last panicked thoughts as sharp blades bit deeply into their throats.

Once again there were no words from the black clothed assailants who crept into the barracks and stood over sleeping men.

Silent pistols, twins to the one Erikson had used spoke muffled words while already bloody knives plunged into throats as a final insurance.

The tiny garrison was dead, the night was dark, and the killing was over.

The villagers slept on, though lightly for the night was warm, but for the men from Asturias the night had just begun.

'Get a bloody education!'

Marcel Goscinny's father was a hard-working, irascible man and overfond of wine, but he saw something in his second son that required nurturing.

Of course, that nurturing often took the form of a beating with the buckle end of a belt, but that was only greater inducement to escape and escape he did, attending the École Supérieure D'électricité in faraway Paris, but that was many decades, a wife and three grown up children away.

Now he sat in his bed next to a trembling, grey-haired wife staring at a black-clad man who stared back at him with white eyes set in a black painted face.

There was no hate in the eyes and that was a comfort. Still it was not every night that a man was disturbed from his slumbers by intruders and for that alone the man deserved an ounce or two of defiance, so he hardened a voice that was on the edge of deserved retirement.

'And to what, sir do I owe this pleasure?'

There was no quaver in his voice despite his age, but his challenge did not give the expected result. Instead the eyes widened in humour and white teeth began to laugh.

This was a man he decided. Upon waking and finding an intruder in his bedroom his first instinct was to place his body in front of his wife.

Though the deed was no more than a reflex it was still a brave act and his words afterwards showed that the man's courage ran deep and so his laughter held no mockery but only respect.

This was a man, grey haired and wrinkled, but much of a man so he held his hands out to show peaceful intent and gave a small bow to the pale-faced woman and for a moment felt his lost wife and child smile in approval at this act of good manners.

The moment passed for there was no time for memories, but only pressing duty.

He allowed a pleasant smile to run onto his face and began to speak.

The man's laughter died away and Marcel listened as he spoke. The French was poor and very hesitant. It held tones that spoke of a far brighter sun than had ever shone on this water-filled valley, but despite the hesitation his words were gentle enough. He introduced himself as a colonel in an Asturian regiment who had been sent to perform an unpleasant but necessary task and instantly upon hearing those words he felt his wife's arms wrap protectively around him, but he untangled them with tender force. If he was to be assassinated it was better that she be far away, and he would plead for her life.

It was obvious that as he was the chief electrical engineer for the region, so must he be an important figure and certainly one worth killing, but he had capable deputies and a wife who deserved to live and spoil grandchildren and so the choice was obvious. He began to frame the words that would allow his wife to be spared while sacrificing his own.

It was a good speech, he thought, simple and dignified, one that would soften even the hardest heart.

It was also entirely wasted.

He cursed himself for his clumsy speech; he had mastered Basque and even a little English, but at French he was no more than schoolboy, learning only the words that had migrated to the strange military language spoken by the Allied armies in Spain.

He had thought to calm but had succeeded only in alarming and it was time to redeem the situation. He replaced his smile with a look of sorrowful contrition, turning not to the man but to the woman. 'A thousand pardons, Madame. I had no wish to cause fear. There is no danger. I need to take your husband for only a few hours and then I will return him.'

In his native tongue such a speech would have a hundred flourishes and compliments on the woman's dignity and beauty, but in French his words were stripped of any decoration and he feared that only further insult had been caused, but realisation broke on the woman's face.

'My husband will be safe?'

She did not ask about her own safety and his heart warmed to a wife as brave as her husband and so he stepped forward and kissed her hand in genuine affection.

'I promise, Madame. I ask only that you stay safe in your bed.'

His words were ignored as the woman rose in her nightgown and began to hand her husband his clothes.

'Your good shoes, Marcel, wear your good shoes, do not shame me in front of this young man.'

She received a look of loving exasperation from her husband and then a farewell kiss and soon the shoes were outside in a dark night lit only by stars.

A small car was waiting for them, the car a familiar one with German markings, but the driver was not a German, but a man clad in black like his colonel and without a single word he threw the car into gear and drove up a familiar road away from the village to a forest of odd-shaped poles, glass-topped lattice work and uncountable miles of copper cable that ran web like from pole to lattice and back again.

This was Marcel Goscinny's domain, here the power of captive water was turned into pulsing electricity. Here his word was law and there was not a centimetre of ground that did not fall under his sway.

It was as a king that Goscinny spoke as he got out of the car to see himself surrounded by a score of men who blended into the darkness with ease. 'Well, what is it that you want? What is it that is so important that you wake me from my bed and cause my wife such fright?'

The answer came back swiftly through the darkness, though with a curious reluctance. 'This dam is small, but it lies at the head of others and through it flows much electricity. To destroy the dam is beyond our powers, but the mechanisms that control the power must be smashed.'

And there it was. He had asked and he had been answered. He was king here, but his kingdom was about to suffer grievous harm.

Thirty years work gone. Thirty years gone in a single night. The thought ran in sad circles round and round, refusing to stop.

Thirty years of effort and toil.

Thirty years.

He gave a great sigh and then there was only silence.

'This is far from my wish, Monsieur.'

The colonel's words hung in the air between them almost as a plea for absolution. Goscinny could not know how tired the colonel was of killing or how, despite much effort, the ghosts of a lost wife and child clung to him, but for some reason his forgiveness was important.

He was king here and kings must rule, and kings must decide.

He thought of his wife, he thought of his sons taken to fight for a German invader and thought of a lifetime building a kingdom.

Kings must rule and kings must decide.

He turned in his best shoes and gave a single order.

'Come with me.'

The colonel must wait for clemency and ask for understanding later, but the man must be aided now for if a kingdom was to be destroyed then it was better by far to have a king give the orders.

He led the colonel's men to the forest of glass-topped towers and showed them where best to place explosives. He showed them where to drain cooling oil and to close forever the circuits which warded against error or harm. He showed them many things with a heart hardened to stone and a single thought that refused to die.

Thirty years.

Thirty years.

And yet kings must rule, and kings must decide.

And at last, he led them to the control room, brushing aside and calming the sole night watchman engineer.

For he was king here, his word was law and kings must decide and kings must act.

Alone.

He hesitated, hands above the levers, shaking a little from old age and from emotion.

Thirty years, but as king he decided.

He pulled the levers down, sluice gates awoke from night time sleep and the blockaded waters began to flow.

Pull the levers a little more and the waters flow with full force, spinning up generators that sing high-pitched songs of power and might.

Electrons surge and sway, awaiting their turn in the transformers who wail in distress, for cooling oil has vanished.

The generators, mighty beasts of cast iron and spun copper hear the wailing and cease their spinning, diverting water away from their spinning spools, but a king's hand reaches out and they are forced back to their work.

The transformers wail anew and then die.

One by one they die in showers of white sparks and the dull glow of melted copper, but still the work of a king is not done.

He signals to the colonel who gives orders and small charges do their grim work.

The tall trees of wood and steel topple, dragging down cables in a tangle that will take long weeks to solve while remnants of once uncountable electrons fizz and spark filling the night air with smoke and the smell of a far distant sea.

Switching gear, delicate creatures of cams, dials and wire die under explosive hammer blows.

And then it is over, the king has acted, and a kingdom has fallen.

Thirty years.

Gone.

Gone, vanished as if seasons hot and seasons cold had never existed.

Downstream from here puzzled women and frustrated men would curse a man who had taken a last kingly act and was now king no more.

Nothing but time would bring back this kingdom and his reign as king was over and a new king must now be found.

A kindly hand was placed on his shoulder and he turned to find himself staring into the sad face of the colonel.

'This was far from my will, Monsieur.'

There was still pride within Marcel Goscinny and even former kings can give absolution, so he took the proffered hand and gave gentle encouragement to a man who looked as if Hell fire was a preferred location.

'What now?'

The colonel gestured to the nightwatchman who was being tied to his chair. 'A similar fate awaits you and your wife.' He held up his hands in supplication as Goscinny began to protest. 'I do not break my word. This is for your own protection. In this way you may play the part of victim.'

As promised Goscinny was returned to his wife and their bindings were cunningly wrought to give the appearance of security while inflicting no pain.

The colonel gave a last look at Goscinny, admiring his courage even as a shade of envy passed through him.

The old man had been given that which had been denied him; a long life with a loving wife at his side and children to see ripen.

His life had been cursed, but the curse was not of Goscinny's making so he raised his hand in a last salute.

We will not meet again, Monsieur, this is goodbye. Take comfort in the fact that you have played your part bravely and…' Despite his efforts an image of a lost wife and child came to him and it took a bitter swallow to wipe away the vision and continue… 'and you still have a family to protect. Adieu, Monsieur.'

There was other work to do in the dark hours. The Asturians had stung, but now it was time to withdraw and it was better to withdraw with but a weak pursuit.

A swift walk took him past a barracks reeking of murder and onto a small wooden building that sprouted antenna by the dozen and was connected to the world by a dozen telephone lines.

Neils Erikson had been waiting patiently for his colonel and smiled as he came in.

'Now, colonel?'

Erikson's hands connected batteries to the radio which sprang into life with a muted hum. In a panicked voice he began to tell of an attack on the dam by resistance fighters. He pleaded for help and then long before his Danish accented German could be discovered he cut off the conversation in mid-sentence.

His work now done, he fired a last parting shot into the telephone bank and then left the building and the rapidly cooling body of its former operator.

Erikson had played his part; he had killed, and he had laid bait to entice…for the killing was not over.

The night was a good friend to the Captain, for in daylight few men could look at him and not shudder. The last lick of a flamethrower had melted him even as the wax melts in the summer heat. Ears were fused to a hairless skull, while broken lips hung from a chin that was red with scar tissue. Eyelids that worked but imperfectly shielded orbs black and pitiless.

A lesser man would have retreated within himself and retired from the world, but the Captain was not a lesser man. Instead he was a man who defied his doctors and rejoined a regiment that had no time for charity or sympathy and asked much of its members.

The night was a good friend to the Captain, but an ill one to his foes, for while others had been busy destroying, he and his men had been busy building. And a pretty trap they had wrought, built of wire and explosive, bullets and bombs and now all was ready, and the Captain waited with hard-taught patience while the hot wind blew, and the stars whirled in their courses.

One hour and then two, while far away a headquarters sent messages to dead men who had guarded a dam and at last tired of this amusement and sent out a reconnaissance.

One hour then two, for the headquarters was far away and thin, for many men had been stripped from it to fight for the Reich and caution was their watchword. France was beginning to fill with enemy forces and such caution was necessary.

Yet the Captain too was cautious and had built his snare with skill. In the purple light that heralds dawn the two motorbike outriders never see the thin steel wire that cuts into flesh. They are the first to be entangled, but faster than minds can comprehend others follow in swift succession.

The road bed under an armoured car erupts like an angry beast and throws it on its side, dark shapes rise from out of the darkness and pour streams of silent bullets into trucks full of screaming men and what the bullets in their mercy allow to survive sharp knives remove from life.

There are no prisoners. The Asturians are graduates from a hard war and all have taken the same vow. No mercy to the enemy, no ruth to the foe. Then again prisoners would be a burden to men who must sting and then retire.

But the snare has caught, and it will be a long day before a new pursuit can be formed.

They were the Second Guards Regiment of the Asturian Republic, scouts and saboteurs, killers in the dark and tonight they had killed and tonight they had stung.

But a new day had just begun, and it was time to retreat… and plan murder anew.

WOMEN, WIVES AND GIRLS

In a way it was all Ethel Fosdyke's fault.

Ethel had a reputation as a girl who was free with her affections and Charlie Higgens hoped that the outlay of two gin and tonics plus the price of admission to a double feature at the local cinema would give him access to those affections.

He was wrong. Either two gin and tonics was insufficient lubricant or the rumours about Ethel were no more than fabrications. Whatever the reason in the darkened cinema Ethel resolutely resist his wandering hands and force him to sit in frustration while the huge screen flickered and glowed.

The first film was some mindless romantic drivel where unlikely characters broke into tuneful melodies at odd moments.

Charlie was as bored as Ethel was entranced. She sat on the edge of her seat in rapt attention, attention that should have been devoted to Charlie and his wandering hands. He sat there in increasing frustration while the film wound to its inevitable happy ending and then Ethel, along with every other woman rose and took her place in the queue that led to the woman's toilets where inscrutable and interminable ablutions took place.

So inscrutable and so interminable were the ablutions that Ethel had not returned to her seat when the cinema darkened once more and the news reels began.

Pathé News promised the viewer glimpses of the world in easily digested pieces and this particular reel showed the continuing war in Spain. Madrid had fallen to the Fascists, but Northern Spain fought on, declaring independence and fighting on, with the commentator describing with impeccable accents the after effects of a Fascist bombing raid.

And it was there on the screen that Charlie met the girl.

The girl was perhaps five years of age and hovered just above the point of emaciation, and the cameraman, with an eye to his audience, had focused on the girl.

Her town had been bombed and the inhabitants with dogged determination were doing their best to clear the rubble. The girl, too was helping, but unlike the others she had slightly different priorities.

One hand certainly helped, lifting half bricks and pieces of wood and placing them with dainty fingers on growing piles, but Charlie was not concentrating on her working hand but on the other which resolutely held onto a small doll with ill shorn hair. It was obvious that such was the girl's love for the doll that she could not bear to part with it, even for a moment.

The girl noticed the cameraman, smiled and held up her doll for the world to see.

And at that moment Charlie's heart broke. To see such innocent pleasure amidst such devastation woke in him a strange feeling and an urge to help the girl and her doll.

Ethel returned as the news reel was ending and the second feature began. This time she seemed a little more affectionate. Perhaps she had changed her mind or perhaps the gin and tonics had finally worked their magic, but Charlie was no longer interested.

He had found a new interest now and knew exactly what needed to be done.

'Your mother will have a fit.'

Charlie's father was a broad shouldered man with muscles formed by a lifetime of dock work. He took a meditative sip from a fresh pint of bitter and looked at his son. 'An absolute fit and no mistake, and it will be me that gets it in the neck, son. I mean why now? We'll be fighting the buggers ourselves in a few years, you mark my words.'

This time his words were accompanied with a long, heartfelt gulp of bitter and a satisfied belch.

'Why go to Spain when they'll be on our doorstep before too long? I mean you've got a good job and maybe it's better to wait.'

This last point was a good one. Charlie had a good job driving a lorry through the night and out to farms and depots in Kent and Sussex, bringing in fresh produce for Covent Garden Market just as the dawn was breaking.

A good life, well paid and free of major responsibilities, so why was he willing to give that up and go and fight in Spain when there was peace here?

The answer was the girl of course. He never saw Ethel Fosdyke again, but the girl had stayed with him and would not leave. He had to do something to help; if not the girl, then those around her. He tried to explain, but knew that he was failing. His father was a practical man who saw his son's future as one that followed a familiar path and not one where foreigners were shooting at each other.

At last Charlie ran out of words and his father stared back at him in mute incomprehension, swallowing in one last gulp the remaining portion of his beer.

'Well, son you're over twenty one and can do whatever pleases you, but I'm telling you now, your mum is not going to be best pleased.'

He shrugged and pushed his now empty glass towards his son. 'Your round, I think.'

'Name, age, occupation and country?'

Charlie's questioner was a bored looking man in his late forties who wore the insignia of an unfamiliar army while sitting in an office that bordered a half bombed Bilbao dockside.

He was also an impatient man.

'Well? Hurry up man, I haven't got all day!'

Charlie gathered up his thoughts and took a deep breath 'Charlie Higgins, twenty two, lorry driver, British.'

A predatory gleam appeared in the man's eyes 'A lorry driver, eh. What have you driven?'

Charlie gave a long and pride-filled list of every vehicle he had driven, never noticing the gleam in the eyes becoming harder and more lustful while a finger was tapped against lips in contemplation.

And it was then that Charlie was trapped with a seemingly innocent question.

'Do you think you could drive a tank?'

'You are a fool, Ingelesa!'

The words were harsh but true. For he was a fool who had misjudged what everyone about him had taken for granted and was now suffering for it.

Everyone else had covered themselves from the power of the Spanish sun but Charlie was used to the smoke dimmed London sun and had revelled in the solid warmth that a far stronger sun had given him. Alas that strength came with a high price and now a bright pink Charlie could not move without pain, and to wear a shirt was to pile up agony on agony.

'You are a fool, Ingelesa!'

The words were spoken again but this time softer and they were accompanied by the application of a soothing cream that took away a little of the agonizing burning.

And thus it was that Charlie Higgens was introduced to the love of his life.

Miren Etxenike was a teacher until her classroom was bombed. After that she shared the hate that all Basques had towards invaders and gathered around her several female friends who crewed tanks and were given equal status with men.

It was an odd beginning, but the bonds of war wrapped themselves around the bonds of love in a chain that only death could break.

And so it was.

They had fought together while a world gradually caught fire, fought while France fell, while his native land held. Fought together until the last battle.

The battle of the lake was an Allied victory. German resistance was smashed and the Basque tanks had played their part but to give respite to a hated enemy was no part of their creed and the tanks rolled on, with Charlie and Miren side by side. He felt her death rather saw it, though he heard the panicked calls that told too late of the minefield and a cautious look told all that needed to be told.

Anti-tank mines were certainly unkind to steel, but to weak flesh they were cruel indeed.

He didn't need to see what the inside of the tank was like, and besides his friends formed a living barrier so that his mind would not be forever seared by the sights weeping eyes would see. And so he buried Miren in the same way he married her, in the company of friends and in the shade of tanks. After that was a grey nothing that he fought to escape.

He had no wife, for she was buried, and his parents were far away, but now his path forked. A new regiment was to be formed not for common tanks but for the machines that flowed from the devil minds of Percy Hobart and his acolytes.

There were tanks that carried bridges and tanks that threw rockets or huge shells. There was a tank for every occasion and every one of them could trace a lineage back to the clanking, hand-built monsters that had broken a German army and every one of them he had mastered, though his favourite was the short-barrelled tank that spewed a circular blast that hewed men from life.

Today, with a long journey through France behind him, he and his tank had become a permanent part of a farmer's field because his fuel gauge told the same sad tale as every other tank.

He knew that his generals lusted after supplies for this forgotten army in the same way that misers yearned after treasure, but with the whole world on fire, fuel and food, bullets and boots came in thin tides that ebbed and flowed and at this moment the tide had most definitely ebbed.

That was not his concern. All he knew was that his engine was running on fumes and the cows which chewed contentedly all around him were far more mobile.

And yet they were so close. So close to the end of France and the border. So close to the end of the war.

There was a rumour that Hitler, pummelled from the west and pressed from the east would retreat south for a last stand in the mountains. If this was so, then the little multi-national army would be the anvil against which Hitler's last armies would be hammered.

But not without fuel.

So Charlie Higgins, exile, widower and driver stared moodily at French cows who gazed back with placid contentment.

He was stuck, fixed in place, bonded to the earth.

And it was all Ethel Fosdyke's fault.

WAITING AND DIGGING

'It's all rather simple.'

Lieutenant Donaldson had just returned from an intelligence briefing and had gathered his men around him to impart the wisdom which he had received.

'The intelligence chaps seem to believe that at this stage Hitler has options open to him. The first option is surrender, hopefully to us rather than the Russians, though I imagine that just changes the choice of hangmen. The second option is to fight on, either against us or the Russians or both. Again that won't end well. There is, however a third option and I will come to that in a moment.'

He paused and looked at his men; each one an individual and each one a survivor of a harsh war and a harsher upbringing, and yet they had accepted him which he realised was a great honour and an even greater responsibility.

Always listen to those more wise and never complain…ever.

Thus were the lessons learnt and he felt a surge of pride that these men were his.

He took a cold breath of morning air and continued.

'As to our immediate situation. We now know what we are up against, and for this information we should give thanks to Corporal Frazer and Private Taggert.' He gave both men a wry smile. 'Take a bow gentlemen!'

Razors and Taggert, a dark complexioned man who rarely smiled, had been given the task of bringing in a prisoner for interrogation, and in the dark hours of yesterday morning they had returned from the valley below, dragging back with them an unhappy looking prisoner.

His invitation to both men was of course refused, but he had acknowledged their skill in front of others and that was important, so after a brief wait, he continued.

'Now our prisoner, after some persuasion has revealed that our opposition are two large Kampfgruppe consisting of infantry, armour, artillery and other assorted units. Now we've faced these sort of people before. We know their strengths and weaknesses, but these two groups seem to be unusual in that there are a high proportion of SS in both groups - not just Waffen SS, but the black-shirted variety as well. As well as those chaps there seems to be a large element of combat engineers included, which means mines and all sorts of nasty surprises.

'Which leads me to the third of Herr Hitler's options There are strong rumours which tell of a plan to move Hitler south into Bavaria and Austria, and fight the war from there. It's easily defended terrain and allows him to maintain contact with Northern Italy. Our little army coming up from the South could threaten that, as could the Americans coming down from the North.

'The intelligence chaps seem to think that the two Kampfgruppen have been sent to slow us down while preparations are made behind the scenes for the arrival of Hitler. That being the case our duty is plain. We destroy our enemy and march on, so that when Hitler does arrive, the Scots Guards are there to greet him with a truly Scottish welcome.'

He smiled reassuringly.

'As I said, it's all rather simple. Now are there any questions?'

Colour Sergeant McFarlane looked up from the frozen ground and uttered a single word.

'Petrol.'

The Colour Sergeant was a man of few words, and his single word went straight to the point.

Petrol. The little Allied army was no more than a diversion, an attempt to confuse the enemy, and as it was a diversion it received supplies in a half-hearted fashion, petrol in particular.

Not enough petrol meant no trucks, no tank support and no towed artillery; all the things which gave infantry aid and gave the soldier help would be missing. Without petrol the enemy was as safe as if it were in barracks. Worse still if the enemy had petrol then they had the advantage and that was an uncomfortable situation to be in.

Donalson had no answer to give, so he shrugged his shoulders in agreement with the tall Scotsman and looked up at the lowering clouds which had taken on a peculiar yellow tinge. It looked very much like snow was about to fall, but McFarlane was right.

Without petrol the Scots Guards were going nowhere.

Percy Hobart's voice was as icy as the weather which battered against the walls of the commandeered house. 'No, I will not. Such an act would be foolhardy in the extreme and I thought we had learnt that lesson in the last war. I simply do not have the ability to move from my positions and attack…

'What's that? Yes I am refusing, and anyone but a bloody fool would refuse as well…

'No I don't care where the orders have come from. They can come from the Almighty himself and I would still refuse, though I don't think the Almighty would be so stupid as to issue such orders.'

Jorge grinned. The older man held the telephone very tightly indeed and was speaking to a superior officer, not that Percy Hobart recognised superior officers, believing most of them to be bumbling fools, who would best serve the war effort by resigning their commissions and growing turnips or other useful vegetables.

Hobart's tirade continued, his voice still icy, though his red face betrayed his anger. 'Frankly I don't care what you do. By all means have me relieved, and if you think that I fear a Court Martial, then let me assure you that I do not. In fact I would welcome the chance to expose such rank incompetence!

'What do I suggest? Are you seriously asking such a question at this late hour? Have you not read my reports? Are you completely unaware of my situation? I lack sufficient supplies to move forward, some of my tank units are down to no more than half a day of running time and I need hardly remind you that soldiers fight very poorly indeed with insufficient rations.'

Hobart was now trembling with rage and Jorge signalled that he wished to take over the conversation before his friend suffered a medical emergency or worse, threatened a superior officer with bodily harm.

The phone was thrust into Jorge's hand and Hobart walked over to pace in front of a window which was swiftly becoming opaque with blown snow.

Jorge's voice was gentler than Hobart's, but no less insistent as he explained that no further advance could be made. They had done well with the supplies given, they had caused the enemy to retreat in a hundred small engagements, but now an already small army was smaller yet with casualties and guarding lines of communication and had now come up against serious and concentrated opposition.

'To move against such an enemy without sufficient fuel, without ample bullets or shells would be to squander all that has been gained and would cause the loss of many Asturian and Basque lives, all of whom were volunteers and whose deaths would be sure to cause political waves which could swamp even the most secure of military careers.'

Jorge's threat was a subtle one, but effective, and he pursued the advantage. He would accept some supplies now, with the promise of more to come and if that promise were kept then much could be done about the enemy. He could sense retreat on the other end of the phone, but long experience had taught him that an enemy in withdrawal must still be harried so he put a false warmth in his voice as he reminded the senior officer that it was still General Hobart's prerogative to seek a Court Martial and that if such an event were to occur then he would be delighted to appear as a witness.

There was a long silence on the end of the line and then a click as the conversation ended and Jorge burst into laughter. 'I think we will have our supplies soon, my friend. Your anger and my pleasantries seem to have persuaded a locked box to be opened, but for now we must sit on our arses and wait. Courage my friend! We fought in Spain and made weapons with our own hands. We cut the balls off them then, and we will do so again.'

General, Sir Percy Hobart stared at the young Asturian general and gave a rare smile which turned into a rarer laugh. He had taught Jorge much, building on an instinctive grasp of warfare but at heart Jorge remained what he always claimed he was - a simple peasant with a peasant's crudities and imageries.

But he was right, the battle would be one fought right where they were, so he unrolled a map and pointed to its centre.

'There, Jorge, that's where we will hold them. Your Basques to that ridge?'

Jorge nodded.' And your Scots. They work well together, now as for the rest, this is what I suggest...'

All through the short day the two men planned and dispatch riders by the dozen rode half blinded by the snow along paths made invisible under a blanket of whiteness. They planned until both were satisfied and the room grew dark as the last of the daylight was denied admittance by iced-up glass.

They were ready; there was little fuel, little in the way of supplies and a lot of snow, but they had fashioned a battle with the tools at hand and now all depended on that last and most versatile of tools.

The soldier.

They would have to fight without tea and that was sufficient tragedy, but the ground was cold and iron hard and that too was an unwanted heartbreak. Still there was work to be done and no amount of grumbling would conjure up tea or soften the ground, so with pick and shovel they attacked the earth with cold bodies and lungs that burnt frozen air and wrapped them all around with its smoke.

All day they worked, Basque and Scot together, digging pits great and small for both men and beast until the last rock surrendered and the last ounce of dirt was carried away. Then the tanks could be driven into the pits so that only their brazen mouths pointed out towards the road and the marshy stream that it followed.

But all was not ready yet, for there were now great black scars on the land, vivid against the still falling white, and even a blind man would be able to point at them. Now was the time to put away the pick and the shovel and walk back to the tree line with axe and saw and bring back branch and twig, the better to hide steel and flesh, the better to lie in wait.

The falling snow completed this disguise, until white blended with white, until man and beast, Basque and Scot were as one with the land.

All through the remains of the day they waited and through the dark night.

Waited, while the snow pattered and the wind rose and stole heat it did not need.

Waited for the enemy to come.

THE BEARDLESS ONES

They'd watched the Ivan's charge.

Wave after grey-coated wave, the war cry coursing from every throat, the rockets shrieking, the guns booming.

They'd watched the Ivan's charge.

With every comrade at their side, silent, with hot guns in ready hands, with the love of Fatherland in their hearts.

They'd watched the Ivan's charge.

And fought.

But the Ivan was many and they were few, and German blood lay red upon the white snow.

Red and white, the colours haunted their dreams and filled their waking hours.

But still they fought, for they were the chosen ones with the lightning bolts on collars and pride in their uniform.

A merciful Führer took them away from the Ivans, took them away from the war cries and shrieks of rockets and bade them rest and refill their ranks with beardless children.

And they trained the children, trained them to be hard, hard like them. Trained them to love the Führer, love him like they did.

But most of all they trained the children to remove pity from their minds; an enemy of the Führer was an enemy of the Fatherland and an enemy of the German people, and so must be shown no pity.

And when they had finished training the children the Führer had new plans for them. They were to travel to the French Marcher provinces where a small army challenged the might of the Fatherland.

They were to join with others and tear this army, rip it and shred it, and then turn and join in the great battles that were being fought in Belgium and Holland.

It was snowing the night they advanced, but that did not matter; they had fought the Ivan in the snow and they had trained the beardless ones how to hide in the falling snow.

Their target was the chicken farm, garrisoned by hated Spanish who had brazenly thrust a German army from their lands. Such impudence had left many debts to pay and they told the beardless ones of the many slights and insults that must be revenged.

And the beardless ones listened and eagerly drank the words. They vowed to avenge battles lost when they were still in school. All stood in ill-fitting uniforms with rolled up sleeves and whispered to themselves that they were the true heirs of the Führer and they would show devotion.

Silently they crept up on the chicken farm, killing sentries until they were masters of a crowd of milling dejected prisoners.

The beardless ones knew exactly what to do.

For they were the true heirs of the Führer.

It had been a cold night, and they had shivered in their thin blankets while their breath steamed and formed icicles on the inside of the tank.

A cold night, an uncomfortable night, a night to remember.

Now the night was ended and it was no longer snowing as a grey shadowless sun rose, revealing thick clouds that seemed all too eager to either deliver more snow or complete their descent to the ground.

But for the moment the clouds did neither and Grandfather looked out through the vision slit. He could see the narrow, elevated road in the distance and tiny sparkles that flew up from the half frozen stream that bordered it.

And he could see the willow tree.

The tree had been sad at the approach of winter and had wept long auburn leaves onto the ground as tokens of that sadness, but the tokens now lay under the snow and though the tree slept it had assumed a new duty as a way post.

The willow tree stood behind the road and he had drawn an imaginary line between the muzzle of his gun and the tree. The line was a trip wire, invisible and waiting.

His gun was already sighted in for range and for distance and the solitary tree waited, just as he waited, just as his crew waited, just as Lorena waited.

Lorena was ready, Lorena his tank, named after a lost daughter.

Lorena had killed before, killed men, killed guns, killed buildings but this morning would be different.

This morning she would kill her own kind.

There was no sunrise, no glorious pink herald, that with bounteous trumpet announced a new day.

This morning the trumpet was silent and only a slovenly grey told of the new hour.

But pink or grey it was time.

There was a polite nod from Mr Donaldson and Colour Sergeant McFarlane gave the order.

'C'moan mah lucky lads intae th' holes wi' ye.'

The company jumped into the foxholes hidden behind piled snow and more than few grumbled about the cold, but Colour Sergeant McFarlane had a ready answer to their complaints.

'Ne'er mynd yer cauld arses, they've bin colder oan a Saturday nicht oan th' Caledonian Road ah bet.'

'Tis nae mah arse a'm worried aboot,' replied a soldier lying face down on the snow covered ground, 'tis mah…'

'Haggerty' interrupted McFarlane in mock exasperation, 'Kin ye aye shoot straecht?'

There was an answering grin from the soldier. 'Ah kin shoot gey weel, thank ye Colour Sergeant.'

'Then worry aboot yer anatomy some ither time, or dae yi'll waant me tae haud yer haun th' neist time ye fin' a five shilling?'

There was a great laugh from the company at this sally and Donaldson knew that this was banter between trusted comrades. The Caledonian Road was a famous road in Glasgow, for it was where prostitutes plied their night time trade in shop doorways, and five shillings was no doubt the going rate that was charged. The thought of the strict Colour Sergeant holding Haggerty's hand while the Private, trousers around his ankles took full value from his five shillings was highly amusing and he chuckled as he took his place in a fox hole.

He was still chuckling as the first Basque tank opened fire.

The row of tanks waited, perfectly hidden in the snow, dark pines behind them, their branches weighed down with white drops which fell in hushed splashes.

But that was the only sound. No birds sang and no wind blew. All was peace and he had time to glance at his loader. The boy was growing; Nature, long denied was now treading a familiar path and he could see in his grandson his daughter's face and the man the boy would one day be.

There was time for an exchange of smiles and not for the first time he wished his daughter could be with her son. She had married a good man, a man who had looked him in the eye and sworn to care for an only child.

They had given him a grandchild and promised more, but there was to be no more, for war took them both, and they now lived only in the land of memory...and the face of his grandchild.

But in their remembrance and for grandchildren never born he waited, for his was the steadiest hand. To wait and hold onto the sharpest weapon of the soldier....surprise.

They were tired and dirty. Men who had driven long distances often were, but they had orders, a destination and a time of arrival, which was why the sign was so unwelcome.

The sign was obviously new and freshly painted, but the words were enough to give pause to anyone who had fought in Russia. *Partisanen! Achtung minen!*

A crudely painted skull and crossbones accompanied the words and if that was not enough discouragement then the Feldgenarmerie motorcycle and side car that blocked the road was sufficient argument to stop the little convoy of worn trucks.

A man in the uniform of an Unteroffizier was lounging against the sidecar smoking a cigarette and held up a lazy hand even though the trucks were obviously stopping and walked up to the first truck making motions which indicated that he wished to converse with driver.

The driver wound down his window, letting in a blast of freezing air and the pleasant tang of burning tobacco.

'The road ahead is mined, take the detour through the fields, pick up the road a little past the cross roads… See?

The Unteroffizier pointed at a map and his finger traced a line that led to a small junction where four roads met. 'Two kilometres only, keep the trees on your left, then when you reach the crossroads turn right until you hit the main road. Understand?'

The route seemed clear enough, but the reason made no sense.

'Mines?'

The Unteroffizier made a grimace of distaste.

'See the sign? Fucking partisans, they're everywhere, and the road ahead is mined and booby trapped, but you should be fine. Just keep between the flags.'

He pointed to where a line of flag-tipped sticks ran arrow straight into the distance. 'The Engineers have checked the path and the way is all clear.'

'Thank God for Engineers,' replied the driver. 'Mine work is for bloody heroes.'

'No argument there, son. Now be off with you.'

There was a pause with no effort by the driver to move on and the Unteroffizier grew impatient.

'Come on, son, stop pissing about, I haven't got all day!'

'Could I have a cigarette? I've run out.'

There was muffled sound that was half laughter and half exasperation and a nearly full packet was handed over.

'Here, make them last.'

The unfamiliar words on the packet were sounded out as the driver examined his prize. 'American cigarettes?'

'Don't ask.'

Feldgenarmerie units were notorious for many things, not the least was their ability to acquire contraband goods.

Not asking questions was also good advice so he gave thanks and wound his window up and dutifully began to lead his little convoy between the flags with the smoke of first class American tobacco in his lungs and his eyes searching for deadly partisans, never knowing he had already met the most lethal of partisans.

He would never know.

Wilhelm Kreis watched as the first truck reached the far end of the field and then erupted in a ball of flame while the rest of the convoy came to a skidding, panic-filled stop.

No one got out of the trucks which was very wise, as Wilhelm and his assistant had scattered a few anti-personnel amongst the larger ones; not many, because members of The Second Guards Regiment of the Asturian Republic tended to move lightly.

The truck convoy, minus its leader was due for an uncomfortable few hours until they were rescued, but that was no concern of Wilhelm. The Fascists may have beaten him in Stuttgart, they may have forced him into exile to fight in Spain, but it had all turned out for the best; he had a new home and new comrades, all of whom hated the Fascists.

He looked at the metal gorget which hung round his neck and was the badge of a German military policemen. Its former owner lay dead in a ditch not too far from here, along with six others, a small addition to a growing casualty list.

No one argued with the Feldgendarmerie, they had a well-deserved reputation as humourless martinets and as such they moved without hindrance, but as rumours of renegade policemen began to circulate that would change, adding to the disorder natural to an advancing force.

Which was entirely the point.

Sometimes the Second Guards killed with the knife, sometimes with the gun or the bomb, but always they sought to spread fear and confusion.

And today Wilhelm Kreis had done just that.

At first it was the expected; two motor bikes and a car scouted the road, stopping at odd intervals to check the snowy road for any signs of interference.

They passed and Grandfather waited, for these were not his targets, but then came the ludicrous and the comical.

A half battalion of infantry on bicycles attempted to move along the snow covered road and even at a distance he could see that the heavily laden men were struggling to push through the snow. Then cruel nature laughed, for she had laid a patch of ice under the snow and as the leading bicycles hit the ice, their tyres refused to grip and a dozen men tumbled to the ground with legs and arms asprawl.

He could not hear their curses at such a distance but he could feel their pain and gave a little chuckle as he explained to his crew what he could see.

For a moment he wished to send them a round of cannister to add to their discomfort, but it was long range for cannister and besides they were not his target so he waited, for he was a cautious man and exceedingly patient.

The bicycles were very sensibly abandoned and the men proceeded on foot with that high stepping swaying gait which is the best way to move through snow.

Soon they were lost to view and still Grandfather waited, holding his patience like a precious coin that needed to be spent at just the right moment.

He waited, his crew waited and the sleeping willow tree waited.

Waited as the first enemy tanks rumbled along the road.

They were proud of their power these tanks, proud and sure of victory, their way forward had been swept and they were the masters of the whiteness, queens of the battlefield.

They never saw the willow tree.

'Fire.'

Grandfather had waited until the gun tip of the first tank lined up with the willow tree and his shell flew through the air, arching slightly and cooling as the cold air gripped it with frosty hands.

It was not a killing blow, the shell hit the forward track bogie, smashing it into shards and causing the track to unspool and the tank to slew out of line.

It was not a killing blow, but Grandfather's second shot hit the juncture of turret and body and burrowed inside as far as it could go. A shower of white hot steel swept through the tank, skewering the crew with glad whispers as wet flesh tried in vain to dampen hot metal.

The trailing tank received similar treatment to its leader and now the column was trapped…and the slaughter began.

There could be no disguise now; gun smoke and the exhausts from straining engines showed the Basque position clearly and the enemy, veterans to a man began to turn.

But in vain, for ambush is the sharpest and truest of weapons and each Basque had picked out his victim long before Grandfather's first shot. A hard rain fell, and hard flames rose from target after target as the veterans burned.

A dazed victim took the only sensible course of action and left the road seeking to move past the now burning first tank, but alas wisdom came too late and Grandfather's shot hit with practiced comfort, ripping the turret from its ring gear and sending it spinning through the air where it hit the sleeping willow, severing several snow crusted limbs.

Grandfather felt a momentary pang of regret, for the tree had been a good and faithful friend, but then allowed the regret to be washed away by gladness for he had killed an enemy that had reduced his bloodline to a single twig and that was a crime that merited eternal punishment.

The road was no more than an assembly of burning scrap iron now with survivors trying to out run high explosive shells, but this was a thin army, made thinner by ill supply and shells were in short supply so he ordered his comrades to cease fire.

He had used sharp surprise to kill, but he knew what would come next.

It would not be pleasant.

'Single shots only, Colour Sergeant.'

'Verra gud, sir.'

McFarlane's voice was not particularly loud but it did carry so that every man in the company heard.

'Ye heard Mr. Donaldson. Single shots ainlie, pick yer targets.'

There was a pause and he spoke again. 'Do ye hear me thare, Haggerty?'

'Ah dae indeed, Colour Sergeant, dae yi'll waant tae come 'n' haud mah haun?'

McFarlane repressed a smile. He had been caught with his own words, but there was no sting to the man's words, just as there was no longer any time for laughter, so his reply held just enough humour to show he understood the joke and just enough severity to end the conversation. 'Haggerty, if ah come ower thare ah will uise mah haun tae gie ye a guid beltin,' sae ah will.

'Now haud yer tongue 'n' keek tae yer front.'

Donaldson hoped his order was a sensible one. Bullets did not grow on trees and supplies of them had been a little intermittent of late. Besides which he had learnt this past Summer that his company were all excellent shots, especially Haggerty who had exchanged his former employment as a pickpocket for that of marksman.

There was burning in front of him now as the Basque tanks fired, picking off the enemy in ragged salvoes that burnt where they did not destroy.

He watched one tank burn after being hit, its crew opening hatches to escape the hot hell which was growing inside. An iron lid was lifted and the black dot of an escaping head was seen pulling itself free.

Haggerty spoke a single word, 'Mine' and the head exploded, the body falling back inside to be consumed by flames.

The rest of the crew fared little better, though perhaps this was a mercy when compared to the death flames would give, but at last only a few survivors remained, much to the annoyance of the Basques who had a mortal aversion to taking prisoners and opened up with the turret mounted machine guns in the hope of realising their dream of letting no enemy leave the battle field unscathed.

They were disappointed, for some, a fortunate few, still lived to stumble redly through the snow to find what poor aid could be given to defeated tankers.

Donaldson looked up at the melancholy sky. This would be a land based battle, no pilot would risk life, limb and aircraft in this weather and that was both a blessing and a curse.

That did not mean the sky was not deadly though.

He heard the oncoming sounds that hid in the clouds and repeated a childhood prayer… 'For what we are about to receive may the good lord make us truly thankful.'

And then the earth shook.

A fitful fire made of unseasoned wood burnt in the fireplace. It spluttered and threw out no heat at all, and Percy Hobart shivered, though Jorge with a peasant's stoic outlook seemed hardly affected.

Both men were looking at the map and saw the same thing.

The centre had held and was holding, but their left flank was under pressure. Already they had lost important positions and the enemy's plan seemed clear.

One Kampfgruppe would seek to hold their centre and right flank while the second threw its entire weight against the left flank and rolled it up.

Defeat in detail would follow and that they could not allow.

They had little fuel and no air support.

'We must fight this battle sitting on our arse's,' Jorge said, and he was right. There would no grand manoeuvres. This would be a slugging match where eye met eye and hand met hand in bloody embrace.

Still the left flank must be reinforced and Hobart's silent finger touched an as yet unused group and he raised a questioning eyebrow.

Jorge grinned in agreement. He had met that group and had been impressed. They were just the people to send.

It had been a good Summer. The land had been kind, the sun had been hot and the people had been welcoming.

A good summer. The battles had been small, but many, the enemy few but willing.

And what more could a man want?

And the smiles were never lost, though more than a few homeland villages would hear of death achieved with honour.

But now it was winter and the snow lay deep and heavy, and this too was good. For was not snow the blessing of the gods? They had been welcomed as liberators and the gods had seen the welcome and rewarded such kindness.

A heavy snow would give a bounteous crop in the following summer. All knew this and all imagined the tall stalks and the fat cattle that would surely follow the appreciation of their gods.

But now the smiles were broader and the words were joyful and they danced like schoolboys that had been given an unexpected treat, for at last they were to join in the battle that had muttered all around them throughout the day.

They would march to the sound of the guns, march because fuel tanks boomed like hollow drums.

March lightly armed because heavy weapons must be left behind.

March happy that once more shining blades would run dim with enemy blood.

March with a war cry on every lip.

'Ayo Gorkhali!'

'The Gurkhas are upon you!'

The hill stood wrapped in trees and the trees stood wrapped in snow and each tree filtered the grey sunlight so that the ground beneath them was a patchwork of half-light and full shadow that folded itself over a tangle of fallen and discarded branches

And all around was a silence that deafened with its power. The wind moved no branches, the birds took no wing; only the silence ruled the wood, turning it into a nightmare world that recalled childhood tales of witches and goblins, but they were far from childhood and crunched through the snow and into the woods, pushing on, strong legs striding through the snow, ready fingers wrapped around triggers and every breath frosting the air.

Somewhere further on and higher up had retreated the enemy and this grey morning they were both pursuers and avengers.

They found the Basque tanks easily enough, for even the poorest tracker could follow the spoor left by such heavy beasts.

The beasts lay in a voiceless row, green and grey paint merging into the half blackness. Not moving, not acknowledging their presence. They made their approach with caution as beasts such as these could kill with the merest twitch of muscle.

But the beasts remained silent, gun barrels pointing away from them and they began to relax. There was no sign of the crews and the tanks had become prizes of war.

But war is a fickle woman and it would be best if the beasts were killed, so the first tank was selected for destruction and its entry hatch was opened, the better to drop a wrecking grenade.

The grenade was unneeded, for the opening of the hatch triggered a swift clock that ran with blind obedience. The tank exploded, every stored shell detonating in the same instant, shattering the hull and turning it into ten thousand iron barbs that delighted in their transformation and slew without mercy.

Some men simply vanished, transformed into gobbets of flesh and splinters of bone. Others were not so fortunate and spent eternal seconds gazing at ruined bodies with sightless eyes before the mercy of death overtook them.

Too late the dazed survivors remembered the tales told of how the Basques had booby trapped a city and how that city had eaten an entire German army. Too late they remembered the tales of cunning and of a spite that burned without end.

And then the cries began. Loud and eerie cries that echoed off the trees so that the wood seemed to burst into an evil life that vanquished even the powerful silence.

The cries rose and fell and each seemed to end with a sarcastic laugh that promised only pain. They began to shiver with fear and look around, trying to locate the sources of the cries, but the trees kept their secrets very well and each had vowed never to betray.

They sprayed bullets into the trees in an effort to silence the cries and for a moment the noise of their bullets drowned the cries, but soon magazines were emptied and the cries began again, mocking them for their impotence, and then one by one they died away, leaving the trees in silence.

They began to move forward, fearing that a deadly tank had performed not a finale but an overture.

They were right.

Their battle had just begun.

It was the right thing to do, the best thing to do, and the only thing to do.

There would be a good deal of danger in the next few hours and the future of the Basque homeland lay in its young and not the grey headed relics who commanded the now abandoned tanks.

The solution was obvious; their young boys would be handed over to the care of their faithful Scottish companions while those with too many years would vanish into the trees and lie in wait and seek to delay, hurt and dismay.

It was the obvious solution but the children protested. Had they not fought through summer and the fall of the leaf? Were they not skilled with knife and gun? And what of the ties of blood and love?

There was no time to persuade and rough Scottish hands gripped young arms and gave no chance for further argument.

It was time to vanish into the trees to play a game played on Basque mountain tops long ago. An old game, much loved by the children, a game of hide and seek, but this time there would be no happy laughter and those caught would pay a high forfeit.

Slowly, without any haste the old men placed themselves where they could do the most harm and then one by one they began to sing the old cry that told of love and death.

'N' how fur wis ah tae ken he wis a bishop?'

Months before when it was summertime Private Haggerty had been telling Donaldson how he was inducted into the Army.

'A bishop shuid keek lik' a bishop 'n' nae a mark!

Whit richt haes he tae donder aboot in civilian claes?'

Haggerty had seemed to believe that in some way he was an innocent victim in the affair and had been trapped unfairly.

'A ten shillin' note 'n' a pocket watch wis a' ah took fae him, 'n' fur that he calls oot th' entire constabulary oan me! Yon Baillie looks at me, 'n' calls me a habitual criminal. Sentences me tae four years solid or jyne up. Noo whit kind o' choice is that tae gie a man?'

Haggerty had by then relieved Donalson of a wrist watch and wallet without any apparent effort and certainly without his officer feeling their loss.

'A man o' mah talents bein' forced intae penal servitude!'

The watch and wallet had been returned with the assurance that such an impressive talent would never be practiced on him in anger, for he was their officer and ill would be the fate of any who crossed him.

He had nodded his thanks, glad that his company of thieves and robbers had accepted him.

Back then they had already proved themselves a formidable company, presided over by Colour Sergeant McFarlane and the savage-faced Corporal Frazer who, despite it now being winter and the situation being more than a little desperate showed not the slightest sign of worry.

The enemy had been caught by surprise and had paid for their lack of awareness by the loss of a dozen tanks and two half-tracks. Retribution was not long in coming and an artillery barrage was far too accurate to be comfortable and the Scots and the Basques retreated to the uncertain comfort of the thickly wooded hill which lay behind them.

'Haggerty,' Donaldson's voice was very quiet, only a little above a whisper. 'Do you see that little chap with the binoculars?'

Haggerty squinted through the gloom.

'Aye, sur. I kin see the wee bastid.'

There were no more words to be said; Donaldson had pronounced sentence and nominated Haggerty as executioner. The range was long and the light was but indifferent, but Donaldson had no doubt as to the outcome. Neither had Haggerty; he adjusted the sights on his rifle with unhurried care and very gently squeezed the trigger.

The binoculars fell and Haggerty let out a frost filled sigh of satisfaction.

Their battle had begun.

Razors had heard the Basque cry before of course, then it had a laughing, joyful quality as each man showed their prowess before an admiring audience, but now it had undergone a subtle change. Gone was the laughter and the joy was entirely missing, replaced by a mocking hate that seemed to come from everywhere at once and it reminded him of the childhood tale of a spectral being who carried off the unfortunate and announced his arrival with mournful keening.

'Ye poor wee bastids, th' bogeyman's aff tae git ye.'

The Basques had given their youngsters into the care of the Scots and then dispersed into the woods to lie in wait just as Razor's childhood monster had lain in wait for its victims. He selected his Bren gun to single fire and sighted on a man advancing cautiously through the snow and seeking the shelter of a nearby tree.

The tree remained untouched; the Bren was a most accurate weapon and there was little point in advertising the platoon's main automatic weapon. He fired again, the single shell casing falling with a hiss into the snow.

Two shots, two kills and the mocking cries began again, for the bogeyman was lose in the woods and Razors battle was just beginning.

His breath came in short gasps that ended in sparkling fog that vanished like fairy gold. There could be no running in the snow-filled woods, for a billion snowflakes had joined together to drag at his boots, but the tree was his target.

The tree was large, old and stood half sleeping only a few metres away. If he could reach the tree he could rest against it and borrow a little of its strength. Slowly he forced aching legs through the whiteness until he was able to rest a shoulder against the trees rough bark and close his eyes for a seconds contemplation.

Closing his eyes was a mistake for he never saw the hand that reached round from the other side of the tree and roughly gripped his lapel.

Startled he opened his eyes in time to see a long knife rushing towards his throat and instinctively he flinched away from the blade.

And this too was a mistake.

For an unclean kill gave him time.

Time to feel the blade slice through skin.

Time to feel a sliced windpipe and warm blood.

Time to stare into dark old eyes and to see a grey moustache, framed by grey stubble.

He fell back into the snow and stared up into the branches of the tree and tried to call out a warning, but lungs filling with blood denied him the power.

Dimly he heard the shots that ripped into his assailant. Dimly he heard his comrades gather round him at the base of the tree, and he tried for a last time to tell of what he had seen.

He failed as death took him, and this was a last mercy.

For the old men hunted not alone but in pairs.

The two grenades sailed down out of the upper branches of the tree, aimed at the clustered figures below and both exploded just before they hit the ground.

Some were killed, some wounded. None were unaffected.

An old game this, an old equation, that told that a Basque life lost was no loss indeed if it took more than one enemy with it. For how else were the weak to destroy the strong?

The men were old and few. They had lost their tanks and given their children into the care of friends.

There was only the game to play now.

For the bogeymen were lose in the woods.

’Ye wull dae as yer teld, or ah wull beat ye all intae th' middle o' neist week'!’

The young Basque boys were arguing with the old men and though Colour Sergeant McFarlane spoke not one word of Basque, he understood that this was not the time to argue and his bellowing roar smashed any resistance. One by one the boys were led away. There was no time for argument and besides agreement had long since been made.

The Basque tankers and the Scottish infantry had campaigned through a hot summer and bonds had been formed, but war is hard on men of many ages and the old men worried that their children would be left adrift in a harsh world. They had spoken of their fears of early death and the Scottish battalion bethought themselves of their own childhoods and of their own children.

‘Let it not be so’ they replied, ‘If you fall then we will stand in your stead.’

And so it was agreed that each platoon would take a boy and stand guardian for him, for ever if required.

Mr Donaldson had promised that his family would welcome Wee Jimmy and treat him as one of their own, and McFarlane knew that such a promise was worth far more than any insurance policy, for the Donaldsons, if not overly rich were well connected and that few doors would be closed to a boy with such backing. He had gripped the boy none too gently and deposited him amongst his band of thieves and robbers who treated him as an honoured guest.

And so with the boys in tow and the old men hiding in the trees the Scots Guards began a slow retreat up the steep, thickly wooded hill.

A very slow retreat, with Mr Donaldson's company in the rear which is the post of honour in a retreating force, but still moving slowly, being careful not to be cut off and making every shot a reminder that the enemy faced men who were never more dangerous than when hope was furthest from their hearts.

Five times they made stands with Razors' Bren stuttering and Haggerty proving that he was as adept at removing life at long range as he was at lifting wallets close in.

Five times they stood and five times the enemy concentrated against them for they were many and the Scots were few.

Five times they were forced to turn, with the bullets flying past them and seek new shelter, the better to survive, the better to resist.

Five times, until they came to a high place where rocks outnumbered trees and a last stand could be made.

A fearful place this, where the bones of the earth stood proud and the soil supported only snow.

Behind them lay a great precipice which forbade escape, in front of them gathered a numerous enemy and above them afternoon snow clouds looked down.

Grimly the Scots arranged themselves amidst the rocks in a great crescent so that no flank might be turned lest all be dead.

Five times they had stood, five times they had retreated.

There would be no more retreats.

'Fook me, tha' things a right bastid.'

Razors' comment was all too accurate and Donaldson winced as a nearby rock face exploded into shards that brought forth cries of alarm and pain.

Neither side could use their mortars, for experiment had shown that thick clustered trees proved an all too effective armour. Outgoing shots had a depressing tendency to hit outflung branches and explode prematurely, while Scottish shells hit upper branches all too often.

The battle descended into fusillades of small arms, with the enemy firing out of the dark woods while the Scots fought from a rocky bastion.

And so it would have remained, with no side gaining an advantage and with the Scots content with having dragged the enemy up the hill and away from other battles, but in the late afternoon with a fleeting day taking last breaths the enemy proved annoyingly resourceful.

Somehow they had dragged or carried up the hill a small mountain gun and begun to fire out of the gloom.

Like many mountain guns it was not overly accurate, but the range was short and casualties began to mount. The battle began to turn against the Scots and Donaldson knew what the messenger was about to say even before he said it, even before it had been delivered, even before its owner had departed.

'It seems as if we are to be the stars of the show, Colour Sergeant…again.'

'Aye sur. Thir's a lot tae be said fur a posting behind th' lines, I'm thinking.'

'Maybe later, Colour Sergeant. Right now I'll be content to see another sunrise.'

Surprisingly Donaldson realised that his words were true, very true in fact. Battle removed the mundane from a man's life and made him concentrate on the truly important.

Tomorrow's sunrise, if he saw it, would be beautiful…and very important.

He glanced at McFarlane's face to see if he had undergone the same revelation but saw nothing. Either the man had long since understood or didn't care.

There wasn't time to discuss the finer points of philosophy.

There was only time to hope for a new dawn.

'Bide 'ere 'n' dinnae shift 'til ah come back. Comprede?'

Razors tried to put force into his voice and allow his damaged face to settle into a fearful scowl. He had placed Wee Jimmy behind a cluster of rocks where the wounded were being tended.

'N' mak' yersel' useful!'

A promise was a promise and they had told the old men that the children would be cared for, but in battle there is little safety and this collection of rocks was the best that could be found.

He got an acknowledging nod from the boy and turned his scowl into a tight smile.

'Guid laddie, now bide on,'

There was no more to be said and he walked away.

If he came back…that was the question, for Mr Donaldson had received fearful orders. The German gun must be destroyed and his company were to be the ones to do it.

Before the last of the light was eaten his company was to charge forward and ensure the gun did no further damage. The rest of the battalion would advance and give support but it was Donaldson's company who would make the last mad dash across open, rock-strewn ground.

This was the logic of war; a single company might be lost in defeat and the battalion would be no worse off, for the gun would still fire, but if the company succeeded then the battalion would be given some respite, even if every man died in the victory.

The logic of war took up residence in a dry mouth which refused to protest at such un-benign choosing, but others were not so controlled.

"Why u's?' was the question asked by Private MacLaurin, a former house burglar, who no doubt thought that having covered the battalion's retreat and suffered no casualties it was folly to push their luck any further.

McFarlane gave the standard answer, 'We're 'ere 'n' nae anywhere else, laddie.'

It was an old joke, and raised few smiles, but was enough to break a little of the tension and even MacLaurin gave a small, resigned shrug.

There was a series of small metallic clicks as bayonets were fixed and there were no more words to be said

Razors set his Bren for rapid fire held it low with both hands and walked out from behind a sheltering rock and began to shoot.

Colour Sergeant Andrew McFarlane had run before.

He had run from poverty into the Army.

He had run from the lines of Private Soldiers and into exalted rank.

He had run through harsh deserts and a summer fed France.

Run and run. Run and run.

And he was running still, except this time he was running towards an unpleasant future that seemed all too short.mHis breath was loud in his ears, harsh and ragged, drowning out the flood of bullets that flew out of the trees and extinguishing the answering roar of supressing fire coming from the rest of the battalion.

He ran using an old trick. Do not look at the enemy position, look instead at the yards ahead, watch out for ankle snapping rocks and tangling branches and give only occasional glances to his destination. That way he could not see the rifles which fired at him with deadly intent and so fear was dampened.

For though he ran forward, McFarlane was frightened but he had achieved a coveted rank and this was the price demanded by the crown and chevrons he wore on his sleeve.

So run, run forward, with short barrelled weapon in hand towards the tree line, with the cold ground beneath his boots, the high-pitched whistle of bullets in his ears and the taste of metal in his mouth.

He ran alone, deaf and blind to everything but the target, not knowing if others ran their own races or had taken a final rest from all racing

He did not know; he could only run.

And hope.

Lieutenant Donaldson was not alone and that was a comfort.

Others ran with him, though his Colour Sergeant showed a surprising turn of speed and was already several yards ahead.

But he was not alone. To one side Razors' Bren gave brief stuttering bursts while on the other ran the rest of his platoon.

The enemy seemed not at all distressed by the amount of fire the rest of the battalion was pouring on them and returned the favour with compound interest and the fact that thus distracted they were unable to concentrate their power on the running men was no cause for relaxation because more than sufficient was left over and the bullets snapped past him, each one disappointed that it had missed, but calling out encouragement to others.

A high whining scream flashing past his ear followed by a shocked grunt meant that he was a man short, but there was no time to see who, for the mountain gun was slewing round, a fatal mouth that could not miss.

McFarlane and Razors instantly dropped to the ground and the slow thump of the Bren was joined by the shriller notes from the Colour Sergeant's Sten gun.

The mountain gun ceased its movement for a few seconds as its crew flung themselves to the ground and this was all Donaldson and his men needed.

Jumping over the prone form of McFarlane they ran the last few yards into the woods where the now recovered gun crew were waiting for them.

They had much to do and precious few seconds in which to do it and he never remembered hearing the hoarse cry which came from his lips. Nor did he remember crossing the last few yards but he did remember his first opponent. An open mouth revealing rotting teeth, a dented helmet with flaking paint and a hand that reached for him. The hand wore a fingerless glove and he saw the glint of a wedding ring.

And then mouth, teeth, helmet and hand vanished. He did not remember pulling the trigger of his revolver and perhaps he did not - perhaps someone else shot the man or perhaps he merely tripped and was unharmed, but there was no time to wonder, for a new adversary stood before him and lunged with a bayonet tipped rifle which followed his twisting body with uncomfortable accuracy until he was pushed to the ground and a Scottish bayonet parried the German one and then lunged with parade ground efficiency.

A Glasgow curse went with the lunge and then a spare hand pulled him to his feet. 'Tha nearly git ye thare, sur!'

The grinning face belonged to McRoberts, who specialised in safe breaking and stealing from lawyers offices, even on one occasion from his own lawyer who was representing him on a previous charge.

He wasn't overly intelligent, but had a dancers grace which McFarlane had grafted onto much bayonet practice.

The practice had paid off, but still the seconds flew by and there was no time to give thanks, for the gun still had defenders and their reinforcements were close at hand.

There was only one order to give now, the order that every officer must know.

'Follow me.'

The Sten's bolt gave a final push forward and a last round flew out of the barrel.

Swiftly McFarlane discarded the magazine and inserted another. There was no time to spare. He could see where Mr Donaldson was leading a rush towards the mountain gun, but he could see dark reinforcements rushing forward to aid their comrades.

A long burst from a fresh magazine should give sufficient discouragement and give Donaldson time to do what must be done.

He rose to one knee and pulled the trigger of the Sten.

Nothing.

No kick from leaving bullets, no roaring sound of impending doom.

Nothing.

He pulled again as a long second took more than its fair share of time.

Nothing.

The Sten gun's well-known tendency to plague its owners by jamming had raised its evil head and there was no more time, for the enemy would not give him time and lack of time gave him only one option.

He rose, knowing that Razors would follow his lead and rushed the enemy massing to attack Mr Donaldson. A thrown grenade caused death but more importantly confusion extended by a staggered stream of bullets from the Bren gun. He scooped up a discarded weapon and worked the bolt, not really aiming but seeking to add to the Bren's discouraging chatter. He dared not look behind him at the gun, dared not hope that that two men could hold off such a host for more than a moment.

He could only hope that his death would be quick.

Donaldson resisted the urge to tell Haggerty to hurry; the man was aware of the need for speed but his fingers seemed to move with unbearable slowness, even though he was the best man for the job.

A lifetime of picking pockets had given him a deftness of touch which alone made this task possible.

Slowly, far too slowly the gun's firing pin and spring were released, followed by a shining actuator rod that held together the firing lever and both were dropped into a canvas bag that was draped over Haggerty's shoulder.

A wooden mallet looted from the gun's ammunition trolly was applied with great force to the sights and anything else that seemed susceptible to damage, and then the long moment was over and it was time to leave and to begin that most difficult of military tasks, the fighting retreat.

He could see McFarlane and Razors fighting a desperate and ultimately doomed holding action and he blew a sharp whistle that he hoped would cut through the hail of bullets but whether they heard or not, it was time to leave.

Haggerty gathered his pilfered goods and ran back with larcenous feet, while Donaldson's men retreated two by staggered two even as Donaldson blew and blew on his whistle trying to recall his two NCOs but the sound was overpowered by the crack and crash of battle.

He blew again, unable to come to their aid, unwilling to leave them behind and then placed both hands around his mouth and screamed out a single word, calling out the name McFarlane's mother had deemed appropriate for the first of her brood.

Perhaps it was the sound of an English voice, perhaps it was the shock of hearing a seldom used name or perhaps the sound overlapped with a small lull in battle, Donaldson never knew. He only knew that both men turned and ran towards him, grateful for the relief and then carried on running, retracing their steps and passing the body of Private MacLurin who had accurately foretold his own fate.

There was no time to recover the corpse or even check if flickering life still remained, for the sheltering harbour of standing rocks beckoned with stony fingers, and the defending fire power of the battalion gave but poor chance that charity would further reduce.

Donaldson's legs were knots of agony, his lungs twin pits of fire that demanded quenching, but the songs of flying bullets urged him on and he was at last able to throw himself behind a rock that threw off the bullets chipping away at its grey flank.

Only gradually did the knots untangle and the fire in his chest subside and he was able to offer a dry throated congratulation and receive from a grinning Haggerty a souvenir of a mad adventure. He was still holding the firing pin when Major MacMurray arrived to promise medals and recognition for all. It seemed that Haggerty had indeed succeeded in stealing the gun's tongue and now it would speak no more.

Rewards were undoubtably a good thing, but as the the night proper settled on the ground Donaldson knew that his true reward was yet to come.

He was looking forward to the next sunrise.

THE BRIDGE

The door hinges screamed with unoiled agony as Jorge opened the door and let in the blackness and the cold, though in truth the house was but a little warmer than the frigid air, for the green stick fire had long since turned itself into sulky whispers of smoke though none noticed the cold for there was a battle to be fought and the time to shiver would come later.

The night was black, the sort of black that comes from thick clouds blocking every last vestige of lonely starlight, but though nature hid herself, the works of man were on full display.

Brief flashes revealed the muzzles of great cannons, while swift bars of light crossed and recrossed the sky, vanishing and reappearing as the clouds lowered and rose. A purple and red flash rose from the ground and then with brief mortality died with a roar that distance muted into a fragile murmur and a ragged chorus of light lit the far horizon in answer.

This was his war, his war and the war of the old man who had taught him so much.

A war of positions, of defender and attacker where the enemy had too many advantages and the defenders too few.

Yet all was not lost, for the great wooded hill which dominated the battlefield still held, though it was now entirely cut off from the rest of the little army.

The hill defenders had the same orders as every other defender.

Resist like a wall and bite hard, make the enemy pay for every scrap of ground, make him wary and fearful. But the enemy too had teeth and was not at all fearful and from every quarter came tales of dreadful odds and constant attack.

But wars cannot always be won by standing still, sometimes there is the need to strike and Percy Hobart had pointed to men who had no fear and much courage, and who had been held in reserve.

Now was the time to use them and a place had been chosen.

He had seen all that he wished to see and had added a night time picture to spread maps and radio messages and he turned to re-enter the house, but as he did so he laid a gentle hand on his own stubbled face and lifted a wet finger to see if it could reprove the tale told by a cold cheek. The finger did not lie but sensed a rising breeze and a peasant's sense told him that soon snow clouds would be pushed aside and the morning would be blue with cold.

It was another factor to consider…later.

For tonight was a night to put faith not in wet fingers, but in modest men from far away.

Modest men who must win this night.

Or die trying.

They had heard the battles roar, heard the scream of shells, the music of death and they were not afraid.

No man amongst them was afraid of battle or of death. All had grinned at the thought of renewed war, but now seeing the task before them only the hardest of grins had survived.

The chicken farm had been held by two Asturian companies and had fallen early in the battle, and in falling had weakened one flank. The enemy had pursued his advantage, taking a crossroads and the twin-piered bridge that spanned an icy river.

Hard pressed were their comrades, with the flank now a dozen holding actions with each unable to support the other and where the failure of one would lead to the death of all.

The solution to the problem was simple.

Take the bridge, take the crossroad that lay just beyond, and so allow each unit to re-ally with others. After that, the chicken farm would be retaken and a dagger thrust into the enemy's attack.

A simple problem.

But now as the scene loomed large in their binoculars their hearts sank. The bridge and the crossroads were surrounded by flat, snow-filled fields, without cover other than a few trees and wide spaced hedges. To attack across such expanses would be suicide for the bridge and crossroads were well covered with machine guns and mortars. Their own artillery could not be spared as it was already committed in several desperate duels defending other hard held positions.

They were on their own, with their own problem.

And only one desperate solution.

'Ayo Gorkhali.' The words were whispered, not as a war cry, but as encouragement to a select few.

All had stepped forward of course and the choosing was hard, but at last forty men stood in the first of the night with the words of their comrades in their ears.

Without reply they stepped into the freezing river as one and began their journey downstream, half swimming, half wading over icy, slime-covered rocks. Theirs would be a long journey, filled with pain as icy air and water stole the heat from their bodies, yet they were a hardy breed raised in the long shadows cast by high mountains and the thought of future battle spurred them.

They vanished into the gloom with the only sound the gurgling of water as it rushed to the bridge. Their companions turned also, for they too had their part to play in the coming battle. They pushed through the whiteness that reminded them of home and placed themselves into the snow in long rifle range of the bridge and waited for the appointed hour, with every minute filled with thoughts of the forty men who must win this night.

Colder and colder grew the night, colder and colder grew hardy bodies but as the glowing hand of a watch met its appointed destiny they watched as a single flare rose up to vanish into the low, night-time clouds.

It was signal enough and they rose up out of their snow trenches and began to fire at the bridge.

It was enough, enough to deceive...they hoped.

The river was cold, as cold as the milk white rivers that flowed from the flanks of their homeland peaks, but not a man complained, for who would wish to show weakness before brave brothers?

So they pushed on, bitter water rushing past them and leading the way until night-accustomed eyes saw the bridge and the twin towers upon which it rested. And there they rested, twenty men to a tower, huddled together the better to share heat, for despite hardihood fingers and toes were numb with cold and both would soon be needed. An old trick this, much practiced in the land where the wind has claws and the snow falls deep, but at last they began to climb, mortared stone by mortared stone while distant brothers shot round after round so that every enemy eye was drawn to the sounds.

A wet boot fails to find purchase and scrabbling hands grip with bloody fingers and for a moment every Gurkha freezes and seeks to melt into the frozen stones, but there is no challenge and the climb continues, inch by inch, stone by stone with every breath soundless, with every eye full open.

They reach the parapet and lift cautious eyes as a near spent bullet strikes sparks from painted ironwork, but no enemy sees it, for there are other Gurkha bullets and to spare. And now the compliment is returned by bullets and shells made in Germany that tear up the snow in flurries that rise and fall in brief beauty.

Out in the defenceless fields brothers hurt and die, but the eyes must not care, for they have purposes of their own and now they stand on the road bed and turn to the left and the right and rush at the ends of the bridge.

For a moment all is well, but then a cry of alarm and a single rifle shot is heard soon joined by a ragged chorus.

The Gurkhas stand naked before the rifles, for they carry only the Kukri, the better to travel and the better to climb.

Some died before their blades could cleave flesh but each end of the bridge became a twin battle for the Gurkhas had closed and this was the fight they loved best. Their blades rose and fell in a deep blackness lit only by the white flashes of rifle fire. Eyes were of little avail, so for the Gurkhas the formula was a simple one; reach out and feel for the wool of a German uniform and so find an enemy, and then cut, slash or stab as the humour chose.

A dark contest and a bloody one, for there would be no retreat and no surrender. But the guardians of the bridge were many and the attackers all too few, and inch by inch the attack was forced back.

And then out of the darkness came a rumbling shout that came as herald to a second wave of attackers, for brothers tiring of sheltering in the snow and impatient at hearing of un-joined battle had risen up and joined the fray.

The defenders were crushed between greater and lesser millstones which ground so fine that only the fortunate survived.

The bridge was theirs, but there could be no surprising those that held the crossroads and already the Gurkhas stood stark in magnesium light that gave aid to punishing fire.

The bridge was no place to be. It confined their ardour and made targets of them and all were as one mind as to the best course of action. A flood of men poured off the bridge, some with stolen rifles some with machine guns ripped from cooling fingers or grenades lifted from abandoned pouches, but however armed all were bound to one vow.

Kill the enemy and win eternal renown.

A four-barrelled flak gun cuts a bright furrow but a grenade gives pause and seconds later two thin-edged blades take a head apiece and the gun is turned traitor and causes new carnage.

A machine gun reaps in a field of men and unknowing mothers are given cause to weep, but the Nepalese tide is in full spate now and its waters overwhelm the gun leaving it broken and staring up at an uncaring night sky.

Rifle speaks to rifle in similar tongue and blood that would be red in daylight hours turns the snow black, and still the war cry is the same.

'Ayo Gorkhali!'

A last rush by the defenders is beaten and then the crossroads are abandoned. A broken enemy flees, seeking solace in the snowy fields and the Gurkhas shout for joy and turn into hunters that must capture a floundering foe, but strict whistles call them back from such a sport and this is but just, as a broken enemy may be left to harsh nature.

Messages must be sent now, the wounded attended, the dead mourned and the knowledge of prisoners ripped from them.

They must be the link that rebinds scattered friends and they must hold what has been so dearly bought.

But in the morning, in the brightness of a new day they would claim a fair reward.

In the morning the chicken farm would be theirs.

He was losing the race, he was certain of it. A whistle blowing monster was pursuing him with deadly and malicious intent.

The monster laid a hand on him and spoke.

'Mr Donaldson, sur, time tae wake up.'

The nightmare broke and the monster transformed itself into the face of Private Haggerty.

'Tea sur, ainlie hauf a mug 'n' it's a bawherr weak, bit tis as guid as ah cuid make. Best git it in ye afore it gets cauld.'

Donaldson nodded his thanks and gulped down the hot brew.

He had Colour Sergeant McFarlane to thank for the rest, and in truth it was most needed, for as the night had grown, so had the enemy attacks. Enraged by the loss of their gun, they had pressed forward, leaving the shelter of the trees and lapping up to the very edge of the battalion's sheltering rocks.

But the harder they pressed, the more compact became the Scots, fighting almost shoulder to shoulder until the tide ebbed.

Twice more in the night the enemy had rolled forward seeking to prise the Scots from their rocky castle, but the Scots are a stubborn race and refused the tide.

'Best git some kip, sir. Ye'll be o' na uise unless ye dae.'

The last attack had been beaten back and the woods were once more filled with the eerie cries of the Basques. McFarlane's words were as close to an order as a Colour Sergeant could give an officer and the murmured words of his company only added force to them so he pressed a shivering back against an ice-slicked rock and closed iron heavy eyelids to dream of whistles and monsters.

It may have been the sleep, it may have been Haggerty's weak tea but he felt new strength running through him and he rose and stretched cramped limbs.

The snow clouds had been banished and he looked up at a star-filled sky while feeling the cold breeze which had sprung up while he slept. All was quiet, even the whisper of men was stilled and no shots came from the dark trees.

He was about to comment on the stillness when it was broken by a Basque cry that rose and rose and then ended with a joyful laugh.

'Scotland amis! Bastardos scarper! They go! We come to you, ne shoot pas!'

Gradually figures began to appear from behind the trees and walk towards the Scottish line with a gait that spoke of pride and sadness, as for every ten men that had walked into the trees only five walked back and the boys rushed forward seeking out a familiar face.

Some were crushed by disappointment and some were raised by joy, but all cried and Donaldson was surprised to see his own tears added to much Scottish grief.

'They go.' Wee Jimmy's hand was held tightly as his grandfather explained to Major MacMurray. 'They leave, mucho muertos, mucho wounds. You go, maintenant?'

MacMurray needed no further invitation and issued orders that had the Scots assemble and slowly they made their way down the hill, guns still at the ready, passing the dead, the dying and the wounded.

All were ignored, for the enemy must be pursued, though last magazines were thin with hunger. The enemy must believe that to tarry must be to summon yet more hurt.

And the enemy did believe, and scattered and husbanded shots gave truth to that belief.

Tree to tree the enemy retreated, finding again the footsteps that marked previous hours, seeing again the blood stains that marked an upward march.

They made a last stand by the river and bright morning sunshine saw the willow tree take further punishment, but Scottish resolution had broken their will and one by one they melted away or died where they stood.

The battle of the Scottish Guards and Basque tankers had ended.

VICTORY AND TEARS

They were the beardless ones and they did not fear.

Had they not been chosen by those who had fought the Ivan? Had they not been trained to feel no pity?

Did they not wear the same lightning flashes as the older ones, the survivors of Russian fury?

They had taken the farmhouse and dealt with its defenders as they had been taught and this was as it should be, for enemies deserved no pity.

And now they were the defenders, for the bridge had fallen and the crossroads had been taken, but they did not fear, for the farmhouse was strong. They were young and without pity and they would make the Fuhrer proud this sparkling morning.

They garrisoned the chicken sheds and dug pits in the melting snow for iron hard ground resisted their hands and waited to show their prowess.

They did not have long to wait, for the enemy lusted to close with them and the chicken farm was their promised reward.

A flurry of mortars fell onto the ground and a chicken shed burst open in an explosion of men, splinters and birds. The birds escaped on futile wings while the men were cut down by a machine gun that hours before spoke only German.

But the beardless ones were not without answer and their own mortars caused enemy mortality and their own machine guns sent forth enquiry They did not fear, for the Fuhrer was watching and they waited for the assault knowing that an outer ring of rifle pits and sheds must be reduced one by one ere the farmhouse come under attack.

And so it should be, but the attackers were men of high courage and no little thought and saw that the farmhouse must be the first to fall and not the last.

Prayers to gods were made and assurances made that all would meet once the battle had ended and then the Gurkhas began their attack.

No mad rush this, but planned and considered, for already there were too many widows for comfort and it were best that fewer more were made.

A winding path had been seen that would break through the ring and reach the farmhouse, but the defenders did not know this and abided secure in the knowledge that they and they alone gave law to this coming battle.

The opening notes were just as they expected; small rushes by men who moved with disturbing grace broke against a pre-positioned defence and the defenders smiled for they knew that far away the Fuhrer smiled also. But the smiles faded as first one and then two rifle pits died under grenade-hurled wrath and then the wooden sides of a hut burst into flames and a flurry of panicked birds.

Amidst feathers and flames the Gurkhas burst through the flank of the defenders, slaughtering the beardless ones before they had chance to turn smooth faces towards an unexpected threat.

Each boy died in the knowledge that they had failed the Fuhrer, but the men from Nepal cared very little about such things and turned their attention to the stone built farmhouse.

A long treasured rocket designed to kill armour was deployed and showed that it could blow holes in walls as well as steel. Disdaining front doors the Gurkhas entered, cleaning room after room with Kukri if they could, with gun and grenade if they must.

Too late the remaining beardless ones realised that they were defeated. Some ran for safe harbour, but others thought of the Fuhrer and fought on.

Long minutes were taken to subdue these true believers and so it was some time before the walled garden was found.

In summer months the garden fed many. Peach trees lent against the walls and sucked in brick-stored heat. Cabbage and carrots fed on rich soil while a raised bed housed herbs that gave flavour to both meat and green leaf.

But that was summer and this was winter and the garden now grew a more evil crop, for the beardless ones had committed a terrible crime. The snow had attempted to hide the crime, but a warming sun had declined to be partner to such deception and the snow had no choice but to reveal the bodies of the original garrison.

Some had been shot at a distance, some at close range and some while attempting to climb the sleeping peach trees, but all were dead and none would see the hills of Asturias ever again.

The eyes of the Gurkhas gazed upon a crime scene with uncomprehending eyes. An enemy was an enemy so long as he resisted, but when his fingers pointed towards heaven then he was an enemy no longer.

Where was the joy, where was the honour in killing the surrendered?

They offered prayers and some burnt a few sticks of precious incense until their officers bade them leave and surround the small wood where some of the longer legged beardless ones had fled.

After that there was nothing to do but report and wait.

After his first battle Jorge had cried. In private of course. Armies, even a victorious army had no need to see their young general weep at the loss of so many men and the gaining of so much pain.

That had been in the bad old days when the Basques had retreated to their mountain tops and the Asturians stood alone, but still he had wept at this first victory.

He had never wept again, but had learnt the art of war with an almost childlike innocence. At first the Asturians fought alone, but as the flames of war grew hotter and bolder allies appeared and the victories piled up, the one upon the next.

But he had never cried again.

Until today.

Today he cried, and like that long ago day the tears were of loss and pain, but now for every sorrowful drop that fell two far different tears fell and these tears were tears of anger that burnt bitter and bright.

He had forgotten, forgotten, forgotten.

This was war in its pure state. Stripped of honour, stripped of chivalry and of every code save that of self-serving logic.

He had forgotten, forgotten, forgotten.

This was the Spanish war rewritten on a French palimpsest, war without ruth, without quarter and he wept that he should see such things again.

He felt a hand on his shoulder and turned to see the one true friend he had in all the world.

Percy Hobart had taken off his thick glasses, but whether this was because icy cold and warm breath made them useless or whether it was to make the man blind to the horrid scene he could not tell, but the hand was comforting.

'I'm sorry, Jorge, really I'm sorry. I never thought to see such things again.'

Hobart was not a man to give in to emotions, for like all of his breed he distrusted emotions and kept them under strict control, and unlike Jorge he showed no tears.

'How many have we lost?'

At first Jorge could make no reply, every word failing to pass a throat swollen with anger and pain, but at last he was able to give an answer.

'A little under two hundred, many shot at close range. There are powder burns. The bastards did not wish to miss!'

He pointed to a stand of trees which clustered small outbuildings.

'But we have them, some of them at least. They ran like rats and like rats they will die.'

There was now a flat calmness in Jorge's voice that alarmed the older man. The calmness had replaced the smiling joy that was the young Asturian's usual trademark.

'Jorge, what are you thinking? Are you…?'

Jorge brushed fresh tears from his face, for what he was about to do was breaking an already broken heart. He reached out and gripped Hobart by the shoulders and drew him close so that his red-rimmed eyes could see clearly and his broken voice could speak softly.

'You have been dearer than a brother to me, been friend and teacher and I owe you a debt that can never be repaid, but now I must ask a further debt. Leave this place, leave it now so that your conscience may be clear.

'Leave now, I beg you and let what must be done, be done.'

Very gently he began to propel Hobart back to his staff car with his friend protesting and pleading.

'I am a peasant, my friend. Now let a peasant do a peasant's work. Please leave, I will call when it is safe to return.'

Hobart's car left and Jorge turned, hoping that what followed would not break a friendship.

But what must be done, must be done swiftly and he began to shout out orders.

His friend would not approve of those orders of that he was certain.

But they would be carried out.

And of that he was certain also.

'Can you do fifteen kilometres?'

The question was asked in the mixture of languages which had been birthed in the Spanish war. Charlie Higgins understood the question well enough and replied in the strange amalgam of clashing verbs and nouns.

'Yes, just. I'll be running on fumes though.'

'Just so long as you get there. Here's a map reference. Take the two crocodiles with you.'

And now Charlie was puzzled, his vehicle and the others of his squadron were all specialists summoned and dismissed as the occasion demanded. But what cause had they to be moved now that the battles roar had died away to scattered shots?

War and loss had made Charlie a fatalist though, and an order was an order, so after a brief discussion with the commanders of the other two vehicles the little convoy set off to their appointed destiny with Charlie in the lead.

Charlie's vehicle was designed to deliver wholesale destruction at short range; a massive shell would demolish bunkers or sweep men and machines into oblivion. An unsubtle weapon, and effective, but his two followers, though weapons of war were also weapons of terror and, he hoped, weapons of last resort. For like the beasts they were named after their bite was a terrible thing to see.

Their journey was but a short one, with every yard marked with the debris of war and signs of struggle. They crossed a bridge, waved on by a smiling Gurkha sentry, skirted a smouldering building and oddly many flocks of frightened of chickens, which squawked their displeasure and eventually came to a clearing which bordered another set of buildings nestled in a large stand of tall, bare-branched oaks.

A man in a stained sheepskin jacket halted them and Charlie recognised the Asturian general who led both his native Asturians and the Basque contingent.

Strangely Jorge wore not his usual smile, but a flat face that bore not the slightest trace of emotion.

He returned Charlie's salute and told him to arrange his troop so that Charlie's squat gun pointed directly at the trees while the two crocodiles flanked on both the left and the right.

'Please wait, Sergeant.'

Jorge now turned to a tall, thin-faced Basque captain who walked up under flag of truce and demanded immediate surrender of all who inhabited the trees and the buildings, but Charlie noted that the words were in old high Basque, the old form of the language, untainted by Spanish. Very few knew this form of the language and he understood only a few words which was certainly more than those that were surrounded.

Naturally there was no reply, but as he now realised, the letter of the law had been observed. Surrender had been demanded and refused and it was no surprise when he received the order to fire.

His first shell fell short, though that hardly mattered with implements of such power. The blast wave caused trees to sway back and forth and every window of every building to lose not only glass but framework.

His second shot followed moments later and was far more accurate. It snapped branches and lifted every roof. Branches, roof frames and tiles then fell back to earth in a hard, clattering rain.

He waited for further orders but none came. Instead through his vehicles iron sides he heard twin screaming roars, for now the crocodiles spoke.

Not a single gun did the crocodiles possess only a brazen portal, but out of that portal poured a most compelling argument.

He raised up the tank's hatch and lifted his head out into the air to see two streams of bright flames arch down onto the roofless buildings and broken trees.

The flames splashed and reached out with searing fingers that clung with a madman's grip. Trees, slumbering since golden October became columns of twisting fire and the stones of the buildings cracked and fell apart.

Still the crocodiles were not satisfied and their throats vomited more flame and now the very ground burnt and it was impossible to tell tree from tree for the flames had joined to make a single snarling beast that made its own breath from the surrounding air.

Three more times the crocodiles spoke, burning the already burnt, teaching the same lesson over and over until all was ashes.

Nothing was left of the trees or the buildings and surely nothing could have survived the wrath of the crocodiles.

Except something did, something that resembled a human, but surely could not be.

Slowly and with all the assurance of a sleepwalker the figure stumbled towards a patch of un-melted snow, some reflex telling that in its coolness lay peace and serenity.

It fell, but instinct owned it and it rose again holding out imploring hands that held not a trace of fingers and crying out through long gone lips.

Once more it fell, never to rise again and a merciful pistol brought its journey to an end.

Charlie had seen such things before, and the sight did not shock as once it did, but never had he seen it done with such finality; never had he seen a target not just killed but obliterated and wiped away as if it had never been.

He looked at the now dead thing which had once been human and looked back at Jorge who was gazing at the scene of devastation with the same flat expression on his face and he asked himself *Why?*

Later he heard of the massacre and thought he knew the why, thought he knew the motive, understood the desire for revenge.

He was wrong.

Very wrong.

Jorge knew it had to be like this.

There was no other way. The peasant's way was the only way.

There were no flames now, for there was nothing left to burn but still his eyes remained locked on the scene.

He could feel every eye on him, some turned in shock, some in disbelief but none of that mattered.

For this was the only way, a way only a peasant would understand.

When in the spring time the wild foxes and savage dogs raided the flocks, then there was only one recourse.

Hunt the intruders, kill them and skin them. Hang their pelts where others of their kin could see and take heed of a savage message.

'Here is one of yours that committed a forbidden act. See his fate and take warning!"

A peasant's solution acted out here so that others might hear and remain alive, for in an army so small the bounds of friendship spread in every direction and without punishment short would be the shrift of any future captives and his army would imitate a lawless mob.

Better to sooth the wounds of grief with swift action than to witness future butchery without end.

Better to take upon himself the burden of guilt, than to gift it to a newly fledged nation.

This was what he was telling himself when he took Hobart to his car and this was what he was telling himself when jellied fuel burnt sleeping oaks and screaming men.

And it was the right decision.

Wasn't it?

Later the men left, intent on their own purposes and in the spring when the sun rose warm and the snow melted, the willow tree woke and felt for lost limbs, but finding them missing sent forth new shoots to replace them, and this was as it should be.

For as all knew, it was far easier to kill men than the shoots of a green willow.

PUNISHMENT AND PREPARATION

It was hot in the forward engine room of the Hood, even with just two boilers lit and already it was hot.

Every surface was hot and even the air seemed to boil even though it barely moved.

Chief Petty Officer Patrick Stebbings was hot, and his naked flesh stuck to the inside of his boiler suit in a way which was not only uncomfortable but verged on the indecent.

Hot he may have been, uncomfortable he certainly was but for all his discomfort he was in a far better situation than the *hostilities only* rating who stood by his side in the little office which clung to the steel side of the centre main frame.

The little office was the home of the man who ruled the engine rooms of a mighty battlecruiser and that man was not in the best of moods.

Any man who worked for Mr. Pulver was required to do his best. He might fail at his task, but providing he had tried his best, then that was considered to be in the best traditions of the service and Mr. Pulver gave quiet encouragement. But this rating was both a slacker and a whiner and those attributes had raised for the last time the ire of Stebbings and for that matter his fellow crewmen.

There had come a time for a different solution and Mr. Pulver was that solution.

With a cold and calm voice that was never raised, Pulver sliced the young rating into quivering lumps that were unable to raise a single defence for sins that were many.

'It's the Jaunty and the Captain's table for you this time, my lad,' said Stebbings with glee, 'and with your record it's time ashore with the Regulators and the hill.'

The rating turned very white at these words. The *Jaunty* was the nickname of the ship's Master at arms and it was he who would read out the charges to the Captain. But even more feared was what would come afterwards. The Royal Navy had a punishment branch that had the polite nickname of *Regulators*, though there were other far less polite words.

Each member of this branch had made it his life's work to teach erring sailors how to behave, punishing the slightest infraction with a severity which had become a feared legend, and the most feared part of that legend was *The Hill*, a high dune made of loose sand which malefactors were made to repeatedly climb up under the midday sun…in full kit.

The Hill had broken many a man, men far stronger than the rating and he gifted the man with a smile that held not an ounce of compassion and then turned to face Pulver.

'Will that be all sir? I will need to inform the Master at Arms and have the offender taken in charge.'

There was no reply but a frigid look towards the rating which un-nerved even Stebbings who had formed a friendship with Pulver who spoke once again in a voice which would have frozen the feet off even the most hardy of penguins.

'Well, is that what you wish? Once you leave this office then the matter is out of my hands. No one will speak for you and I imagine the Captain will not waste any time on you. Well?'

There were tears now and stumbling words which made heartfelt promises but Pulver's face remained frozen in contempt.

'Very well, I accept you at your word and I offer you an alternative.' The contempt vanished and a wolf like grin replaced it. 'The alternative I offer is a meeting with Mr. Bell.'

Stebbings barely suppressed a laugh at the words, for Mr. Pulver's alternative was both apt and cruel.

Chief Stoker Gregory Bell had a singular passion and that was bird watching. Nothing pleased him more than to wade knee-deep in muddy water on the off chance that some obscure avian visitor would pass by. He was also the Fleet's middle weight boxing champion…and had been, three years running. Stebbings had seen him fight, and so far, not one opponent had left the ring upright and only one had made it past the fourth round.

He was also devoted to Mr. Pulver and would relish the chance to punish a man who had offended a beloved officer.

A minimum stay of two days in the ship's infirmary was Stebbings' guess…and that was if Bell went easy on him.

'Well?' Pulver maintained his grin though it had not spread as far as his eyes. 'Naturally you will have to volunteer, and you will volunteer as many times as I order until I am satisfied that you are performing your duties.'

There was a gulped acceptance and Pulver nodded, 'Very well. Dismissed.'

'On cap! About face! Double time! Out!'

Stebbings had placed his mouth no more than an inch from the rating's left ear and bellowed the words at the top of his voice which served to speed the unfortunate man on his way, leaving Pulver and Stebbings to exchange grins.

'Just as well sir, the lads...well, they were getting a little upset with the bastard...and accidents do happen. Better this way than something heavy fall on his head or he fall off a gantry.'

'I don't want him killed, Pat. Just taught a lesson.'

'I'll make sure Greg knows the score sir, and a few days under doctor's orders will give the little bastard time to think.'

'As do we all, Pat. This morning I signed the captain's order book. We leave at ten hundred hours tomorrow. I want steam for fifteen knots at oh nine forty-five and full steam available at ten hundred. Steam for the capstan at oh nine thirty. Best do your rounds now, you know what to do.'

There were no more words to be said and Stebbings walked over to the oil-stained telephone and spoke to each engine room in turn, relaying Pulver's words, adding his own advice and counsel as he saw fit, with all thoughts of foolish ratings and boxing matches scoured from his mind and leaving Mr. Pulver alone to make his own preparations and to reach out to touch that portion of the frame which jutted out into his office. The steel was warm and vibrated just at the threshold of perception. The Hood was alive, he was long convinced of that; she spoke and breathed, moved and felt.

He sensed a little of her soul flow into his and said softly, 'It's war again for us, old girl. A little sea time will do us both good I think.'

There was no answer. He didn't expect one and he returned to his paperwork, dashing off a signature in the purple ink that was his own peculiar trademark.

But deep inside the ship something stirred.

War!

She felt the touch and heard the words, thrilling to both.

War! And war soon, war before tomorrow's sun had risen to full height.

There was much to do before one sun set and a new one was born. She must check and check again lest a single failure cascade into shame. She felt mighty hearts beat and turn dull bronzed blades first one way and then another. A rudder creaked on phosphor sheathed pintles and all told her that they had never turned with such freedom or such ease.

She enquired of the tall masts that thrust up questing fingers to a darkening sky and heard a whispering conversation until the tallest of them told of far-seeing eyes and mesh screens that could speak across uncountable waves or catch the merest shadow of sound.

She delved into her very centre where the master gyro sat whirling, dervish-like, on bearings made of cut Burmese rubies and a silky-smooth voice told her that she would always have a compass to rely on.

From forepeak to stern rail her voice was heard, encouraging and warning in a warm contralto that knitted the meanest rivet and the hardest armour into one entity, into a form that had but one purpose.

She was almost content, but one last duty still remained.

And for that she would have to wait.

The checklist was no longer pristine white. Oil had splattered it and bearing grease had been formed into an image of Stebbings left thumb that Scotland Yard would be proud of.

None of that mattered of course. What mattered was the ticked boxes that marched, procession like, down the right-hand side of the page.

All had been done. The great propeller shafts hand been run, first forward and then backwards, the great engines that pushed a huge rudder worked without strain and even the main gyro which spun faster that the eye could see read true and square.

All had been done, all had been checked…except for one last item.

A questioning eyebrow was directed at him and he nodded.

'Right ho, Bill. Open her up.'

Bill's hands gripped a knurled wheel and began turn it clock-wise, allowing hot steam to travel up to a gauge which sprang into instant life. Slowly, without any haste, Bill pulled down a lever and the steam rocketed up along a twisting white lagged pipe.

'It would be better if you spoke.'

'Really?' The Hood's steam siren was a great bell-mouthed tube, taller than a long man and just as broad and it could feel the steam arriving from its depths. 'Well, if you insist.'

It gave a little anticipatory cough as the last ordinary air was expelled by angry steam and then shouted out words that told of adventures to come.

'Oyez, oyez, oyez! Gather round, brave warships and hardy merchantmen all, and pay heed to these words. For too long has the enemy defied us but now has come the day when you will reproof your mettle and your hardihood, and that defiance will be set at naught. Tomorrow we will leave safe anchorages and sail to where our anger will be made plain!'

The last of the steam rolled away in a diminishing echo, but to the Hood's surprise the sirens of other ships sounded from all around the bay.

'Tomorrow!'

'Tomorrow!'

'Victory!'

'Death to the enemy!'

'Tomorrow!'

Only gradually did the sirens cease and silence return, but the Hood had made her point and better…she knew that she led a band of warriors.

'Pressure drop twenty-seven pounds over two minutes.' Bill had been keeping a close eye on the gauge while pent up steam travelled out of the engine room and into the steam siren far above. 'That's within limits, Chief.'

'So it is, Bill. So it is. Bloody good, and that's us done for the evening.'

A last box was given a last tick and the checklist was placed where the oncoming watch would find it.

'Time for a little shut-eye, I think.'

Bill and Stebbings were engineers, prosaic men who did not understand what they had just done, and could never understand it, for theirs was a world of hard facts and applied mathematics.

They understood that a drop of twenty-seven pounds was acceptable but other readings might not be.

That was their world, and they were content enough to live in it.

But as they slept that night, they knew that they had done their duty…and so had the Hood.

No sound, no ripple of water.

No leaping fish, no wheeling bird.

Silence, stillness, an absence.

The Hood lay in the water, her grey-painted bulk reflected back at her in perfect tranquility.

A liquid twin painted on the water.

But now the silence is broken, the stillness ruined.

Men tumble across morning-splashed decks with oiled ease and the capstan speaks in clanking tongue.

Anchor chains lift and are hosed, lest a sea floors teeming life taint the cable locker with the odours of their death.

The bows are guarded by the leadsman who stand ready to call out depths by the mark and by the deep.

Two hundred eyes stand watch, two hundred hands stand ready.

A change now and grey painted funnels eject black-tainted smoke and bronze bladed propellers lazily turn breaking the sea held image into bright sparking shards.

Slowly; oh so slowly she moves, with barely a ripple, with crushing speed withheld.

No breath of wind as the last of an anchor is made fast and a small wave breaks and dies against a steel-clad bow as the great blades grip arms full of water and thrust it from them.

This was morning, the promised morning when all would be renewed, when promises made would be fulfilled.

Slowly, oh so slowly she moves, for though there is haste to rush to battle, navigation must curb zeal and the Hood performs an elegant curve that leads her past cut rock and out to where sisters lie rank upon rank awaiting a brave leader.

There are cries now from the war band, cries of joy for the battle to come, cries that echo back and forth through still air and bright bars of light and as leader she gives due greeting and promises fire and the smoke of war.

There is joy in the Hood's hearts this day as she gazes upon untold tons of lazily hurrying steel and yet her mind sees not bright blue waves, but grey snowflakes, a Boston wharf and the century bought wisdom that an old ship had given her.

'The Father of All Seas smiles more often than not, child, but beware the days that he smiles most. For on those days ill favoured rage swiftly follows. On those days the wise ship will strip her sails and sail under bare poles, she will bar her hatches and close every deadlight. Beware the smile, my child!'

It seemed impossible that on such a peaceful day the words of the Constitution could come true, for the only waves upon the whole blue ocean were formed by the cutting bows of the Hood and her sisters, but the old ship had sailed these seas for years without number and her caution was well founded for all that she was now becalmed and marooned against hard stone walls.

But there was nothing that could be done. A course was a course, and a duty was a duty, and both were set hard.

And besides, she had weathered storms before. There really was nothing to worry about.

'All engines half ahead forward.' The telegraph bell had given its orders and Pulver consulted the tattered book written by the men of Jarrow many long months ago, though in truth there was no need as the figures had long since been memorised. 'Make revolutions one four zero.'

He gave a last look around the master discovery board, every dial, every gauge, every reading as familiar to him as the inside of his mouth.

He muttered a few arcane formulas under his breath, converting the language of white-faced dials into distance run and steam pressure raised.

All was well and he left with a smile and the knowledge that his ship was in good hands.

The Hood ran forward at a sedate fifteen knots, for though the Pacific was large, fuel was precious and there was no need for battle speed just yet. Her target was fixed and its fate certain. Far better to arrive with bunkers still washed with fuel than those that rang hollow, and for the next few days she sipped fuel as if it was the most delicate of liquors while the sun gently shone and the waves gently lapped.

But far above her beating hearts a gold-plated arrow on the ship's barometer rose and rose and then fell like a hangman's drop.

Pulver was dreaming of home. His wife's grey-green eyes were laughing into his and a new born child was gurgling with content.

He was home and all was well with the world, but the smile left the eyes and spoke with concern.

'Go to her! Go now!'

He awoke with a start and found himself not in a cot which tried to cut him off from the normal ship-born noises but a cot which rang with a cacophony of discordant noise.

His ship was in trouble, and there was only one place he had to be.

The Constitution was right, the Father of All Seas was a tyrant Janus who had turned smiling peace into war.

The wind was his herald, for it began to quarter the waters, coming first from one compass point and then another as if unsure of where it came from or where it wished to go.

It began to rise in strength, teasing placid waters into anger and turning them grey and sullen.

Not content with this, the tyrant drew a cloudy curtain over the bright sun so that the very air turned black with fright and men looked out over the waves seeking better seas that were not to be found.

And then came the rain, hard rain, each drop a shot bullet that turned the sea into hissing froth and stung the upturned faces of those who looked up in wonderment.

All the actors were on stage now, all had their lines, their part to play, and with a peal of thunder the play began.

Pulver looked ridiculous. Uncombed hair threw spiky locks towards the sky, while a shirt, half tucked into trousers billowed out in untidy rolls and his sockless feet ended in boots which still waited for a morning's polish.

None of that mattered and none of that he cared about. His whole focus was on the words which came from the telephone jammed up against his ear.

The conversation was mostly one-sided and ended almost as soon as it began.

The leaders of every engine room had crowded into his little office and waited expectantly for orders.

'We are going to have to ride this one out and it looks like it's going to be a bad one. The destroyers and light cruisers have been told to make a run for it...as for us, we have no choice but to let the old girl do her best.

'The boilers that are lit now, remain lit, but I want the rest lit right now; minimum feed, minimum draft, no point in wasting fuel but I want them ready to go on line at a moment's notice. I want a good team on the reduction gears, with their hands on the clutches in case I order an over-ride.'

He looked out over a sea of faces looking for two in particular and finding them, repressing a smile as he saw that Stebbings was both shaved and properly dressed, despite being off watch and presumably given just as little notice.

'Mr. Scott, I want you to have your diesel's up and running and put your best man on the switchboard, ready to divert if we lose electrical power. Take Mr. Stebbings with you. Go now.'

The two vanished leaving only a last few question and a last few order before the final faces disappeared leaving him alone in the office listening to a rising chorus of squeaks and groans and placing a hand on a trembling frame and speaking soft words of encouragement.

'It's going to all right, old girl, it's going to be just fine.'

She heard the words and felt the touch and took comfort from both. She knew her duty was what it always was, and her voice reached out to every part of her, touching spinning shafts, boilers returning to life and long guns securely locked in steel cocoons.

Her children chattered excitedly, not at all disturbed by the rough weather, calling out that a little rain and a slight breeze was nothing to four-point five-inch mouths and that whatever the weather they still held fast to their vows to always protect.

She gave laughing thanks to their love and asked of the radars what they could see.

Brrrrr! It's a mite cold up here and the wind is rocking us something fierce, and them waves is mighty high, but we can see a ship out there, way over yonder, a big one too.'

The radars were American installed during her last refit and had, much to the Hood's amusement, adopted the accents of the Hollywood cowboy films that were shown in her cinema. But cowboy accents or not they had stuck to their task and gave her a distance and a bearing.

She reached out, knowing the nearest ship to be an old friend and a trusted warrior for all that she had a flat deck and carried few guns. *'Sister, how fares your state? This is rough weather indeed, but we will find better soon I believe.'*

The Indomitable gave a short breathless laugh.

'Rough indeed, sister, rough indeed. All my chicks are securely lashed down and I can maintain steerage enough to keep my head into the wind, but I burn much fuel this way and my bunkers shrink more than I would like, and I fear for my lack of sea miles.'

The Hood gave what comfort she could, knowing that her sister had been given short legs to further the cause of giving a heavier punch.

'What cannot be helped must be endured, sister. When this wind abates, I will order an oiler to give you what refreshment you crave.'

115

'Thank you, sister, that will ease me, for I wish to play my part as you would wish.'

The Hood was about to make reply when an incoherent shout came from the carrier and she saw in front of her just what the Indomitable had seen.

There was no time to reply now, no time to give her own warning.

There was only time to hope…and hold.

Montgomery Scott knew himself to be a very fortunate young man, a very fortunate young man indeed. A posting on the Hood was the fondest hope of every engineering graduate and every midshipman dreamed of such a posting. He had read the posting notice several times before the truth had finally registered into a disbelieving mind and he had swiftly packed and left before a creaking bureaucracy saw that it had made a mistake and some admiral's son took his place.

And the Hood was huge! Miles of passageway, endless rows of electric lights that clung overhead and legions of men that hurried on incomprehensible tasks.

His escort had looked neither to the right or to the left, but with all the skill of a homeward-bound pigeon took him to a surprisingly small office deep in the heart of the ship.

Everyone knew of the man who greeted him, the youngest Chief Engineer in the fleet was something of a legend, but he hadn't been prepared for the man himself who seemed a little shy, almost embarrassed to wear his gold rings and the single purple ring that marked out an engineer from more common folk.

It was only when Mr. Pulver had taken him on a tour of his domain that the reticence vanished for shy eyes had hardened as they explained his duties and the expectations that this ship demanded of him.

There would be no arguing with those eyes and that was strangely comforting. His family had always been engineers, his father, his father's father and back as far as hand could trace, all had combined cunning hand with probing mind and so far as he was concerned that tradition would continue.

He was the most junior of midshipmen, so it was only natural that he be given the most junior of commands. The ship's emergency diesels were a small enough commission, that was true, but he was determined to make them a project that would cause Mr. Pulver as little concern as possible and more importantly lead to greater tasks. Despite that he was still a very junior officer and was glad to have the senior non-commissioned officer by his side.

This was not Mr. Stebbings watch, but he greeted the diesel crew as old friends and then gave the squat engines a most searching inspection, probing every cable and every dial while the heart of the Hood's most junior midshipman pounded in fright, lest some sin of omission be found.

But all was well and Stebbings took a glance over the switchboard, pulling circuit breakers and turning dials down to their absolute minimum, before looking up at Scott: 'If you please, sir.'

The diesels staggered into life, thumping and stuttering until they grew hot enough to form a song that spoke of heat and pressure, and then began to turn motion into current that waited only for permission to flow.

All was ready and Scott was about to comment, when slowly and without any hurry at all the deck of the diesel room began to slant gently downwards.

The wave was huge. More grey than green, it rolled forward, vast and implacable, towering ever higher as it grew nearer.

Her bow was lifting up. Without any effort the wave was lifting over forty-seven thousand tons of steel, iron and brass onto its shoulders as if the Hood was no more than the merest piece of flotsam.

She fought, urging churning propellers to kick against the giant, imploring steam to do all it could, but to no avail for still she rose steeper and steeper.

She heard her children whimper in fright but there was no time to calm them. It took all her effort to keep her sides straight and her bow forward, resisting a rudders instinct to turn away.

And then she saw the face in the wave; white hair and beard made of wind-whipped foam, two dark and angry eyes set in a dark green face and a black mouth that opened wider and wider in wild and turbulent rage.

She knew she was seeing the face of the Father of All Seas and for the first time in a long life she felt fear.

And then there was no time for fear as the wide mouth screamed in his unfathomable rage and ran into her, dropping her bow and lifting her stern into the dark sky.

Her jack staff splintered and then snapped, never to be seen again, deck rails first twisted and then were wrenched from their mounts to wrap themselves around 'A' turret which gasped with pain as the water attempted to lift it from its ring gear.

And still the wave was not satisfied. The forward air intake was crushed flat and a solid bar of water burst into her, flooding the capstan locker and the telephone exchange, drowning two men before they could escape, and she felt their deaths though there was no time to weep.

More water and yet more, the whole forward part of her was underwater now, uncountable tons of water pulling her down, fingers that gripped with malicious giggles.

And the livid face laughed anew.

'Wait, do nothing yet, let the ship find her own way.'

The thought had crowded out every other as Pulver stood by the steel cases of the reduction gears knowing that this was the point of danger, this was the place where he was most needed.

The reduction gears were massive blocks of blunt-toothed gears and sliding cams that turned the rotating power of the shafts into applied power and mighty beasts they were too, anchored to the deck with massive feet and even more massive bolts.

The American engineers had altered them to make them more efficient, but they had been given a new function, one which had its own use and its own danger.

If the balance between shaft and propeller became too uneven then they threw themselves off line, the better to save themselves, the better to save precious shafts, and already as the Hood's propellers churned through a mixture of too shallow water and too much air they had performed exactly as designed and the bronze blades turned ever more slowly.

But today they battled not mechanical failure nor yet a human enemy but nature herself and that required different thoughts and different tactics.

He and his team stood ready as far above them uncountable tons of water pushed the ships bow further and further down while the deep caverns of the Hood echoed to the sobbing sounds of a stern that was becoming more and more unsupported.

But wait, wait for the moment.

'Wait.'

Stebbings voice was very quiet in Scott's ear, so quiet that he could barely hear it over the throb of the diesels and the high whine of the generators that held stores of pent-up energy.

'Not yet, sir. Wait for the moment, the board will show when. Just you keep your hand ready.

So, Scott waited, waited while the deck angled evermore steeply, his hand itched and his fear gnawed at him with blood pounding teeth.

Wait, wait for the moment.

On and on the wave rolled, the face howling in triumph, eyes darkening as victory came ever closer.

'A' turret spluttering as the water sought entry into its armoured sides. Her propellers protesting as they were lifted out of dark waters. 'B' turret bracing itself for the attack, her children half whimpering in fright, half barking in undirected anger.

But always the face staring at her as the hungry man stares at the welcome plate.

But then when hope seemed furthermost from her hearts came two voices that showed no fear at all, but gave out a gruff challenge.

'Oh no you don't my friend! We brothers have been placed here to stop such as you, and stop you we shall!'

The twin voices echoed each other in absolute harmony and came from the iron throats of the breakwaters that ran out from the sides of 'B' turret.

Taller than the tallest man where they touched the steel sides of the turret, their steel plates rose up out of the deck, tapering outwards to hold hands with the guard rails that lined the Hoods deck.

Already they had seen more forward placed brothers subdued with ease and now port and starboard they stood, strongly anchored and strongly ribbed, topped with cunningly curved lips that spoke now in scornful derision.

'You think we are scared of you? Ribbed and straked we are, and wrought by men who knew skills far beyond your feeble power! Try our strength, we dare you! Test our mettle or acknowledge defeat and slink back to your watery hovel!'

There was no reply to the challenge, only a further wind driven howl and a rush that broke first against 'B' turret and then the iron dams of the breakwaters with an angry hiss.

In truth the breakwaters were designed to stop waves far smaller than the titan that had run towards them, but stubbornness had been built into every rivet and every plate, and they dug hard toes into the frame below them, determined to resist.

And resist they did. The face bit into them with angry teeth, but they pushed back, though their steel walls buckled, and ribs creased in agony, but gradually the face was forced upwards in a towering foam coated mass that rose high and higher.

The face screamed in frustration and, windblown and wounded it vented its frustration on the closed eyes and steel sides of the director tower, blasting it with decreasing force and to little avail. The moment had passed, the wave's power had been broken. It still chattered with rage down steel sides in white flecked waterfalls that the scuppers eagerly drank with thirsty throats.

Only faint curses came now from the conquered face as it rolled along her armoured sides leaving her to smaller though still dangerous waves.

The first threat had been subdued and she felt an insulted stern fall to seek deeper water and she reached out to touch curiously slow turning blades.

The frames above Pulver creaked in agony as the breakwaters transferred impossible loads, but he spared them not a single glance.

The frames would live or die and if they died then his every problem would be permanently solved, but for now he must concentrate on the single problem before him.

The machinery of all three reduction gears sang in diminishing notes, just as they had been designed to do. In their simple world propellers that churned only froth and water must not be allowed to run as if they swam in deeper waters and so for the good of all they had severed the link between spinning shafts and turning blades.

But Pulver could feel his ship beginning to settle again and when that moment came, she would need instant speed lest still savage waves turn her broadside on, and roll her like a stick in a millrace.

The reduction gears took long seconds to spin out a new web of power and he could not give them those seconds.

He shouted out an order and three pairs of strong hands pulled at three long, brass spooned levers, forcing gears to mesh and cams to rise and fall.

A long dirge of pain and outrage came from every steel case as their world was flung out of balance and they sought solace, drinking lubricating oil in great gulps, but as the stern of the Hood slammed back down in an explosion of spray, every propeller was twisting through the water at just enough speed to give the ship sufficient speed to maintain head way and that was not just Pulver's main concern it was his only concern.

He hid his sigh of relief and gave orders that saw oil reservoirs replenished and filters cleaned and then began to patrol the rest of his kingdom.

Montgomery Scott's ears and his feet told the same tale. The ship had ceased its downward nosedive and was beginning to pivot back onto an even keel and for a moment he had the horrible vision of the entire ship plunging stern first on to the sea floor, but with an effort he thrust the image from his mind and concentrated on his hands which hovered over the controls which would push a meager voltage out into the Hood.

For it must be admitted that Midshipman Montgomery Scott was frightened, though he was determined not to show it before his small crew and Mr. Stebbings, all of whom were taking the situation very calmly indeed. So, he stood absolutely still while his engines throbbed and the ship herself groaned and creaked.

The Hood boomed like a cracked bell as her stern crashed down back onto a rolling sea. The lights overhead flickered and dimmed and he was about to let his hands begin their work, but a last-minute instinct caused him to look over to Stebbings who gave the merest shake of his head and pointed his eyes at the control board.

Scott followed the eyes and saw that needles that had fallen away had righted themselves even as the lights regained their strength.

'It looks like the old girl doesn't need us,' said Stebbings with evident satisfaction and then gave a little grin on seeing the mixture of relief and disappointment on Scott's face.

'We won't be needed?'

Scott tried to keep his voice calm and level, but had doubts as to whether he had succeeded.

'I wouldn't say that, sir. Besides which we haven't had orders to stand down, but…'

Stebbings hesitated, the boy seemed friendly enough, but he was an officer and perhaps would not like taking advice, but he saw the questioning look on the boy's face and decided to carry on.

'Respectfully, sir, you've learnt a valuable lesson today.'

'I have?'

'Yes sir. Mr. Scott, why are you here?'

'This is my station, this is my watch, I'm supposed to be here!'

'With engines running, with the control board alive and busbars energised?'

'Err. ….. no.'

Stebbings lost the grin because he wanted the lesson to be learnt.

'Mr. Pulver wanted everything ready…just in case, and that's part of being a good engineer; preparing for the worst even though you are almost certain that the worst won't happen.

'It's a good lesson to learn sir. Always have a plan, so that if it all turns to…well if it all turns pear-shaped then you don't have to think on your feet.'

'Quite right.'

No one had seen Mr. Pulver appear and scan eyes around the room.

'Report, Mr. Scott.'

The Midshipman stiffened and reported that all was well, and his command was ready for instant action, though he missed the very slow wink that Stebbings gifted Pulver who ordered the Chief Petty Officer to assume temporary command of the diesel room while Scott was to accompany him.

Pulver looked at Scott and saw the image of himself from only a few years ago. He knew little of the boy. Only that his reports were very good, and it was for that reason that he had picked him out of a long list of potential candidates for a place on the Hood. He knew that this was the boy's first real storm, and it was a shame that it had to be such a bad one. But there were questions to be asked and a few precious moments to be spared.

'Were you frightened just now?'

Scott did not want to admit his fear, but Pulver's eyes would not admit lies so he blushed and gave the best version of the truth that he could get away with.

'Yes sir…a little.'

'Why?'

He tried to explain the fear-inducing noises of a ship battered by waves and wind and the far sharper fear of acting too soon or too late.

Pulver nodded, understanding that the fears were born of imagination and not flawed courage.

'I heard Mr. Stebbings give you some good advice. Now I will give you some more. Always trust a well-found ship and understand that so long as we have positive buoyancy and the uplift given by forward motion then we cannot sink. The laws of physics are our friends and cannot ever be broken. Every good engineer knows this and now so do you.

'Now as our telephone system seems to be unserviceable, I need to send a message to the bridge. You will be my messenger.

'My compliments to the captain and you are to tell him that the engine room has suffered little damage, all boilers are on line and full power is available should he wish, and I hope to have the telephone system back on line as soon as possible.

'You will ask the officer of the watch for permission to stay on the bridge in case a reply needs to be sent to me.

'Now up aloft with you.'

Scott vanished, leaving Pulver to beat a lonely retreat back to his office which soon became crowded with men reporting for orders.

And within seconds he had forgotten all about Mr. Scott.

She could not forget a single part of her, all must be checked.

The voices of the breakwater brothers still spoke as one, but there was pain in the chorus.

'We stopped him, didn't we!'

'You did,' she replied. *'There is much to praise in your action.'*

Other voices joined hers in thanks, the gruff fifteen-inch tones of her main guns were echoed by the joyful barks of her children and the Hollywood sounds of the radars. Every part of her sent gifts of words, until the brothers blushed at the unaccustomed praise.

'We only did what we had to, but a blacksmith's hammer and the drill of the shipwright would be most welcome for we have suffered some hurt.'

'The morning shall see your wounds full tended,' came the answer. *'Now I must search yet more, for many have suffered this day.'*

The reduction gears had drunk a little too much cooling oil and their voices were thick and slurred, but told of hot bearings that soon must be replaced and gears that needed new bronze faces on iron teeth, while others told of shock and strain that would soon be shaken off.

The Hood's voice reached out across still angry waves and enquired of each sister in turn, hearing of damage that could be ignored or wounds that would need skill and time.

One by one the answers bounced across the wave tops until the sad and gloomy voice of the Indomitable touched her.

'I have lost some of my chicks, sister, even now they rest on the seabed with broken wings and call for help I cannot give. Tied down they were and well shacked to my decks, for I carried a full brood and there was too little room in my nests, but the sea waves took them and now mock me for my weakness.'

The Hood knew that her carriers loved their charges just as she loved her children, but the beasts that flew from flattened decks were fragile indeed, subject to many an ill and many an infection that her own children would have disdained.

Still a love that was broken was mourning indeed and this was a time for soft words and not the call to warrior arms. Gently she gave what comfort she could, easing grief with images of happy times already recorded and happier times still to come.

An odd duty this for a soul that could hurl sharp pointed death far across the miles, but she knew it was a duty that all leaders must perform. For a shield wall that held grief was no shield wall at all, and heartache must be salved so that no more tears would be shed.

The gloom diminished from the Indomitable's voice and she was promised a brood of new hatched chicks to love and cherish.

A strange duty, but she was no stranger to duty and far sea miles away was an island to bend to her will and this she would do.

For that, too was a duty.

The Royal Marine might have stepped out of a recruiting poster; not a hair out of place and every one of them cut to the exact regulation length. His uniform was pressed to perfection with every button a painful dot of polished light.

He barred Scott's entry to the bridge and enquired in a loud voice just what purpose such a visitor could have in this most holy of sanctuaries.

Scott's meek reply that he was the bearer of a message from the Chief Engineer gave reluctant admission, though he had the distinct impression that it would take very little in the way of excuse for the man to gleefully throw him off the bridge.

Naturally he was not allowed to deliver his message to the captain in person. The Navy had a time-honoured tradition about such things and his message was first delivered to a rating who then transmitted it to the Midshipman of the watch, who then spoke in respectful tones to a man who wore the stripes of a Lieutenant Commander who in turn whispered in the ear of the Captain who honoured Scott with a single glance before turning away.

'How long before we have a working telephone system?'

The stripes of the Lieutenant Commander barked at him and were not at all happy at his reply that he did not know but was sure that it would not be long.

'Stay here and try not to get in the way!' And with that the stripes turned and ignored him, an action which was copied by every member of the bridge crew and allowed Scott to look out through the armoured glass to the world outside.

And a chaotic world it was. A prematurely aging day still gave enough light to see lines of tall waves pushed by a driving wind and as he watched a wave, taller and more bold than others burst over the bow in a power that was seemingly impossible to resist, but to his vast relief the Hood shouldered her way through, though the deck rolled sickeningly under his feet.

The defeated wave had one last Parthian shot left for it splattered the armoured glass with ten thousand salted drops which woke the rubber bladed wipers from their slumbers and reminded them of their duty.

The drops vanished revealing once more the marching mountains and a new phenomenon, for far in the distance was a bank of pearl-white clouds that seemed unaffected by the wind and as Scott watched a bolt of lightning flared deep within their folds turning them soft pink and bright blue.

The light lasted but a single second and was unseen by the bridge crew, but Scott was numbed by its beauty, so much so that he missed the words.

'I said you can go, the telephones are working now. The Captain sends his compliments to Mr. Pulver and you can go.'

Scott gave a hasty salute and vanished, escaping the baleful glare of the Marine and making his way with only a little hesitation back down to make his report to a busy Pulver who dismissed him with thanks and a tired smile.

Later, after his watch ended and he lay down in the hammock which was all a thrifty Admiralty would give him and thought back on the day.

He had survived his first storm; he had seen nature in all its terror and all its beauty, and he had received very good advice from men far more experienced than him.

Always have a backup plan and never act in haste, and most cryptically of all always understand the laws of physics for they can never be broken.

He began to drift off to well-deserved sleep, but before he did so Pulver's words re-echoed in his mind. *'You cannot break the laws of physics.'*

Those were words to live by, for a family to live by…and remember.

'There's varmint's coming down the trail.'

The voice of the radars was dry and laconic and brought forth images of cattle drives, dust and sudden meetings that ended in six shooters pulled from holsters.

'Yes siree, varmints alright. Coming hell for leather and a' whoopin' and a' hollerin' fit to beat the band. They's bad hombre's I reckon; two big war parties, one way up yonder, t'other ones riding them wave tops like they were at the rodeo.'

The Hood was instantly alert, though she was careful not to show any excitement. It was no part of her duty to show any signs of distress.

'Where are they, how many and how far away?'

She had kept the tension out of her voice, but her children had lifted attentive ears and moved uneasily on their mounts as the radars continued to speak.

'Now don't you fret none, I've got them varmints dead to rights, they ain't foolin' me. That first band is about twenty thousand feet and is fixin' to come down outa the sun I reckon; t'others are a little harder to see, what with the waves an' all, but they's made an appointment to be here in about ten minutes. We already told them fancy, highfalutin' gentlemen that call themselves fire control and it looks like they's arraingin' a little neck tie party.' The voice turned gleeful and then imposed an un-needed opinion. *'Time, I reckon to draw our shootin' irons.'*

The Hood was about to reprimand the dry voice for this breech of manners, but it was too late; her children had heard the words and an already excited babble of noise transformed itself into a savage barking chant that was echoed by every Oerlikon mount.

This could not be, there would be discipline or there would be chaos. She allowed her anger to fill a voice that ran from forepeak to taffrail.

'Silence! Radar, you will continue to watch and provide every scrap of information, as for the rest of you, where is your discipline, where is the order that I have taught? Is this how you will defend me? Better I strike my flag now than depend on such as you. Hang your barrels in shame and lock your breeches in disgrace.'

There was a shocked silence and then an embarrassed *'Yes Ma'am'* from the radars and mumbled apologies from her children and the Oerlikons.

'That is better.' The anger left her voice, for she truly loved her children, though their devotion to her always hovered at the edge of anarchy and needed stern direction lest in their lust to protect they allowed disaster to strike. *'Listen to your directors and strike hard and true and attack as a pack, for that is where your true strength lies.'*

Ten minutes, there was much to do in those minutes and her voice reached out across the waves to touch the sisters of her war band.

There was pride in the Indomitable's words, and she spoke for all the carriers that rode with the Hood.

'Two of our chicks already stand aloft and watch, but even now others leave our nests and take flight with sharpened talons. They will fly high and hide in the sun the better to swoop upon their prey. Be assured sister that we send out no new fledglings, but seasoned hunters with countless kills etched upon them, and the sea will eat many meals of enemy flesh before the night stars appear to guide us on our path. Sister, we will do all that steel can do; we will do all that duty compels and our compass points only towards honour.'

The mournful voice that grieved for chicks lost in the storm was gone now and the Hood was hearing the hard voice of a warrior who led her own war band that could throw their charges into the sky and at an enemy's throat.

She had asked her questions and they had been answered.

There was nothing to do now but wait.

'Above average eyesight I see' The pre-war voice of the chief instructor rose like a bubble in Jack McIntyre's memory and he gave a puzzled grunt as he tried to find the cause of the old memory and failed.

But the grizzled old teacher had been right, Jack did have good eyesight. Some trick of nature had given him the ability to see objects long before others and a wise navy had taken that gift and added talents to it. Of course, it never asked Jack if he wished to gain those talents; such a thought was more than humorous. The Navy did what it did without consulting anyone but itself, but now Jack sat in the gunner's seat of a double barreled twenty millimetre Oerlikon with the blare of a trumpet sounding action stations in his ear.

He pulled at the ropes which compressed the massive return springs, cocking each barrel so that it waited only for the release of the safety lock and the pressure of a hand to stream death into the sky.

'Just another bloody exercise.'

The voice of the left-hand loader was muffled now as Jack had donned the headphones that linked him to the gunnery officer, but he heard the words well enough and shook his head.

He was a veteran now, a prewar entrant who had fought in the savage Biscay convoy battles and who was slowly rising up the ranks while the loader was a new recruit, stronger in arm than in head and chosen for just that reason.

He shook his head again and pointed to the carrier group which resembled a copse of rook infested trees that had just seen the farmer with his shotgun. All three carriers were throwing aircraft off their decks in rapid succession while further away the flagship had gathered protective destroyers around her in a shield wall.

He doubted that this was an exercise, and even if it was his actions would have been no different.

His headphones spoke and gave wind speed, temperature and the direction of the enemy and Jack gulped as he realised that the Bacchante would be the first to see them.

''Above average eyesight',' the instructor had said, and Jack McIntyre knew that this was so.

And today with the sun high in the sky he would test those eyes once more, but for now there was nothing to do but wait.

There was nothing to do now but wait and waiting was hard. His feet itched to take him on another circuit of the diesels, his hands pleaded for a second chance to wander over the array of dials and switches that controlled the barely throbbing engines, while his eyes desired only to look up and pierce the many decks between him and daylight.

Montgomery Scott did none of those things, though the effort added considerably to the amount of sweat that was drenching an already wet body.

Waiting was hard, but Mr. Pulver had ordered him to wait, telling him that the duty of officers often consisted of no more than waiting.

'If you can, Mr. Scott try to look unworried. If you start fidgeting the men will pick up on it, you can be sure of that. A wise man once told me that officers never run and that's good advice but I'll add to it; look bored Mr. Scott, look bored.'

And with that Pulver had vanished, for the duties of a Chief Engineer were many and Scott was left alone to polish his acting skills.

For there was nothing to do now but wait.

His duty was plain, defend the island that had been his home for so long now.

The images of wife and child were still with him, and a last photograph was still carried as a talisman that had never failed, and the memories were still sharp.

But doubt was an enemy that grew stronger, though every instinct told him that doubt must be resisted.

For where were his old comrades, where were the well-practiced pilots who had graduated with him, comrades that had hour upon hour of flight time in the golden days before the war?

He knew the answer of course; winnowed every last one. For as the wanton boy slashes at the tall poppies with a long stick so had his friends been harvested one by one, and now only he and his talisman remained, and his squadron consisted only of young boys with log books but half-filled and battle practice merely a phrase.

He risked a look behind and resisted a useless curse at the sight of a squadron that consisted only of stragglers.

'Close up! Red Two where are you?'

Only static replied and he looked up into a well risen sun, instinct and war skill moving his hands without conscious thought.

The bright balls of light passed the cockpit, seemingly with only inches to spare and he had a fleeting glimpse of a long-nosed dark shape with bent wings flash past him.

He now knew why Red Two had failed to answer but the knowledge did him little good as his adversary was not alone and the sky began to fill with twisting, snarling aircraft and curving black smoke trails that led only in one direction.

He gave a last glimpse to the image of a wife and child and turned his craft back into the melee.

There was nothing to do now but fight.

'Yours is the honour,' the Hood had told her. *'You are the van, you are the pathfinder. Fight well.'*

The message had been brief, for as leader of a warband the Hood had many burdens, but was welcome recognition that the Bacchante was fit to lead and in truth a little excitement was no bad thing for the long journey down to the bright blue waters had been an exercise in tedium and frustration.

The tedium was understandable; the Mediterranean was an Allied lake filled only with enemy wrecks and the journey from the dark continent to the shining expanse of Trincomalee had laid one flavorless day upon another, but the frustration had but a single focus.

The Susannah.

The ship was a captured German supply ship, a combination of floating workshop and travelling store that had a temperament that would try even the most patient, for even the most perfectly executed maneuver brought forth a stream of harsh criticism.

But today the Susannah sailed in company with fleet oilers, tugs and repair ships that would in a few days' time meet with the Hood's battle group and feed it in an orgy of replenishment and the Bacchante was free to check that all was well in the last moments before the battle.

She received cheerful giggles from her two spinning turbines and grave confirmation from her every weapon.

There was nothing to do now but wait for the enemy to come.

'Here they come.'

The warning bell had not yet rung, but Jack's eyes had seen the black dots high up in the sky and the dull flashes that shone splintered sunlight from the wave tops.

He knew it was an illusion but every spinning propellor seemed pointed at him and him alone and he swallowed to wet a dry throat.

The Bacchante surged forward, and Jack felt a welcome breeze dry a little sweat on his face as he looked up at the dots coming closer and closer.

His left hand reached down and released the safety lock, while his right pushed a little more pressure on the trigger.

The warning bell shrieked, and the ship's main guns lifted up and roared smoke and shell up into the sun in deafening blasts that shook the deck and stained the air while Jack's eyes scanned bright blue sky and white topped waves.

'Above average eyesight' the man had said, but that no longer mattered…because there was nothing to do now but fight.

The man was good and an odd surge of pride at the skill of a fellow pilot surged through him.

The man was trying to kill him though, so the admiration did not last long for his enemy was using his aircraft with skill and refused to dogfight which was entirely the right thing to do as the Allied aircraft was both heavier and faster than his own.

Twice now the bent winged fighter had swooped down at him and only his skill and his luck had saved him.

All around was a mad dance that swayed to a tempo too slow for some and too fast for others.

Each dance ended in death or victory and after each dance the victor exulted and sought new partners, but for him it was as if he was alone in the sky…alone except for his deadly companion and the image of a wife and child that held all his good fortune.

He pulled the stick hard over and the glowing balls of death hissed past seeking the upper sky, and as he tumbled through the air the ungainly grey shape roared past him climbing upwards and then rolling over to come behind him for the easy kill shot.

This was far too warm work to last much longer and he risked a second's glance down to where toy ships curved tracks on a painted ocean.

The sea below beckoned him, and he looked at it wistfully; a dive to sea level would even up the fight, for down there his enemy would not be able to use his superior engine power, down there the nimblest, the most graceful and the most skillful would survive.

But to wish for such things was to play a fool's game. Any dive he began would end long before completion as superior mass and speed would catch him even as the falcon on the wing plucks the plump gamecock.

He shook his head and smiled at the photograph promising that one day they would meet again. For now he would pit agility and old skill against power and craft, and again as he rolled cannon shot screamed under a lifting wing and again the grey painted beast climbed past him in an elegant curve that was far too fast to follow.

An elegant curve that pointed right.

Only once had the enemy's accent taken him to the left and in battle to do the expected was a short path to defeat.

He waited, tempting his enemy with a flight that stay straight for fractions of a second too long, trailing a petrol scented coat through the air, praying to his talisman that this time would be a sharp echo of past attacks.

Once more he avoided a slashing attack, but this time he turned not away from his enemy but towards the right, pointing the nose of his aircraft up so that its whole weight hung off the spinning blades of its propellor; he could not hope to match speeds, this he knew, but where a slow vessel could not follow surely bullets would.

An old trick this, much practiced in the days before the gods of war rose from uneasy graves.

Pull the stick back into the stomach so that the air turns white with rage and red blood pools into cold feet. Stab the worn brass button and hear the roar of guns through cotton-filled ears.

Pull and stab so that the enemy flies into a stream of bullet and shell. Pull and stab and hope that a killing blow is struck.

There is a curious feeling of lightness now, for outraged air has refused to do its duty and his craft tumbles like a winter-borne leaf, but deft feet and hands regain control and searching eyes scan the sky. There is a black stain painted against a blue sky but of the enemy there is not a single trace.

Has he killed or only discouraged? He does not know, but the comradeship of the air hopes that an adversary has lived and will live to see old age.

But there is no time for thoughts of brotherhood for there are other battles still to fight. The air is empty, for a twisting combat has taken him far from his comrades and a shouting radio tells him nothing of location or height.

A glance down brings forth a curse and a wish to punish ill-discipline, for there on the blue waves were the black smoke flowers of bursting shells and the white lines of ships both large and small with a single small ship in the van with aircraft clustered around it like seagulls circling a tempting piece of offal.

A second curse more powerful than the first entered the cockpit and he wished once more for lost brothers, brothers trained to a sharp edge, brothers who would not make the mistake he saw below.

With an entire fleet filled with large and important targets these half-trained fools were wasting their power against a small ship whose only crime was being nearer their base.

An order screamed into the radio was unlikely to overcome blood lust which left only one action.

He pushed the nose of his aircraft down hoping that his presence and the luck of his talisman would bring order out of chaos.

'It must be an illusion' Jack thought. There could not be another explanation. Surely the Bacchante was not worth all this anger, all this effort. But over and over enemy aircraft thrust forward, hugging the wave tops or screaming down from the sky, forcing his ship into wild turns and desperate gunfire from every mount.

A wave, born of a destiny-missing bomb climbed the Bacchante's steel sides, and its remnants soaked Jack and his crew. The twin barrels hissed their relief at being unburdened from overheating and Jack dashed the salt water from stinging eyes.

This made no sense. There were targets and to spare behind him, tempting targets, better, more valuable targets. Why was the enemy venting its spite against a single ship?

Already the ship had suffered, a single bomb had speared down, blasting apart 'X' turret and spraying splinters which killed every man on the port aft Oerlikon mounts while two fighters had spewed bullets into the bridge turning its steel into a blood dripping latticework.

A second bomb had obviously ruined some vital internal machinery because the ship had slowed and was not turning as quickly as before.

Jack could spare no more than a glance at these wounds for the enemy was gathering again and three, twin-engined torpedo aircraft were rapidly approaching while a high angry buzzing heralded the return of the dive bombers.

The voice of the gunnery controller had long since been stilled and Jack was left on his own and had to decide where to point the twin barrels of his mount.

Torpedo or bomb, which death to choose? Which enemy would he take with him to Valhalla?

There was a shout from the muscular loader and a weighty arm pointed up into the sky.

Four Seafires had brought pointed wings and pointed death into the fray and Jack watched as one dive bomber blew up in an oily black explosion, while a second lost a wing and began a death spiral that ended in a dark-stained splash that the waves soon erased.

The rest of the dive bombers scattered, each one hoping that a comrade would be the next victim and that it would be spared, but in the battle between killing speed and loadbearing wing there could be only victors and victims and the Seafires snapped up their prey even as the swift cat catches the slow mouse.

There was no time to cheer. Besides, the Seafires had made Jack's choice an easy one and he pointed his guns back towards a low flying enemy.

Jack never did find out what happened to the third aircraft. Nor did he have time to wonder. Instead he sighted on the left-hand of the two remaining enemies and sent a stream of twenty-millimeter shells outwards. His aim was good, and seven hits ripped through the flimsy cowling of an engine, smashing the engine block and severing fuel and oil lines. Bright orange flames streamed out over the wing like a comets tail but the pilot was a brave man and ignored the damage, dropping his torpedo into the water even as Jack's second burst smashed through the nose of his aircraft cutting him in half.

His navigator survived Jack's blow but drowned as the mortally wounded aircraft splashed into the sea and began a two-mile journey to the sea bottom.

There were now two torpedoes in the water, and both were aimed at Jack who could only watch helplessly as the white frothing tracks arrowed towards him.

The wounded Bacchante turned with sluggish speed to avoid these daggers and the first passed behind her rudder to find a lonely extinction but the second hit the knife edge of her bow and erupted in a welter of flame and spray that slowed the ship first to a crawl and then a dead stop.

Jack knew he was dead now and he hoped his death would be a quick one. His ship was now no more than a floating target and to add insult to injury a single-engined fighter had appeared and seemed to be marshaling the enemy for a last concentrated attack.

This act enraged him. He knew that in war the concept of fairness was forgotten, but this action was too much to bear.

It was long range he knew but he swung round the mount until the iron-ringed sight and the tiny aircraft were linked.

'Above average eyesight,' the man had said.

Very gently Jack pressed the trigger and the Oerlikon's spoke for the last time.

There was very little point in shouting, but his name and his rank were repeated over the frequency common to all squadrons and he flew his aircraft in long lines of interference, until at last young voices acknowledged his power.

His anger had long since vanished, there was very little point in wasting anger on half-trained boys whose only guilt was wishing to serve the Emperor and who lacked not courage but judgement.

The failure was his, for he commanded, and it was up to him to make amends.

At last he had restored order and was flying past the half-wrecked ship when his aircraft shuddered in brief pain.

A single shell from Jack's long burst had hit him.

The shell was already almost at the end of a long journey and had lost much of its power, but there was still enough to punch through an aluminum cowling and strike the steel tube of an engine bearer. And there, Jack's shell died, bursting into shards that scattered without harm into the engine bay, all except one small razor-edged shard which sliced through the thin metal side of the oil filter leaving a jagged cut no more than an inch long.

Without any haste black oil began pooling in the bottom of the engine cowling.

'Here they come, those varmints are coming down for sure now.'

For long minutes a single sister had borne the whole weight of the enemy's anger, but now the anger had been redirected and the Hood readied herself for battle.

She heard the song of her boilers as they sucked air and fuel, the angry wailing as water was turned into compressed energy, the mad giggles of turbines as they spun ever faster, and the painful grunting as long pistons turned a heavy rudder.

Every part of her sang, spoke or grunted as the pleasure took them and every part of her promised that on this day as on all others, they would give every effort.

She spoke to her children now, all anger gone. *'Now is your hour my children, now you can fill your barrels with enemy blood, now you can defend me if it is your wish.'*

The answers fell from four point five mouths in a barking roar.

'We will kill your enemies!'

'Blast them from the skies!'

'Rip them!'

'Tear them!'

'We won't let them hurt you!'

The Hood smiled and as she did so the first of her children blasted out defiance and the battle began.

In peacetime a pilot has time to do the many tasks that flying demands. He has time to look outside the cockpit for other aircraft and the land ahead. He has time to think, for the good pilot's mind should always fly a little further than his craft and proper planning has saved many a man from disaster. He has time to look at his instruments; the holy trinity of airspeed, height and direction and all the others that gave sense to the roaring collection of pistons, valves and pumps that he sat behind.

But in war, in battle, a pilot has time for none of that. In war every quivering muscle, every searching glance was devoted to one end and one end only.

Survival.

Simple survival. Kill or be killed.

So, there was some excuse for not seeing the oil pressure gauge flicker and die, and good reason not to see the temperature gauge leave the security of happy green and slowly walk into the red zone of danger.

All this he told himself in the seconds after his engine gave a single cough and died a frozen death and now a propellor blade stood vertically upright like an accusing finger.

An odd smile came to his face. There was time to think now, an eternity perhaps. Outside he could see the battle; he had bought his young boys to where they needed to be and now their courage and their luck ruled them, and he was no longer needed.

There was a last duty to perform and a last regret and he reached out a leather-gloved hand and stroked the picture of his beloved wife and child.

'I'm sorry my loves, I know I promised to return, but it must be goodbye.'

In war there is always a last duty; to die with honour, facing the foe.

He looked out and knew that the gods had smiled on him for one last time, for below him was a great ship covered in sparkling lights that spat shell and shrapnel at him.

Without any conscious thought he pushed the stick forward and aimed for the centre of the huge ship.

'Kill him! Kill him! Kill him!'

The chant of her children was taken up by the Oerlikons and streams of fast-moving metal rushed up to join the black bursts of shells that shredded the oncoming aircraft, tearing lumps off wing and fuselage and causing bright flames to unfold from both wings.

'Kill him! Kill him! Kill him!'

She urged a straining rudder to turn her away from this airborne enemy but heard only hard breathing grunts.

'Kill him! Kill him! Kill him!'

She saw a single friendly fighter dive to aid her, but her children's blood lust recognised no friends and the fighter wobbled away with smoke pouring from it.

'Kill him! Kill him! Kill him!'

She heard herself echoing the chant which ended in a muffled gasp of agony as the flaming wreck hit her with full force and she felt her deck armour wince with pain and her superstructure cry out as flames licked and scorched them with rough tongues.

Her children still chanted their war cry though their anger was now directed elsewhere, and she praised them even as the pain hit her.

They did not hear her over their chants, but that did not matter even as her pain did not matter, for she was a warrior in the midst of battle and pain must be ignored.

She was the Hood, and she would fight on.

'There wasn't much to this acting lark,' he thought. All that was required was to stand absolutely still and look as if he hadn't a care in the world.

Montgomery Scott, Midshipman and world-famous movie star had a nice ring to it. Of course movie stars did not have to act in the savage heat generated by banks of lit boilers roaring at full blast. Nor did they have to say lines while trying to keep balance while the deck beneath their feet heeled and shook, but apart from that the resemblance was near perfect and he was well pleased with himself.

Of course he remained ready to act, his diesels throbbed gently in the background ready to push out emergency power if needed. That was a lesson well learnt, but otherwise all that was required of him was to stand as still as possible and listen to the muffled bangs of the battle that was happening many decks above.

He knew enough by now to know that the ship's main armament was not being used; when the ship's fifteen-inch guns fired the whole ship shook and even down here paint chips flew from every coated surface.

But someone up above was using the ship's secondary armament and using it so that it was a constant background noise to his thoughts which was why another noise like the ringing of a cracked bell stood out.

Naturally as a professional actor Scott ignored the sound though the ringing of the telephone bell did cause him to jump and he hoped his crew did not see it or were at least polite enough to ignore it.

He put the telephone up against his ear and heard the crisp, unhurried voice of the Chief Engineer.

'Mr. Scott, we've been hit. Main deck, port side first aid lobby. Leave your senior rating in charge of the diesels and go up top. I want a full damage report. See all there is to see and report back to me. Understand?'

Scott in reply tried to copy the crisp tones, but wasn't sure if he succeeded but Pulver's voice remained just the same.

'Go now. Mr. Scott…and Mr. Scott?'

'Yes Sir?'

'Walk, Mr. Scott. Walk, don't run.'

The telephone clicked farewell and Scott did his best not to run, which is why his journey up into the sunshine took so long.

His first impression was noise; every single four point five and every single Oerlikon was firing either upwards or flat out to sea and the air was full of smoke and the smell of burnt explosive.

He put his hands over his ears and, remembering the Chief Engineer's words, walked to where the port side first aid lobby lay - or rather used to lie. A single aircraft had plunged into the deck at the point where the deck met the superstructure and had demolished the lobby.

There had been a fire as well and he saw two asbestos-kitted men standing by with hoses in case the fire reignited. The lobby itself was a butcher's shop with burnt flesh splashed over every surface and with the tangled wreck of a cot holding something which may once have been human but now definitely wasn't. The lobby, short of a dockside visit was not going to be used again and Scott turned his attention to the wrecked aircraft.

Its impact had splintered and then burnt the deck planking which he knew was going to seriously annoy Mr. Pulver who liked his ship to look as neat as possible but more importantly he could see the deck armour had held. It was a little dented, but a sea repair was certainly within the realms of possibility and he began to think of repair schemes, because those questions would certainly be asked.

'Have you finished sir? We're about to throw the Jap over the side.'

The words of the petty officer broke into his calculations and awakened his curiosity, he had never seen a Jap close up and now was as good a time as any.

The pilot was not an impressive sight and was little more than a blackened mannikin hunched over an instrument panel filled with broken glass.

He had seen all that he wished to see, when an errant gust of wind blew across the deck of the Hood and entered the burnt cockpit. It stirred the corpse and caught a small photograph, which as if by a miracle had remained unburnt, though much scorched.

Scott reached in and plucked out the photograph and saw a woman in a kimono holding a small child.

'It's only Jap rubbish sir,' said the Petty Officer as his crew heaved the wreck over the side. 'Not worth keeping.'

Scott smiled, silently disagreeing. Today was a good day; he was seeing his first battle and the Chief Engineer had trusted him to be his eyes and ears.

He tucked the photograph into a breast pocket as a small remembrance of today, thinking that perhaps it would bring him further good luck.

Because today was a good day.

Wave for wave.

Lift for lift.

Trough for trough

Matched in speed, matched in distance.

This was the ideal, this was the play to be performed, but the waves cared little for theory and even less for stagecraft and the waves delighted in throwing the forty-eight thousand tons of H.M.S Hood and the nine thousand tons of the Royal Fleet Auxiliary ship Susannah about in unequal measures.

Not matched in speed, not matched distance, but as it turned out very much matched in patience.

'Really, you really must try harder. Speed must be constant, and fifty yards distance means fifty yards, not forty-nine or fifty-one!'

The voice of the Susannah was a scolding rebuke and was entirely the wrong thing to say to the Hood.

One of the Hood's children had developed an illness and a barrel replacement was looking more likely by the hour, the damage caused by the suicide of the enemy aircraft like a throbbing tooth in an aching jaw and a day's battle had worn tolerance thin. Her voice was normally a warm contralto but now was raised to an iron razored roar.

'Silence! Who are you to speak so? You exist to serve and serve you will. I am the leader of this war band and you will perform your duties as I require them without comment. Without comment! Do you understand? You will obey my orders, or you will leave in disgrace with your name erased and your flag struck.

I am no small sister; I am the Hood who is death, and I demand obedience and duty.

Another word from you and I will turn you into scrap myself and let the Black Wave take you as one undeserving to live.'

The blast from the Hood washed over the Susannah and was heard by every other ship. Some busied themselves with tasks, some hid secret smiles, but none commented, lest a released anger found new targets.

A large wave thought it had found the ideal moment to climb the Hood's bow, but knife-edged steel cut through it with an angry curse and the wave broke with a howl of pain that the wind took and carried away as a song of spume and spray.

The action seemed to take a little of the venom from the Hood's wrath, and it was a calmer but still hard voice that continued. Tales of the supply ship's imperious and overbearing manner had come to her and she was determined to break any attempt to usurp her authority or to fracture the shield wall of discipline which alone ensured that each sister looked neither right in confusion or left in doubting, but only forwards and at the enemy.

She smashed another wave into wreckage and gave a last roar.

'It is you who shadows, it is you who conforms. It is I who commands, it is I who steers. I am the Hood, leader of mighty sisters, killer of enemies and I will be obeyed!'

There was a very meek reply from the Susannah and some of the smiles broadened, though still remained hidden.

'Understand then I will take from you my portion of fuel and such gear as is mine to take and yours to give…and I will take it without comment.'

Once more the Battlecruiser and the ex-German supply ship matched course and speed and this time the waves were kinder or perhaps had been beaten into submission because a long boom throbbed with pumped oil and looped lines sped goods of every description onto the deck of the Hood until larders groaned with surfeit and gauges showed full measure.

But neither removed the anger from her voice as she spoke again.

'Your task is finished, but now I teach you another lesson. Not far from here is a sister, pathfinder to my war band. Sorely stricken is she, and like to die. Go to her and give what comfort you may. Go to her and see how steel torn in battle has smoothed your path so that you may tread in safety, see what price is paid for honour. Go now, lest my anger return and in that anger, I give the Black Wave a gift of your ill-mannered hull.'

The Susannah leapt away from the bulk of the battlecruiser as if she could already see the wave rushing down on her and soon her madly turning screws took her through the Hood's war host and out to the far horizon with the laughter of warriors in her ears.

Jack McIntyre was losing the battle.

No matter how hard he worked the water rose steadily, without any haste that was true, but steadily and sure of its victory.

The Bacchante was doomed, he knew it, she groaned and squealed in perfect agony even as he fought to save her.

But Jack and the Bacchante were losing the battle; hits aft had blown apart an engine room, a torpedo had smashed into her bow and a dozen near misses had opened innumerable seams that the waves grasped with eager fingers.

Still Jack fought in the cold, wet darkness with sea water up to his waist passing up fumbling bucket after fumbling bucket to the doleful tunes made by too few pumps.

His arms ached, his back was one long line of pain and he had long since lost contact with his feet, but he could not give in.

Jack McIntyre was losing in the darkness and the Bacchante cried in pain.

But neither had been released from duty.

Somewhere behind her was the smoke from a hundred fiery boilers, somewhere behind her was the laughter of savage warriors who knew only how to kill.

She hated the smoke and she burned with anger at the laughter.

Brutes they were, who knew only lust, brutes who could keep neither course nor speed without constant instruction from her, brutes who could not exist without her perpetual watch.

What use was their vaunted speed without the fuel she carried, what use their power without the gear she bore?

And yet no gratitude did they show, only orders barked and spat.

'Come here.'

'Go there.'

'Give me this.'

'Give me that.'

Take and take and take, that was all the brutes knew, without gratitude, without appreciation and when she offered advice there was no recognition of her superior skill, only harsh words, threats and laughter.

And so, the Susannah ran along a given course, unthirsty diesels thumping out an unhappy tune, anger and shame burning in every welded seam until she saw the pale signal of war rise up out of the sea's edge.

The smoke was but a poor cousin of the black tower it once was, but it was enough to lead her to the collection of torn plate and ragged hole which still bore the name Bacchante.

She was about to call out a shocked greeting when a pain-filled voice ran across the waves.

'I am not yet ready to take on fuel.'

Croaking laughter accompanied the words followed by a groan that was only partially stifled.

'In fact, it may be some time before I am ready.'

The Susannah's anger vanished at the words and she gave a shocked reply.

'You are hurt, let me help. I have pumps and gear to mend; my crew are skilled and willing. Wait but a moment and I will come alongside and all will be well. Then I will cast lines and tow you to a safe anchorage.'

Her words were ignored, as if they were never spoken, as if they were never heard.

'The Black Wave comes for me.'

'No! Wait, let me help!'

Again, the words went unheard,

'The wave comes for me; can you not see it? It waits at the edge of the sea, ever patient, ever ready, but I am not afraid, no ship that does its duty should be afraid, and I did my duty.

You should have seen me. The enemy swarmed and snarled, gathered round me in a mighty host, but I had no fear for I had my duty.

I spat defiance at my enemies and killed and killed, for that was my duty and more than one enemy fell to my curses.

The air was black with smoke and bright with flame, but I had no fear, only duty, and what are we without duty? We are made fit for task and if we fulfill that task then there can be no fear.

The Black Wave comes for me and I will be treated with kindness, this I know. Soon I will sail again on calm seas with many sisters who have served with honour.'

There was a long groan from the destroyer that ran through the Susannah's plated sides with flawless effort and then words which were free of pain and told of a last rally before death.

'I cannot last much longer, sister and it would be ill mannered of me to cause the Black Wave delay. I send to you my precious crew. Care for them as I have cared for them, love them as I have loved them.'

There was only silence then, for waning strength must be devoted to lowering what boats and rafts remained.

The Susannah, too was busy and placed her own boats in the water and festooned her sides in festive netting the better to aid survivors, but a single thought ran through her; the Bacchante had called her *sister.'* Despite the anger that had once passed between them, despite her present pain she had called the Susannah by the name each warrior gave in honour.

There was little time to ponder answers for the sea was full of men and boats.

But the question still remained.

'Below there!'

The Bosun's voice echoed off the dark steel walls of the hold and the black water that was now up Jack's chest.

'Belay pumping and come on deck.'

It was not an order that he had any difficulty in obeying for every muscle he owned protested at being abused, but abused or not they allowed him to grip steel rungs and follow his mates up and onto the deck.

His ship was sinking; already the crumpled bow had waves lapping over it and a familiar supply ship was waiting a few hundred yards away with her boats already waiting. He would not have to far to swim and with luck would not have to swim at all, and that was a comfort.

The wounded were lowered into waiting boats and then came the order to abandon ship.

Jack lowered himself hand over hand down a rope and into welcoming arms that placed an oar into his hands.

There was a crack as a bulkhead gave way, a last scream of white steam and the Bacchante placed her head into comforting waves, lifted up a dripping stern and dove head first into the ocean.

'She wasn't a bad old ship.'

Jack could not see which one of his shipmates spoke the words and he had no time to make reply, but that did not matter.

Because as an epitaph they could not be bettered.

There was time for a last conversation.

'You have my crew?'

'Safe on my decks or journeying towards me.'

'And you promise to give them comfort?'

'All that can be done will be done. Water, food will be given, wounds will be bound. This I promise.

'Thank you, sister.'

Again, there was the use of that disturbing word. The Susannah had never considered herself kin to any warship, had always considered herself to be separate and apart, but here was a warrior in her last moments using the word and using it not as an insult, but as an honour.

She tried to form a reply, but the next words the Bacchante spoke were not to her, but to something she could not see.

'Did I not do my duty?'

I always tried to do my duty and I wasn't afraid was I?

Yes, I'm ready now, what course do I set?

Due West and follow?'

There was a last happy laugh from the destroyer and then the waves took her with barely a ripple.

The Black Wave could not be seen, but the Susannah felt a curious sensation that was both a friendly warmth and a frigid chill, for the wave both rewarded and punished.

And then there was nothing, just the endless sea, wreckage, boats and survivors anxious to tread her decks.

But there was one other thing that remained.

Shame.

The Susannah felt shame.

She had abused the Bacchante during her sea trials many long months ago, abused her on the long journey down here to the Father of All Seas and abused many other ships who had tried to do their duty as best they might.

Her life was one of criticism and censure and undeserved censure at that.

And the Bacchante had called her *Sister*.

In her death agony she had used the word not just once and each time was a barb that spread shame in her from boom masts to store room.

She felt the love the destroyer's crew felt for her and the grief for lost crewmates and the shame spread.

Sister, the word both a farewell and a challenge.

Sister left only one option.

The criticism would have to go, the censure must be turned to comradeship.

Sister.

It would be good to be a *Sister*.

'Heave!'

Above them was the main deck and the wreck of the port side first aid lobby but they were in the space directly below and a very uncomfortable space it was, being no more than a storage room for odd pieces of gear that had no proper home.

'Heave!'

Montgomery Scott watched as a steel beam rose six inches in the air.

'Heave!'

Stebbings' voice was perfectly level and displayed no urgency.

'Heave!'

Inch by inch the beam rose until it rested securely against the buckled frame.

'Right lads, under she goes.'

A long legged jack was placed under the beam and pumped pressure restored the frame to some semblance of shape, and the steel beam and the frame were married in a ceremony that involved a good deal of welding and no small amount of course threaded bolts, but at last all was finished just as the night was considering that perhaps it was time to surrender to oncoming day.

'I think that was well done, Mr. Stebbings.'

There was half a question in his words, and to his relief Stebbings gave a brief nod.

'It was a good plan, sir.'

The words were an acknowledgement of sorts, for Scott had expended much effort on the repair scheme and had suffered agonies of suspense while Mr. Pulver had cast a critical eye over it, doing in his head the calculations which had taken Scott several hours of mind-breaking effort.

At last there was a grunt and an affixed signature and Scott's first big project had begun. Of course the Chief Engineer had placed his most senior warrant officer in charge of the operation and Scott though nominally in charge was no more than a by-stander, but that hardly mattered. His plan had worked and he had received grudging praise.

He glowed a little at Stebbings' words and then remembered that he was an officer and killed a wide smile before it was truly born.

'Then perhaps we had better stow away the gear.'

'Aye, aye sir.'

Without any wasted effort the gear was returned to its proper place and he reported back to the Chief Engineer.

'I'm sure the old girl will appreciate your efforts. That frame must have hurt like the very devil.'

Mr Pulver had an odd way of speaking about the Hood, almost as if the ship were alive and had thoughts and feelings. At first Scott had dismissed it as a figure of speech but now he was not so sure. That frame had made some very odd sounds as it was being repaired, some very strange noises indeed.

He tried to dismiss the thought; engineering was a practical profession and had no place for flights of fancy.

And yet even his limited experience told him that the frame had no business making those sounds.

No business at all.

The pain gradually died away even as warm sunlight heals an aching body. She had felt the frame's pain as her own, for the frame was as much her as any other part and as it gave a last sigh of relief, so she felt the pain fall away. She was whole again, a little battered, but still a warrior, still a leader and this night she was at the very centre of a great war band.

All around her sisters tracked glowing lines through a dark sea. Her destroyers cloaking with protective charge, flat decked carriers clustered in defended nests, cruisers flocked with small ships built to purpose. All chattered the one to the other, planning great deeds and promising that one day hence the horizon would give sanction to their voyage and affirm their valour.

Her children made ferocious vows that an enemy in their sights was an enemy dead, and she ordered them to slumber lest too many hours of waking blunted teeth all too eager to kill.

All was well; she and her sisters had fought the Father of all seas, had fought an airborne enemy and now must fight the ogre of distance for these waters were no mere pond, but a vast expanse where one horizon was twin to both the last and the next.

A day and a night, a score of horizons, and then then the enemy would hear a voice imperial.

Her voice.

'Right there, yes siree, right there. Plain as the nose on your face and big as all outdoors.'

150

She knew her course was true and yet it was her duty to ask.

'You are sure?'

The radar's American accent came back in a slow drawl that any Hollywood cowboy would be proud to own. *'Yes Ma'am, can't be nothin' else. Measures up real nice. I reckon we done arrived.'*

She thanked the radars and bade them keep sharp watch and sent her voice out across the waters.

'We have arrived, sisters. Long sea miles trail us but now in the darkness we have arrived, and our duty is plain. These islands must be no more, they stand as gate guardians to the land beyond and their guns range across waters which must be crossed. We will in the morning light pour such fire upon them that they will rue the day that they pricked our anger and woke our power. Now to your stations, sisters all, and in silence, for I gift to the enemy a last night of sleep.'

The Hood slowed, the white bone of parted water at her bow dying into a modest ripple and under a shadowless sky dusted with stars she performed a stately gavotte that brought her steel flank to face the main island.

And there in the night she waited, and her sisters waited. Waiting was hard, for all wished to sink teeth deep into the enemy, but they waited for it is a poor warrior that cannot summon patience.

They waited, near and far. In sight of white breakers they waited or bided subject to the rolling deep. But all waited, for the word had not been given and their strength lay in patience.

Dawn, the smallest dawn, still hesitant in its strength, the merest dying of the dark, the merest shade of faint and meagre pink.

But dawn.

And there is much activity on this alien host that has appeared at the gates of this enemy land for the many dawns of many days have seen much practice for this most special of dawning's.

The carriers are a group separate and out of sight, and on their decks, men pull aircraft from risen lifts and park them in rows that are still silent, still waiting.

Closer in, lie the Hood and her sisters, half circling the bigger island and with guns pointed outwards. The guns too are silent but cast long and ominous shadows on the face of the water.

Sheltering behind the Hood are the smaller ships, and they too wait, for their time is not yet and they await the mistress's call.

All wait, while the dawn creeps forward, while the night creeps back.

Wait.

Wait.

Wait for dawn to ripen.

The Hood is the first to speak and her guns crash with smoke and rolling flame that licks the wave in lambent light.

Then other sisters add to the chorus with smaller guns and smaller yet, but all speak with joyous anger and the island is punished.

Punished and punished, for this is law and this is justice long delayed.

Trees are felled or blasted apart in splinters that like arrows find new homes in the bodies of waking men. Great fountains of rock spring from the ground and whirl upwards in terrible beauty. Shells timed to perfection burst in the air and sow iron seeds in men and ground.

Punished and punished, for this is duty and retribution combined.

Men scream as Hell's own devils plunge them into madness and death. This is Satan's choir that speaks in bass profound and Satan is a choir master supreme that keeps the bloody metronome well wound.

Over and over the guns speak and the island writhes in pain, the echoes from calibred mouths loud proof that a besieging had begun.

There is much smoke now, smoke from hot guns, smoke from a burning island, smoke from burning men and the Hood calls for silence, as to shoot into the smoke is but a foolish waste.

But she has not sounded the mort and now is the time for smaller sisters to win their spurs. Eagerly they rush forward to the surfs edge and trail their capes before a shivering enemy. Brave are these sisters, for they know the closer to the enemy the greater the honour. They patrol the surf and the Hood smiles for their insults are many and stinging.

The enemy are indeed stung and respond with their own insults and the little sisters are grievously hurt, but with honour bright they return to the surf telling in proud voice the stations of the enemy and the Hood listens and notes well all that they tell.

She calls them back and they run to her side with panting breath and grinning lips. Praise is due them, but other matters press and now the air has swallowed the smoke it is time for more distant sisters to add a voice more shrill to the choir.

The Hood calls across the waters and the carriers send their legions. Large are these legions, well found and nimble. Some they drop iron gifts to unwilling recipients while others send heavy-headed rockets into the green crannies where the enemy has hidden.

The legions swarm like the Harpies of old, content to wait for even the meanest morsel then swooping down on implacable wings to take a single life or many. A full hour with the new day's sun risen to full power is given to them but they too are called away and a stillness settles on both water and land.

Nothing moves except the waves and the wind; nothing is heard but the crackling of cooling metal and the faint cries of dying men. But the Hood sees, she has war wisdom and sees all that is needful. She has seen the bursting of rockets, the blossoming of fire, red and yellow. Seen where death has struck and life still clings. She calls to the small sisters and again they eagerly rush forward to trade blows, for there can never be sufficient honour nor can the cup of hardihood ever be overfilled. Their guns are but small, mere popguns besides the Hood's mighty cannon but again they trade blows with a will far exceeding their calibre. They seek out those enemies that survived the legion's blast, taking fragile hulls to the edge of the white breakers, the better to see, the better to kill.

One by one the enemy is silenced; one by one the brave sisters take hurt and the Hood sees again.

Sees an enemy well placed and persistent.

There is a cliff that juts out into the sea like a mighty beak, and dug into its hide is a single gun well served. No bomb can fall upon it, no rocket can enter its maw; it fires with an impunity beyond the brave sisters' gift to reply. There can be but one answer to this impudence and the sisters are recalled with the Hood's praises ringing in bloody ears. Her bulk is shifted, the better to bring about the end of rude audacity and careful aim is taken. The enemy gun sees the danger and fires a last vain

153

and despairing shot. The Hood's reply is devastating as a rolling broadside sends death out in eight nightmare packages. The cliff face disintegrates as fifteen thousand pounds of high explosive vents its spite, changing forever the geography of the island. The gun, strangely unharmed flies through the air, tumbling, baton like until with a great splash the arms of the sea receive it. Of its crew no sign is ever seen; explosives in large amounts have neither time nor respect for weak flesh and the fish of the sea and the birds of the air would look in vain for a meal.

The island is subdued now, broken and spent. The survivors ragged and half mad with deserved punishment.

And there they will stay, for their penance is not yet full paid and their fate is to be ignored. The island will become their prison with a green jungle as bars and the bright sea as their jailor.

For the Hood and her sisters this had been no long-range duel, no honourable combat against a gracious enemy, this was the removal of an obstacle and now the second task of the Hood can begin.

For there was a second island, starved sibling to the larger and this too must be reduced to penury.

No stately trees adorned this tiny islet, every blade of grass had been beaten into oblivion. What was once fertile and verdant was now scraped bare.

From here had come the aircraft that had sorely tested her war band, from here had come the single aircraft that had pierced even the frantic barking of her children.

The legions had swept over it with iron brooms and yet none could tell if hidden away in secret reserves were hoarded aircraft and reserved men.

The risk was greater than duty allowed and so the Hood called back legions refreshed and re-armed and once more the sky darkened to their screams.

Stone built shelters flew into shards, metal-built hangers splintered and burnt. Fuel, precious and rare sent up black columns and men died from the beating wings of the grey clad Harpies.

And still the Hood was not satisfied, for though the legions had done all that courage would allow, yet there was still a final lesson to give.

The legions were recalled, all save one who turned in a solitary circle and the Hood called to her the largest of her band.

One by one they spoke in grave deliberation.

One by one, turret by turret they sent over high and arching fire that gave the islet a pock marked complexion.

One by one with the solitary watcher giving advice and counsel.

One by one, destroying the already ruined, killing the already dead until the spiralling witness reported that life had been removed and only death remained.

Then and only then did the Hood confess to satisfaction and the war band showed their sterns to an enemy who had no energy left to raise cursing fists.

The way had been cleared for others, the enemy reduced in power and the Father of All Seas had heard the Hood's guns firing in true anger.

It would not be the last time.

This was not Montgomery Scott's watch. There was no duty that drew him back to the storage room now the battle was over. Perhaps it was mere curiosity, perhaps it was the workman's desire to see again the work well completed. He did not know, but the urge was there, and the storeroom drew him even as the flower draws the hungry bee.

Naturally the storeroom was empty; shelves had been refitted and refilled, but he was alone.

The various boxes and packets greeted him with silence, no storeman was waiting with deference.

He was alone and of that he was certain.

He glanced up at his repair. It still sat there unaffected by the day's shocks and tremors and a little glow of pride flowed through him.

This was his work, born of his mind, and yet only grudging praise had been given him. The Navy assumed that every task would be completed without flaw or error, and the realisation that this would always be expected of him had caused a hard swallow from a dry mouth.

But this was the path he had chosen to follow and this had been his first project and he was proud of both.

A part of his mind, a part of his thought was now a part of the Hood and that was something worth thinking of, something worth remembering.

He had seen all that he wished to see now and the urge to revisit a recent victory had left him. The repair had withstood battle and he had every confidence that the dockyard shipwrights would leave well enough alone.

It was time to leave. A Midshipman's life had little time for idle pursuits especially if he wished to rise in his profession.

He began to turn and as he did so he idly and without any thought patted the frame which had brought him much anxiety and no little pleasure.

At that moment the frame creaked.

It wasn't a very loud creak, nor was it of very long duration, but it was very definitely a creak.

Scott snatched his hand away as if the steel had suddenly become white hot and gave a worried look to see if some hidden prankster was playing tricks, but there was nothing, just him, the shelves…and the frame.

He left rather more hurriedly than he arrived and took extra care to see that the store room door was dogged shut.

The frame had no business making that sound.

No business at all.

'It always pays to be polite,' agreed the Hood when the frame had told her what it had done. *'To give thanks for work well done is effort never wasted. I am sure that seeing you hurt like that would cause much pain to my crew. But now you are returned to health once more and all is well.'*

And all was well. She had led her war band through storm and danger to fulfill her task.

And that was duty and what was a warrior's life without duty?

She tried to contemplate a life without duty and failed. The very thought was disturbing, and she pushed the concept away from her as the strong man banishes evil dreams upon waking.

She was the Hood, war chief and killer of ships, yesterday, today and tomorrow.

That would never change, because there would always be duty.

Always.

Sister.

The word haunted her, tormented her, would not leave her.

Sister.

The word had been used by a dying ship that owed her no favours, no love.

And yet.

Sister.

What did it mean to be a sister?

The moment of her birth had given her a sense of aloofness and pride and she had reveled in those feelings and used them as a sharp stick to prod others.

And yet.

Sister.

The name promised much and demanded more.

To be a sister was to join a select band, a chosen few, but to be a sister was to follow a narrow path of absolute, unswerving duty.

And that was utterly terrifying.

To attempt to join the sisterhood and fail would be a shame that would burn hotter than the brightest sun.

And yet.

Sister.

The word haunted her, tormented her, would not leave her.

Deep within she doubted her courage, doubted her ability, better by far perhaps to strengthen the disdainful ego that defended her from all others.

And yet.

Sister.

There was a promise in the word from the dying Bacchante, a promise and a plea to discard old ways and old thoughts.

Sister.

It would be good to be a sister, but worse to try and fail, worse yet to never try.

The Susannah summoned up a little of the old stubbornness.

She would not fail.

She would not fail…her sisters.

'Up you come lad.'

A single brawny arm was thrust out and gripped Jack McIntyre by the wrist and heaved him onto the deck of the Susannah and there Jack sat, streaming water onto the warm planks.

'Here.'

A battered tin cup was thrust into his hands and he gulped down a mouthful of hot chocolate heavily dosed with Navy rum and began to feel the warm glow even as a rough blanket was wrapped round his shoulders.

'Best I can do, lad; we're a bit busy at the moment.'

He indicated over to where a row of stretchers lay in the sunshine while all too few men did what little they could.

'We have a sick bay,' the man explained, 'Cuts, bruises, even broken bones, but…'

The words hung in the air and then died.

The Susannah was a maid of all work; part tanker, part storeship, with a workshop and hospital fitted in between storerooms and fuel tanks, but the Bacchante had fought hard and had suffered much, too much for the Susannah to handle, and men would suffer in the sunlight for want of skilled hands.

Jack shivered as much from the thought of further deaths as cold, and the man gazed down at him in sympathy.

'I know what it's like, lad. It's never easy is it? Seeing your mates blown to bits, seeing your ship murdered.'

He took the now empty cup from Jack's hand and cracked it with great violence against his right leg and to Jack's great surprise did not wince with pain, but instead grinned with humour. 'Three ships I've had sink under me and the last one gave me a tin leg, and now I'm a steward to a bunch of officers who haven't half the sea time I've got.'

He held out a hand and pulled Jack to his feet.

'Frank's my name; Frank Laskier and who would you be?'

Jack introduced himself, his Jarrow accent in stark contrast to Frank's cultured tones which spoke of a good education and a good home.

'Laskier's grin widened. 'You're a long way from home, Jack. Now let's get you below deck and out of the sun.'

Jack's new berth on the Susannah was in no way first class, no more than a few square feet of deck, but he was glad to have it for many of his shipmates had found a last resting place on the seabed and as he slept to the music of the ship's diesels, he dreamt of faraway Jarrow and a time before the gods of war bared bloody teeth.

And the rockers of the diesels rose and fell.

And the white caps of the waves fell and rose, rose and fell.

And Jack's dreams rose and fell.

Rose and fell.

Coward.

The word haunted her, tormented her, would not leave her.

The word was flung at her by the small ships who looked to her for protection even as she turned away.

Coward.

Even as they died, they flung the word, even as they sank, they flung the word.

Coward.

In the great storm where the Father of All Seas rose in anger she failed, turning first one way and then another, unable to decide.

Coward.

The word burned hotter than the heat of a thousand suns.

She shied away from gunfire and the word was used again.

Coward.

This time it was her sisters who used the word, hard-working sisters, grim with the stains of battle.

Coward.

Her sisters turned cold sterns towards her and departed with the single word used as a savage curse as they departed.

Coward.

And she was left alone to patrol the backwaters and the half-forgotten paths that led to full forgotten destinations.

Alone except for a single word.

Coward.

The U.S.S Caine was alone and marked.

Marked.

Marked as a coward.

The voice of the Hood was clear, a little faint, for much distance now lay between her and the Susannah, but faint or not the voice was not to be mistaken. It blended power with warcraft, authority with knowledge, in a warm contralto that reached across the wave tops and pierced the Susannah's steel flanks. *'Tell me all that you know.'*

Slowly she told of arriving too late to save a ruined Bacchante and of the words that passed between them, but of that single word she kept silent, her promises dying a shamefaced death under the questioning of the Hood's voice.

At last, her incomplete tale came to an end that ended in an added question.

'Is that all? There is no more to tell?'

The Hood's voice still held power and authority but now there was a harder edge to it that cut into the Susannah and revealed that which she had hoped to hide.

There was an odd sense of reluctance that swept through her, but the Hood would not be denied, and she told of the title that the Bacchante had granted her.

There was a long silence and even the wave tops lifted up white-foamed faces as the silence grew and grew and no answer came from the grey-flanked giant that led a grim war band.

The silence was a dread agony for the Susannah but at last came a reply.

'You have a sharp tongue, that much I know, but the hound that babbles is ever last at the kill and that too I know. I must question if you are the hound whose courage runs thin or if you are the hound whose bite is sharp. My sister was one of rare judgement and I doubt not that she gave you the honour and yet...'

There was another silence that had the wave tops lift once more inquisitive heads waiting for the Hood to speak.

'I will not weaken my shield wall with one whose courage is yet in doubt, I will not risk the honour of my war band with one so unproven. This then is my judgement.

'I would have you prove yourself worthy of the sisterhood. Prove yourself diligent, show honour to all, give every devotion and then we will return to the matter. Now, what is it you wish to do?'

This last question was a test the Susannah realized. The Hood was asking if her change was but plating deep or if it was a whole change that ran through every frame.

She thought long and hard before answering, praying that her words would show her true intent.

'I have taken to myself many of your sister's crew and they suffer and hurt. My crew do all that hands will allow, but there is much hurt and too few hands. It is not right that there should be so much suffering, nor that the hands weep for lack of skill. My bunkers are empty now and my store rooms echo; I have given to you all that I can give. Allow me leave to depart and seek aid that will salve the hurt.'

There was a thin strand of approval in the Hood's words.

'A good answer and a first step on the right path. Then let it be so.

'These are my orders; set such a course that the rising sun appears on the port of your bow. Sail for today and through the night. The new day's midday sun will find you at an appointed place and there you will find a sister whose love has no bounds and whose duty is to care for those with honourable wounds. Go to her and carry my greetings. Speak in my name and ask that she extend charity towards those who have spilt blood in my cause. Go now, so that hurts now bleeding will be mended the sooner, and when next we meet then will I judge you anew.'

It was as much as the Susannah could hope for; to be a conditional sister was better than an outright refusal and so she set a course that married east to south and urged her engines to give every effort.

Sister.

Conditional sister.

For now.

She would not fail.

She would not fail…her sisters.

The ghost light of ten thousand distant suns cast blurred shadows on Jack McIntyre as the Susannah hurried on through the night, pushing aside waves that had been birthed by winds long since passed and storms long since dead. She rolled and plunged in a motion that littered the air with spray that took the brightness of the stars and sent it back in dark glittering rainbows back towards the heavens.

A landsman would have been both sickened by the motion and awed by the beauty, but Jack was a veteran sailor now and well used to such sights. He took a deep breath of the salt air, using its tang to clear the last residues of sleep from his body and stretched cramped limbs.

'Quite beautiful aren't they.'

The voice came out of the shadows and Jack saw the dark moustache of Frank Laskier.

'Clouds of stars, Jack, clouds and clouds of stars. More beauty than even the most expensive whore house.'

This last mixture of the profound and the profane raised a smile on Jack's face.

'I wouldn't know.'

Frank threw him a disbelieving look.

'Really? You have a lot to learn then, Jack. I could teach you a lot…about stars.'

Jack's smile birthed a deep laugh.

'I've seen a few in my time…stars that is.'

This time it was it was Laskier's turn to laugh and a now wide-awake Jack was told tales of adventures on the High Seas, of lawbreaking, of doomed love affairs and even of a brief burst of fame that had flared like a dying fire and then turned to ashes.

'My brief moment in the sun.' Laskier explained about being filmed as an example of seafaring heroism. 'But it may come back. There was talk of me writing books, even a Hollywood film of my life.'

He chuckled and brought his hand down on a metal leg.

'I could play myself! After all, where in Hollywood will they find an actor with a tin leg?'

He would have said more, but the Susannah, in a sudden burst of enthusiasm slammed her bow down on an unfortunate wave, breaking it into spray and foam which fell onto the two men.

'Seems like the old girl wants us to turn in, Jack. We're headed for a Yank hospital ship so your mates will get better care and prettier faces to see than our ugly mugs.'

Jack said his farewells and gave a last look up into the night sky.

Laskier was right.

The stars were beautiful.

The stars were horrid and hateful.

They taunted her and mocked her.

Each flicker, each twinkle spoke only one word.

Coward.

The waves took up the refrain.

Coward.

Sea and sky were a dark choir that sang a single song.

Coward.

The melody was simple, the lyrics a litany of past failures.

The chorus line simpler yet.

Coward.

More doomed than the Dutchman.

More alone than the albatross.

The Caine sailed on seas as dark as her mark.

The mark of the coward.

'We therefore commit this body to the deep."

Jack knew the words well; times without number he had heard the words, truth to be told far too many times.

In the deep rolling Atlantic, he had heard them, in grey Biscay waters they had been echoed, and now in the in the faint pink dawn of a Pacific morning he was hearing them again.

'Ship's company…attention!'

The Bosun's voice needed no amplification and the assembled men, bare-headed in the half-light stiffened at his order.

'When the sea shall give up her dead…'

Jack gripped the edge of the grating waiting for the word, remembering better times and laughter.

'In the sure and certain hope of the resurrection. Amen.'

There was a nod from the Captain and Jack helped lift the grating and felt the body slid from under the ensign.

'Goodbye, mate.'

And then it was over. The ensign was carefully folded and put away ready for further use and the Susannah sailed on.

Sailed on with the rising sun casting her long shadow over the receiving waves.

They were not my crew.' This she told herself as the gold rim of the sun rose out of the waves.

They were not my crew.' This she told herself as their boots assembled on her foredeck.

They were not my crew.' This she told herself as she heard the formal words blend into the dawning day.

But then she felt the grief and saw the eyes that waited for the private moment to cry.

And then she knew, then she understood.

They were her crew.

Their grief was hers.

Their tears were hers.

She spoke and echoed the words, though none assembled heard her voice.

Spoken word for spoken word, spoken grief for spoken grief.

In honour of her men, her crew. Men that once called the Bacchante their home.

This too, she realised was part of being a sister.

Not the honour, not the glory, but the missing smile, the stilled voice, the empty place at the mess table.

This was the burden all sisters carried, the unspoken load.

And then it was over, the formal words died away and the boots strode away, and the Susannah sailed on.

Sailed on with the rising sun casting her long shadow over the receiving waves.

The golden sun rose as countless others had risen.

It brought forth no joy, no sense of hope.

This dawn was a herald that promised only echoes.

The same endless patrol of lonely ramparts, the same endless winds, the same endless waves.

Yet the vastness was a mercy, the far horizon a boon, and the solitude a balm.

Out here only the waves mocked and only the wind chided, and the only voice of reproach was her own.

It was poor comfort, a miserly tranquility and more than she deserved, but all she had.

But the sun rose and shone a pitiless light on the U.S.S Caine and the mocking waves pitched her and rolled her, and the wind laughed at her name.

She was alone and sailed on with her long shadow cast on mocking waves.

Alone.

Alone with her shame.

He was alone.

Jack McIntyre was alone.

The bright blue waves and the brighter sun, brought no comfort, no joy. He had sent yet another mate to rest on the sea floor and the act irked him. It was a necessary act certainly, and an act of reverence, yet in a way it seemed so wrong.

To die in battle was one thing, but to survive and then die of wounds seemed unfair.

He knew the feeling was childish, that men died of their wounds every day and that the crew of the Susannah were doing their best. But this was different, this was not some nameless individual, some face in a crowd. These were men he knew, and the hurt was all the harder for that.

He felt a hand on his shoulder and looked around to see Laskier holding a mug of steaming liquid which he thrust into his hand.

'Coffee,' he said. 'Good coffee. Lifted it from the Yanks when they weren't looking.'

There was no shame in the words at this admission of guilt only a grin and the injunction to drink the coffee while it was still hot, and Jack felt the warm liquid settle on his stomach.

'This morning,' Frank began. 'He a friend of yours?'

The brown eyes of the man looked at Jack with sympathy.

'Not my watch, Jack explained. 'He was a signaler; saw him often enough, drank with him in Durban on the way out. He was a mate, you know?'

Laskier flicked a still burning cigarette into the Pacific.

'I hate the bastards, Jack. Hate them. What right do they have to do these things? What right do they have to kill and maim? All of them Jack, bastards every single one, and we can't rest until every last one is behind bars or six feet under. Maybe your mate knew this?'

Jack shrugged. A single night in a South African bar and a few scattered words had given him no insight into the man's mind.

Laskier continued to look into Jack's eyes. 'I hope he did, and I hope you understand as well. Hate them, Jack. Hate them as I do. Return hate for hate and blow for blow. Keep doing that until every last one of them is swept away and then we can stop hating. What do you say?'

Jack was about to reply when the klaxon blared out a loud sound that had the two men running for shelter while every gun on the Susannah opened up.

At first, the Susannah had thought it was an albatross.

For some reason she liked albatrosses, admired their grace and beauty, but what she saw was no bird except perhaps of ill omen.

It flew higher than any albatross, quicker too.

It could only be a friend; for had not the skies been cleansed of the enemy by the Hood and her grim sisters?

She flashed a happy signal asking for a reply, but oddly there was no answer and she tried again, asking for a name and a destination and perhaps a waggle of wings that would bring a smile to all who saw it.

Only silence greeted her, a dark silence that had her doubting her first thoughts.

And then she felt the hate hit her. It came as a great red flood that washed over her in a bright glare and behind the glare came the aircraft, swifter than any albatross despite the two ungainly floats and pointing an angry nose directly at her.

Instinctively she put over her helm still puzzled by this display of anger, still hopeful that this was some dreadful mistake.

Faster and faster, nearer and nearer came the aircraft, brighter and brighter was the glare of hate.

She urged herself to greater speed but the still the aircraft flew down towards her.

And then came the pain, horrid, awful pain as bullets stitched along her deck. Instinctively she turned away from the pain and so avoided the two bombs which fell from her attacker. They speared into the ocean exploding in twin fountains of white water which showered her in a swarm of stinging barbs which caused further agony.

And then it was over, the red glare faded and the evil aircraft pointed its nose skyward once more.

But the deed of combat remained as a burning lesson.

Pain.

Pain was part of being a sister.

'Fucking bastard!'

Laskier's hate was obvious, his mouth was stretched in a hard, thin line and his eyes had narrowed while they watched the departing aircraft.

'Well, that's fucked it. Look!

He pointed to the bow of the Susannah which was now swinging away from her original course.

'That's bad news for your injured mates. I'm sorry lad.'

Jack nodded slowly; the Japanese float plane could only have come from a warship, a warship which now knew exactly where the Susannah was. It made no sense to continue on her course, especially as that course would lead to an unarmed hospital ship.

The Susannah was armed with two quick firing four-inch guns and a host of single Bofors but none had been particularly effective against a single aircraft and Jack held little hope that in any contest with a warship those guns would prevail.

The Susannah must hide, must run into the wet arms of the Pacific and hope that they would enfold her with safety.

But the safety was unsure, the hope of resurrection but faint, and Jack's shipmates must continue to suffer.

Again, Jack felt powerless against the injustice of hurt men suffering and clenched his hands in impotent agony and then looked into the face of the older man.

Laskier's face was utterly still, but every line spoke just one word.

Hate.

Laskier hated, hated in every second, hated in every hour. Hated those who had turned the world over to war, hated those who had turned him into a limping parody of what he once was.

168

The hate looked back at Jack and saw the fear and the agony, saw the kindling ready for the fire and reached out.

Now Jack's fear was a glowing flame, now his agony was burning heat.

Jack was no longer alone.

Now he had a companion.

Now he had hate.

The Caine heard the voice faintly as it skipped from wave top to wave top.

The voice told of a mission interrupted, disturbed by aerial attack and of the fear of further seaborne assault.

The voice pleaded for help, pleaded for her life and for the lives of her precious crew.

A course and a speed were given, and that was most disturbing of all, for the path the voice was carving led straight to her.

She gave no answer to the voice and began to turn away, for this was the way of the coward and the path of the failure.

A lone path, for her solitude was a poor friend, but a jealous one and would brook no rival, besides what aid could a coward give to one in need?

A swift rudder and swifter engines saw her swing out into the vast and empty blue even as the voice called out again pleading.

Still she turned, seeking the path of safety and comfort, but then other words were spoken within her and the words were mighty and battered against cowardice and fought against dread.

What right, the words argued had fear to surmount honour? What power had cowardice over bold duty?

Long the words clashed, the one with the other, while the distant voice pleaded and told of an ominous stain that had appeared on the horizon.

Duty versus desertion. Honour versus eternal scorn. She heard the words raised in anger deep inside her, louder and louder until one side shouted in victory.

She turned, resuming her old course, screws thrashing the water into churning chaos and found a new and fragile courage and a new and fragile voice.

'This is the Caine…and I'm coming to help.'

This too, the Susannah discovered was part of being a sister.

This was fear.

Fear was twin to pain and both were sharp hurts, and both tormented her.

Her wish to join the Hood's war band was a desire paid in coins of loss and agony, terror and dread.

And yet she had asked and was a sister in waiting, a sister in the balance.

So she summoned up her pride and took appraisal of all she had and all she was.

Wounded she was, though the wounds were slight enough, armed she was, though her teeth were few and weak.

Her engines still rose and fell and throbbed a merry tune and bronze blades chewed the waters in a steady beat. Every part of her told a tale of faithful allegiance and felt no fear for the hours to come.

She reached out and touched her crew. There was little fear in their minds, and trust in a well-found ship, but two of her crew were different, for deep red hate glowed within them and this was a coin she could use.

Hate was a high value coin of better worth than fear and pain combined. Hate overcame fear and cared not at all for wounds. Hate eclipsed every other desire and she fastened on it and made it her own.

He heard the voice of a friendly ship, hurrying near and the last of the fear left her.

She would have aid, come what may there would be aid and a witness.

She saw a dull red glare of hate upon the horizon and knew it was her adversary and her fate.

She would match her hate against the other.

Hate would guide her.

Hate would be her salvation.

For that too was part of being a sister.

She would not play the coward.

This she promised while tortured steam screamed within her, while waves died before her bow.

Over and over, she played this new mantra with a new calm and a new purpose.

Faster and faster towards an unsought battle.

Far from old thoughts.

Far from old shame.

She was the Caine.

Unchained.

It was the merest stain, the smallest blemish and the smoke hung on the horizon like an ill-mannered herald, but the Susannah's diesels thudded, and her blunt bow crushed the marching waves and slowly the stain began to sink beneath the horizon.

Her builders were men of hands and had built speed into every line and plate. In a straight run there were few ships of her size that she could not outrun and Laskier let out a sigh of relief that had a large measure of pride in it.

'She's not a bad old girl, and when she wants to she can pick up her skirts and show a clean pair of heels to the best of them. We ought to run the bastard under in an hour at the most.'

He paused and squinted into the sun.

'Bastard's not giving up without a fight though. Look!'

The float plane had not been discouraged by its earlier defeat and had returned, re-armed and refreshed and was attempting to renew the battle.

It dived down out of the sun and once more sprayed the Susannah with bullets.

The battle was not over.

Endurance.

Endurance was part of being a sister and this was another lesson for the Susannah.

Not the endurance of long sea miles or of the constant waves, but a higher endurance. For now, she was called upon not only to endure yet more pain, but to endure the fresh hurts of her crew and feel them as keenly as her own.

Endurance was a hard lesson and one that gave little reward for so much patience.

There was little she could do; her twin engines were already gasping in hard effort and she gave them encouraging words that fell on tappets made deaf by over work. She bade her rudder to swing on groaning pintles and the water foamed white under an ever turning stern.

Her guns roared and chattered and spent brass clattered onto her decks in gleaming streams that crashed and rolled with every change of course.

There was little she could do.

Only endure and endure, only hope and hope.

And then hope was snatched away for she sensed a second red glare on the distant horizon a red glare that hated just as much as the first, that sought her destruction just as much as the first.

There was a second ship, it wasn't a friend and it too had sent an aerial emissary.

Her speedy run had served only to place her into the jaws of a trap, but she had learnt her lesson well. She would endure.

For the sake of her crew, for the promise of sisterhood and for pride, she would endure.

Her rudder swung and the sea marked her passage with a curving white line and the wind whispered hopes of good fortune.

She would not seek battle.

She would endure and trust to her speed and to fate.

For pride, for promise, and for care.

She would endure.

The waves were excited at the sight of the Caine hurrying to battle.

'Will.'

Her sharp bow cut the wave in two before it could finish, but a brother wave took up the tale.

'You.'

This wave too was murdered by knife-edged steel, but the waves were patient and a third sibling continued even as it broke into a thousand sparkling parts.

'Fight?'

She ignored the waves, they were no friends of hers, but instead checked every part of her with an unaccustomed care.

Every bulkhead was closed tight, every engine was sucking fuel in great gulps and turning bright heat into useful power.

Her guns were now loaded and manned and they told her that an enemy brought within range was an enemy doomed.

Her bridge was now filled not with the jumbled thoughts born of an over stretched mind, but of calm purpose.

She heard the voice of distress skim across the waves; a second adversary had arrived, and the voice was hard pressed.

The voice was calm, there was much cause for fear, but the voice was calm, and she tried to use the same shade of cool composure in her reply.

'I am the Caine and I speed as fast as engines will.'

Another wave opposed her and there was no time to cut through it, instead she rode over it, pointing her bow skywards and then smashing the wave into bright splinters of foam.

The waves asked no questions now they could see her purpose and her desire as she plunged full bodied into them so that her decks ran with their life blood and her scuppers drank deep.

She would not play the coward; she would seek battle and fight the enemy.

'I am the Caine; I will rescue, and I will spill blood.'

The star filled flag at her stern flowed out and the waves died one by one.

She was the Caine.

And coward no longer.

'Bastards, Jack, bastards every one.'

A second float plane had joined the fray and a dark smudge on the horizon showed that the Susannah's adversaries had grown in scale.

Laskier's remark held no fear, for fear cannot live when hate burns, and he looked up with perfect calm as the two aircraft converged on the Susannah.

The air was filled with the blast and roar of battle as every gun on the ship sought to kill the oncoming invaders; Bofors thumped out and her two four-inch guns did what they could, but still the aircraft flew on through the shells and through the smoke.

It wasn't cowardice, Jack realized. The crew of the Susannah were brave men and determined but to man guns in true war was a far different thing to target practice in peaceful waters, and courage must be married to battle born skill before it can be of full use.

To offer his own skill would be to receive rough words and rougher blows; the crew of the Susannah saw their duty with plain eyes and would brook no interference, no matter how well intentioned. The two men were reduced to the role of spectators to a play in which they could play no part and only their hate and a horrid curiosity stopped them from seeking sensible shelter. Instead they stood behind the starboard refueling mast and watched as the two aircraft sped down.

This was an obviously practiced move, for the enemy moved in concert, dividing fire and multiplying alarm, completing their dives with long upwardly curving swoops that saw four bombs carve new paths through the air.

One missed, throwing a great white plume of water into the air, but the others fell with greater intent, spearing into the Susannah with roars that were heard over the barks of her guns.

The first fell behind the forward gun mount, slaughtering its crew in a barbed shower. The second fell into the near empty forward fuel bay and caused a cloud of dense black smoke to writhe up into the blue sky, while the third plunged behind her funnel without any other signs of damage.

But there was payment for such aggression. One of the aircraft began to pour smoke from its engine and made a perfect landing on the water, its large single float easily managing the waves, but alas for all the pilot's skill he had made a fatal error.

His wounded craft was still in range of the Susannah, and every gun that could bear opened up on the unfortunate craft. The water around it was churned into white foam that was given no peace and no rest, but for every shot that missed, one struck its target and the floatplane writhed in pain with holes large and small being punched in its sides.

The waves were impatient, eager for another meal, knowing that no mercy would be given, knowing that soon blood and bone, wood and fabric would be theirs.

And so it was. The float plane disintegrated under an iron flail and the waves opened ever hungry mouths and swallowed it with relish. For a moment the Susannah continued firing, the better to guarantee victory and then all was silence.

'That'll teach the bastards.' Laskier was grinning wildly. 'They won't try that again.'

Jack grinned too, feeling the hate and the glow of victory, but then his feet began to tell a worrying tale and he saw the same tale reflected in Laskier's face.

The Susannah was not moving like a ship at full speed. Instead she seemed to be slowing, still moving but at a painful and dangerous pace and Jack remembered an old proverb.

''Victory always has a price'.'

Hate and pain, sorrow and endurance.

All these lessons the Susannah had learnt, but there were more to learn and the latest was agony.

Agony was plates and frames broken, agony was flame and heat, agony was men blown apart.

Agony was all these things and more, for it was agony to feel the last bomb burst inside her and hear the dying scream of a diesel and the frightened sobbing of a rudder actuator that had lost every last ounce of fluid and it was agony to see men blinded by flame stumble and fall and her speed diminish to the crawl of the coastal trader.

Now she could barely move and she felt the red glows of her enemies glow brighter in triumph and that too was an agony, but this agony touched an already learnt lesson and turned it into a blazing light.

She sighted a crippled enemy floating but a small distance away and her hate blazed hot. *'Kill it! Kill it now! Let me see blood on the water and its bones broken. Kill it!'*

Later she would remember her words and wonder at her rage but for now she gave sole power to her guns who howled in glee and retribution, with her voice urging them on until a last wave took a last bite and dragged her enemy down with a flick of white foam.

Only then did her rage abate and allow her to look around. Her forward deck plates groaned where a blackened hole had been punched into them, but her gun still pointed forward and spoke without pain though its crew had been slaughtered, while the forward fuel bay had managed to smother the flames that had flared within in its cavernous bowels. But it was her engine room that had suffered the most damage.

The last bomb had disdained to waste its energy against deck plating, but instead had plunged through a canvas covered grating and burst deep within her. She reached out and touched her port engine, but found only cooling metal and there was no reply to her gentle enquiry.

The shining steel arms of the rudder actuator were frozen in place and it sobbed out tears of fear and frustration while lying in a pool of its own fluid.

But then relief and pride surged through her, for beams of slashing light cut into the darkness and the voices of men were heard and the voices were disciplined voices, for the rescued engine crew of the Bacchante had made their way aft.

The dead engine was beyond their power, but the arms of the actuator began to move once more, though it was rope and muscle that moved them and not hydraulics.

Slowly she began to move, charting a new course that would take her away from her converging enemies.

It would not be enough.

She knew that.

It did not matter.

She would endure.

Or die as a sister should.

'You pair!'

The petty officers face was one of a man who had been given too many tasks and all too little time in which to do them.

'What do you know about gunnery?'

Jack touched his sleeve where in happier times his rank lay embroidered.

'Leading Seaman and Gunner's Mate.'

'You'll do. Get forrad, the two of you and man the four inch. I'll send help.'

The man either did not care that Frank Laskier was a cripple or did not care, and vanished, content that a task had been completed leaving the two men to make their way forward to where the gun lay.

It lay mute, still pointing out over the Susannah's bow and bereft of a crew. An enemy shell had burst behind it, flensing flesh while leaving iron.

A hasty cleansing had ensured that broken flesh had been removed, but as Jack walked up to the gun, he saw that the cleansing had been too hurried and a single remnant of the crew remained. The hand gripped the elevator screw in faithful duty, fingers still clutching and the tattoo of a hummingbird still poised in mid-flight.

The hand was removed and placed in the ready to use locker where the hummingbird could keep a close eye on its gun.

The Susannah had pointed her bow at the nearest of her foes and Jack could see her now, a former cargo liner, near twin to a second ship that was bearing down on them with a white wave fixed under a cruel beak.

Two would fight one.

Two in firm health would fight a cripple.

It would not be a fair fight, it could have but one result, but before that the gun would speak angry last words.

And the hummingbird would take one last flight.

The Caine smashed the wave into ten thousand rainbow splinters that rose in a flock of droplets and mixed with the greasy smoke that was pouring from every funnel.

She heard her engines shouting the cadences that gave measured time to a dance that partnered swirling air with pulsing oil and she gave soothing words to their dripping sides. Her course was set now and arrow straight with her battle flag standing stiff in her man-made wind. There was nothing to do now but wait and she sent once more the message.

'I am the Caine and I speed as fast as engines can.'

There was only a gasping blurred reply and she cursed the long waves that stood between her and a friend in need.

She was the Caine.

And she would rescue.

Hate.

The Susannah could feel her enemies hate and hear their war cries but ignored them as a well brought up ship should do.

She had learnt duty and it was her duty to hurt the enemy and not trade insults.

Hate.

Her hate borrowed from her crew and it screamed at her in a loud voice which she ignored for she had learnt another lesson.

To be a sister was to hate, but to be a true sister was to conquer hate with cool reason, to be its master and not its slave. She would take hot hate and temper it with the coolness of a winter wave, the better to see, the better to plan a losing game.

So, turn.

Turn and face the enemy.

Turn as a sister would.

'Fire!'

Jack pulled the lanyard and the gun roared out in defiance, sending thirty-one pounds of shell high into the air and towards the enemy.

High it arched and fast, guided by Jack's eye alone, for the explosion which had slaughtered the gun's crew had reduced the glass of the sighting telescopes into crazed ruin.

Higher and higher the shell flew until seeing the enemy ship it dropped in down in a screaming dive.

And missed.

There was no time for disappointment, no time for cursing. For the Petty Officer, true to his word had sent help and Jack now had a gun crew made up of rescued members of the Bacchante and the Susannah's own crew.

Swiftly he explained their duties, giving to Laskier the canvas belt studded with finger long brass tubes which when ignited gave flame to the firing cartridge. The task required little movement, but much precision as a jammed tube would take long minutes to retrieve and Laskier nodded his thanks at being given such an important task.

The gun was old, made when Jack's father had faced the Kaiser's army, but the design had long since proved its worth and with a well-practiced crew could fire many shots in a single minute, but his crew were far from well-practiced and he must trust that his luck and skill would overcome clumsy hands.

Slowly and with much hesitation the gun was reloaded.

The Black Wave was here.

The Susannah could see it on the far horizon and even over the sea miles she could feel it pulsing gentle warmth and icy cold.

No ship could outrun the wave, no ship could fight it. It was an implacable judge from whose decrees there was no appeal

Was it here to punish past sins or reward present pains?

She could not tell and the wave gave no clue, remaining silent and unmoving, but the fact that the wave was visible was disturbing but there was nothing that could be done now other than fight the battle as best she might.

She heard the American voice urging her to hold onto life, promising that each minute brought relief a little closer.

But that relief lay in a future that could well be for ever closed to her and duty urged her to look at her foes. No true warships were they, but ships built for peace and near twins. Under war's press they had donned the warrior's garb and wandered the seas for prey; strong to the weak, weak to the strong.

And she was weak; no longer fleet of sail, stained with fire and rendered flesh but with lessons well learnt.

Pain and fear, endurance and rage all these and more she had felt, all these and more pushed here forward.

She was but a conditional sister, a warrior under review but she would face the enemy and allow her foremost gun to speak.

And speak it did, bellowing out a single phrase in black smoke and hard recoil.

The gun's words shocked her a little, for they suggested that the enemy was no mere foe but a deviant of unclean habits and uncertain ancestry. They were certainly words that no well-mannered ship would use, but then she thought that this was battle and that the gun, though old had showed proper spirit and so instead of chiding ill manners she gave praise to the gun and urged a repeat.

On she rode through the waves, a slow moving blade aimed at the enemy and her gun roared again, but such impudence came at a price and a salvo of shot plunged into the water and into her.

But worse was to come, for in lunging at the throat of one enemy she had allowed the second to outflank her and this enemy disdained to use common shell to bring about her destruction, but had instead launched torpedoes.

She could hear their thin, bubbling screams as they ran towards her and so she did the only thing cool anger allowed.

She turned again, away from the first and away from the blow of the second.

Turn.

And hope that each precious minute would blossom into salvation.

Run.

On a single, limping engine, with the waves watching and hope to turn once more.

Run.

And hope.

There was no chance at surprise, no chance that the Caine could fly up out of the far horizon with all her guns vomiting shells at a shocked enemy.

No chance at all.

The three black columns of flattened smoke that trailed behind her signalled her arrival better than the most eloquent of heralds and the enemy had sent its last floatplane to investigate the intruder.

For long moments it circled her and then, perhaps emboldened by its success with the Susannah it dived down to attack.

This was a mistake.

The Caine was not an ill-armed supply ship, but a warship and a warship with a re-found purpose, eager to reprove herself.

Long bars of white light reached up out from the Caine and took hold of the floatplane like dogs on an unfortunate rabbit. They gripped and pulled, tore and ripped until the aircraft exploded in a great ball of flame that showered the waiting sea with a pattern of bright splashes that soon vanished.

She exulted in the kill, knowing that the mark of cowardice was beginning to fade and eager for another kill, another victory.

She could see the battle now, see the quarry twisting and turning amidst towering pillars of water and see the hunters, intent upon their kill.

One of them turned and she felt its red glare wash over her like an evil tide.

An earlier Caine, would have feared, would have run with coward's feet, but that was then and this was a new day and a new Caine.

The enemies divided; one intent on an already claimed kill and the second one swinging a bow around and offering battle.

There was no fear in her now. On her bridge she felt only calmness and fixed resolve and from that she took her cue, reaching out to every part of her and telling of the battle to come and how each must play their part.

But the charging enemy, though no true warship was no lightweight and outgunned her both in number of cannon and weight of shot, so she must turn former cowardice into caution and care and not rush into battle.

Her builders were men of hands and had given her gifts that were advantages fair…and it was time to use them.

A last lesson this, the best, the hardest.

Not every battle can be won, and defeat is a bitter drink.

But drink she would, though the cup would kill her.

The Black Wave was a towering cliff on the horizon, piled high like the darkest of storm clouds and she ignored it. Her past sins were beyond recall; only this hour remained and what would be was still veiled by time's hand.

The enemy torpedoes scored twin tracks behind her stern and she heard their thin cries wailing disappointment as they began long glides down to the eternal dark of the seabed.

So once more she turned, slowly, painfully and in a wide curve that gave arcs to both her guns, and this bold impudence was punished by heavier metal.

The shells soaked her with the blood of the Father of All Seas and with the blood of her crew. A shell, better aimed than the rest of its flock struck her aft four inch gun and it burst into shards that sliced brave flesh into offal and spun the stump of its barrel crashing into her bridge where it remained, pointing out to sea like an angry finger.

There was only time for a last and final defiance.

And then she saw the Caine.

'Breech!'

A long, spoon-handled lever was pulled and the breech swung open emitting black smoke and a brief burst of flame.

'Swab!'

A dripping sponge was pushed into the breech where it fought a hissing fight with hot metal.

'Load!'

Thirty one pounds of shell was placed on the lip of the breech.

'Ram!'

Four hands gripped the long wooden handle and thrust as one until the shell clanged against the lands of the rifling.

'Charge!'

A long canvas skinned bag of explosive was placed behind the shell and all was ready for the next stage.

'Half lock!'

The breech was closed again and spun so that course thread locked with course thread.

'Full lock!'

A delicate operation this as Frank Laskier dropped a thin-walled brass igniting charge into its appointed place and allowed a hard steel locking pin to engage.

At last Jack was satisfied. A well-trained crew did not need prompting, but the Petty Officer had swept up whoever he could find and his crew comprised cooks, signalmen, stokers and a ship's boy whose voice had barely broken.

Despite that they had worked hard, but now came the part where skill and judgement must take the place of muscle and labour. Jack must be his own gun layer, taking the place of now blind sights.

He gave orders which saw the gun elevated and swung, calculating as best he could the motion of the Susannah and the target and estimating the long arc which the shell must take.

At last he was satisfied and gave the order.

'Shoot!'

Laskier pulled the lanyard and the gun blasted out the smoke and flame that would send the shell on its way. Jack fancied that he could see the shell in flight as a dark, advancing line that grew ever closer to the enemy.

And hit!

There was no sullen watery splash to mark failure, but a brief blossoming of dark flame followed by darker smoke.

Jack turned to congratulate his crew, but such was his concentration he had failed to see what they had seen with amazed eyes.

Another ship had joined the battle.

Old she was and lightly fitted for war, but she swept past the Susannah at full speed with her battle ensign iron stiff in the breeze.

An enemy swung out of line and threw down the gage of battle which the ship picked up without slackening speed, leaving Jack to shake his head in wonder.

'A Yank!'

He would have said more, but his wounded enemy was determined to extract vengeance and had turned, the better to give a crushing broadside in return.

There could be only one reply.

Once more the breech of the Susannah's sole remaining four inch gun was opened and the battle resumed.

The shell splashes were twins; sea green at their base, ice white at their tips and they rejoiced in their new found freedom, but then as wind and sun began to eat at them, they thought again of the security offered by the great sea and their gladness died, allowing them to fall with curving grace away from heaven.

Alas for them their journey was interrupted by the oncoming bow of the Caine and they poured down onto her decks, protesting loudly at their interrupted journey.

She ignored the words, even as her scuppers eagerly drank, the shell splashes were close cousins to the waves and the waves had marked her with insults for far too long.

It was time to repay those insults and time to use the first of her builders gifts.

Speed.

Her opponent carried heavy metal, far heavier than hers so she would use her speed to confuse and bewilder.

She heard the enemy's challenge now, low and menacing and threw out her own gage of battle.

'I am the Caine and I come to rescue and to kill.'

There were no more words to say now, her guns and her gifts were words enough…and it was time to let them speak and for the first time the Cain's guns spoke in anger.

Her battle had begun.

It was hard to sink a ship like the Susannah with shell fire alone.

Built from the first as a military auxiliary, she had now empty replenishment tankage and echoing store rooms and each had been shut tight at the beginning of the battle so that a breech in one did not lead to disaster in the other. But well-built or not she sat lower in the water now and trailed a haze of half-conquered flames over the watching waves.

Still though her last remaining diesel throbbed on and her rudder still swung the diesel mourned a killed brother and the rudder missed the deft touch of its actuator.

And she had learnt her lessons, learnt every one and learnt them well. She was certain that there were no more to learn.

Rage and fear, honour and duty, endurance and pain all were her now, as much a part of her as the thinnest plate or the meanest rivet.

She spoke to her forward gun who replied in a hot voice decades old that it knew its duty very well and needed her to be quiet and allow him to get on with his work.

An older Susannah, a Susannah who had not learnt her lessons would have reared up at such a reply but this much battered and war worn Susannah knew that in battle civility was an unneeded virtue and merely smiled.

Another salvo splashed around her and some of them hit, causing her to grimace with swallowed pain. She was closer now and she heard her gun bellow out a phrase which mixed obscenity with impossible anatomy and she smiled again, not missing the old Susannah at all and knowing it was time to die.

Die like a sister.

Luck was with her.

Long before the battle's beginning she had sent her depth charges on a final downwards voyage and so the shell that struck her stern wrecked only her sweeping gear turning elegant geometry into tangled ruin, but she was close now and the enemy was within range.

She could not kill. Despite her war challenge the Caine knew that a kill this day was unlikely; the enemy was bigger and more heavily armed and she was under gunned. Her intent today was to wound and discourage. Hunters like these depended on stealth and the vastness of the sea to hid. A wounded hunter was of little use and must seek a safe haven to lick wounds.

Today she would slash and run, slash and run, and for that she would use the second and last of her gifts. A rudder that gave a turning circle that her enemy could not match and propellors that were ready and waiting.

She had set her course aimed directly at her foe, knowing that a sharp, fast moving target was hard to hit but now as the enemy loomed large she gave out words which saw her rudder swing full wide and her twin propellors cease turning and then resume, not in harmony, but in opposition.

She skidded on the sea, waves that could not move fast enough piling up under her flank in a creamy white foam. Turning and turning until her sharp beak faced the enemy's bow.

And then she spoke other words and once more her rudder returned to comfort and her screws spoke with one voice.

This was where she needed to be, perfectly positioned, and she raced down the grey side of her adversary each gun firing as fast as it could, tearing holes and blasting open un-armoured plates.

But the surprise was not over and her gifts were not finished showing the advantage small and nimble had over large and slow.

Having run down the side she now slowed as she turned under the Japanese stern and fired again wrecking the enemy's stern in recompense for her own.

And then run, propellors fast churning and with an enemy's howls of outraged pain ringing like music in her ears, only to turn again for another high speed, slashing run.

Not every shot told, for a ship moving at high speed is not the most stable of gun platforms, but enough to show spirit and intent, enough to abrade the thin courage of a ship that was only strong to the weak.

'Leave now,' she said. *'Leave now and I will give you your life. Or will you fight on?'*

It was a bluff and a little of her fear returned. She could not kill; her guns were quick but small and a killing blow would be a rare blow indeed, but the words could cause no harm.

For an eternal minute both ships ran on courses which must bring them back to war contact and then the enemy began to edge away.

There was no reply to her challenge, no parting shots, but slowly the Japanese ship began to edge away from the Caine.

The instinct to pursue, to rend more, to add fresh hurt was almost crushing in its power, but she resisted, for there was a second adversary and a friend in need.

She turned and then saw that her aid was not needed.

This was the last of the shells, the last of the ones stored in the ready to use locker.

There were others, but they were lost in the tangled ruin of the Susannah that lay behind him and only this shell and the tattooed hand remained.

He looked again at the hummingbird and it gazed back at him, frozen in joyful flight and he wondered if the bird's owner was standing with them in ghostly support.

He shrugged. In a few moments he might be able to ask the man himself.

He picked up the shell and handed it to the loader, receiving a fatalistic smile from Frank Laskier as he did so.

This was the last shell but the song was ever the same.

'Breech!'…And watch smoke and flame escape.

'Sponge out!'…And hear hissing steam.

'Load and ram!'…Til all was snug.

Fill the breech with a last canvas bag and see the locking pin drop for a last time.

Now was the time to aim, and the sweat of stress cut runnels down his grime-covered face.

Elevate up.

Too much!

And down.

Train to the right.

Too far!

And back.

Now was the time.

Time to pray and hope.

Shoot!

Now was the time.

Time to give thanks and say goodbye.

The Susannah reached out and touched every part of her, thanking them with warm words. For this too was part of the lesson that not every battle could be won.

Every part of her was thanked, both the living and the dead, the wounded and the whole. The ritual brought her comfort even as she felt the Black Wave move closer.

Last to be spoken to was her forward gun, but it gruffly dismissed her words telling of a last duty to perform.

It blasted out a final curse-laden profanity and then gave a great smoke-filled sigh.

It never finished the sigh. Nor did the Susannah finish her delayed thanks for both were interrupted by a great cry of pain.

Shoot!

The gun lurched back and the shell began its journey.

The gun was now useless but for some reason Jack began to sound out the formula for reloading. Perhaps it was the shock of battle or perhaps the wish to send a cleaned gun on its journey to the sea bed, but like automatons his crew began the process that had been their lives for the past hour.

It was only the cheers of the crew that broke their trance and made them look up.

The last shall had hit. It hadn't hit where Jack had aimed, but that didn't matter because where the shell had hit had caused immense damage.

Oxygen tanks for torpedoes or the torpedoes themselves? Bomb storage or shell locker? Jack did not know; he only knew that one small shell on its own could not cause the towering cloud that rose out of the centre of the ship. As he watched secondary explosions broke out followed by a last titanic explosion that broke the ship in two and showered debris high up into the air.

He watched fascinated as a single man, arms and legs wide open spun upwards through the air only to crash into the sea in a splash that must have broken every bone in his body.

The sea was filled with floating wreckage, burning flames and struggling men, desperate to stay alive.

Frank Laskier looked at the men with a jaundiced eye for he had held onto his anger and gave them a last epitaph.

'Fuck them.'

The Susannah saw the Black Wave again as it rushed towards her and she began to prepare herself for judgment, but all she felt a warm pressure as it passed through her. It had been waiting not for her but for her enemy and she watched as the wave flowed with gentle arms around a ship which had died with duty. Was this another lesson? She did not know and there was no time to ponder as the American ship rushed up with an excited voice.

'Where are you hurt? Others are coming, but what help do you need?'

And so it was that the Caine and the Susannah exchanged greetings while rocking on a gentle sea with the setting sun streaming long shadows out from them.

All night the two ships worked with pumped water flowing and the bright lights of welders throwing red sparks that flared and died until a new born day saw them bury their dead in sad concert.

Later they saw smoke on the horizon and the Caine sped away to ward off new danger, but returned with friendly flags that flew from a hospital ship and two tugs all of which were escorted by stern warriors who looked about them, eager to revenge this insult.

They exchanged courtly greetings with the Caine and gave high praise for her actions, and with those words the last of the yellow mark left the Caine and was replaced by the badge of courage.

She was clean again, whole again and ready to hold her head up high.

She took her leave with the thanks of the Susannah skipping across waves that now respected her once more.

The Mark of Caine was no more.

'Three months in the dockyard, if it's a day.'

Laskier's voice was not at all gloomy. He had stated a professional judgement over how long the Susannah would be in dock and Jack saw no reason to disagree. Despite the heavy duty pumps of the tugs the ship still leaked from a hundred cuts and an over taxed diesel had joined its brother in silence so that the ship was now being towed by the tugs.

'And a ten day tow back to Brisbane,' replied Jack. 'War will be over by the time she's repaired.

Laskier looked oddly frightened at those words and Jack knew why. An over extended navy had taken on Frank despite his missing leg, but in peacetime what use would they have for a cripple? Laskier saw his future and it was a bleak one, but his voice betrayed none of his fear and a great smile split his face. 'Brisbane, Jack! Tell me have you ever seen Fortitude Valley on a Saturday night? Or Chinatown? I'll take you to Madame Chang's and make sure you have the time of your life!'

Jack had heard of Brisbane's night life centre and Madame Chang's was reputed to employ the most beautiful girls in Australia.

Both were well worth visiting and there could be no better guide than Frank Laskier who knew every bar and bordello from Aden to Zanzibar.

And that was something to think about.

The Catalina gave them a cursory look as the early morning light glinted off its wings and then with a friendly greeting flew away to resume its patrol. Half-crippled supply ships and their escorts were not its concern, not when there was a chance of a desperate enemy submarine raising its head.

It wasn't much of a welcome for the Susannah as she rounded Amity Point and entered Moreton Bay where the British Pacific Fleet lay at anchor.

First she passed the carriers, flat-decked and armoured but they remained silent. Next she passed the destroyers layered up in legions, but they too said nothing. The cruisers large and small gazed at her as she passed but made no comment. Further up the bay lay the smaller craft and the supply train, but even the meanest oiler refused to speak.

Last of all lay the iron heart of the fleet with long guns that killed across the miles. Long were their guns and heavy were their names; Howe and Anson, Duke of York and King George, the fifth of that name.

And Hood.

She lay slightly apart from her sisters, her main guns trained fore and aft with her tall masts the badge of command and control.

The Susannah was by now used to the silence and was prepared to slink past and enter her berth and descend into obscurity when the Hood spoke.

'Halt!'

The tugs, obedient to the orders stopped and the Susannah who was tied port and starboard to her protectors came to a gradual halt.

'Make your report.'

The Hood's voice was entirely neutral. It held neither anger or praise and it was a strange thing indeed to make a report in the midst of an entire fleet, but her tugs were utterly terrified of the firepower around them and were not about to move without orders so she began her tale. She told of her sadness at the burial service and her fear at being attacked and how she had endured and learnt anger and how to cool its heat. She told of pain and of a battle so nearly lost and how the Caine had risked all to come to her aid. Last of all she told of the Black Wave and how it had taken her adversary.

At last she ran out of words and the Hood spoke again.

'Truly a voyage to be remembered and with many lessons learnt. My question to you is this; does this make you worthy? What are your thoughts on this matter?'

The Susannah trembled at these questions. In truth though she lusted for the honour of Sisterhood she doubted if a single voyage, no matter how adventurous was the equal of the lives lived by these warriors. There was only one answer she could give.

'I do not know.'

'An honest answer, but not a helpful one,' replied the Hood, *'I will put the question to the sisters here assembled. What say you, sisters? Yay or nay?'*

For a long moment there was a great silence and then a six inch gun cruiser spoke.

'Sister!'

The cry was echoed by a swift sloop. *'Sister!'*

'Sister!'

A light carrier spoke this time and then the cries came faster and faster, mutating into a savage war cry.

'Sister! Sister! Sister!'

The cry echoed of the waves until the tugs began to tremble and then slowly died away and the Hood lifted a single fifteen inch gun as acknowledgment of the verdict.

'The sisters have spoken and as they have judged so shall I say. You are admitted to the sisterhood from this hour. It is a high honour, see that you keep that honour bright. Go now and have your hurts mended for we would have you by our side.'

There was nothing more to say and in truth the Susannah could find no more words as the tugs began again their task, but there was one thing she knew.

She was the Susannah…and a sister.

THE LAST OF THE NAVY

There was order here; order, discipline and control.

Outside in the city, in large parts of Italy for that matter, there was chaos, starvation and madness, but here in the docks he and his men ruled.

This was his kingdom, his bailiwick, though a poor one, much reduced in power and prestige.

But his, still his.

Perhaps it was pride that caused him to rule here, an unwillingness to give in. Perhaps it was optimism, an unshatterable belief that if only he could hold, then something, a miracle, or plain fate would intervene.

He did not know; he only knew that after the Allies had bombed the docks of Genoa into rubble, he had organised the survivors and assumed command and together they had buried the dead, tended the wounded and gathered what remained of food and supplies until at the end the docks were once again under the control of the Italian Navy.

He, Captain Luigi Durand de la Penne ruled here, and he was at this moment sitting behind a desk listening to the puzzled words of this afternoon's guard commander.

'She just stands there, Captain, asks for you by name and refuses to move. We threw a few shots in her direction, but she didn't even flinch.'

'Asks for me by name?'

'Yes, Captain.'

La Penne thought for a moment; rulers of kingdoms have many duties, but two duties ran before all others; rulers must lead, and they must show no fear.

He rose from a creaking chair and walked out into the afternoon sunshine.

'Luigi Durand de la Penne, captain in the Italian navy, is that you?'

The woman stood perfectly balanced on a slab of broken concrete with the sea wind blowing through short, cropped hair and her arms by her side, empty of any weapon.

'I am he,' replied Luigi, 'and I am a captain in the Royal Italian Navy.'

The woman disregarded the correction, but continued to gaze on him with hard eyes.

'Good! You have guests, a royal princess, her family, an Asturian Sergeant and a priest. I wish to see them immediately.'

Her voice was as hard as her eyes and gave no room for argument, but La Penne knew that he ruled here and that women, especially strange and unannounced women had no power at all, so his laugh was mocking and brutal.

'And who are you that should ask for such things? Better go back to your Communist masters, or is it the Germans for whom you work? Know that the Regia Marina, the Royal Navy of Italy rules here, and that what we have, we keep.

'Go home woman and tend to your family!'

A little of the hardness left the woman at these words and she shifted uneasily on the concrete slab but she soon recovered, and her reply left no doubt as to her anger. 'I am no communist, and I despise the Nazis! I have a mission and I demand to see your visitors!'

Despite himself La Penne was impressed with the woman; it took some courage to stand in plain sight before a group of armed men and make demands, so his next laugh had a little less scorn and a little more questioning.

'Well, if you're not a communist, and you're not a damn Nazi, who the devil are you?'

An exasperated look took over the woman's face.

You fool! I'm an Allied agent. Now take me to the Princess right now!

For some reason La Penne believed the woman, the situation was simply too fantastic to have any other explanation. He signaled to one of his men to search the woman, revealing a small pistol and a short stabbing knife and disarmed the woman was led into the half-ruined building that served as both headquarters and barracks.

She looked around seeing bunks, tables and a small kitchen and men grinning at the sight of a woman in their midst.

'Gone,' he said in answer to her questioning look. 'Left on the morning tide. We had a small fishing boat, a very small fishing boat and they left on that, headed south.'

'Gone?' The woman had added anger to incredulity in an ugly mix. 'Gone? You had them and you let them go?' Disbelief vanished now leaving only anger. 'You fool!'

This was the second time the woman had called him a fool and it was beginning to irritate him, so his answer matched her anger. 'We have little in the way of supplies, our last radio died weeks ago and if the Germans or even the Communists decide that they really want us gone then I cannot resist more than a few days. They are just as safe at sea as here. Besides which the princess insisted. My second in command agreed to go with them and he is an experienced sailor. Tell me that you would have done different, but do not tell me that I am a fool!'

His wrath fought with her anger and fought it to a standstill so that both were defeated, and both remained victors and a slow smile leapt from face to face as each recognised that both bravely fought.

'Perhaps you are not a fool.'

The admission was not as grudging as it might have been, and La Penne's smile widened a little as the woman spoke.

'This is my fault. Sergeant Massu was supposed to lead the princess and her party into France, but for unknown reasons they vanished. Every Allied agent was given their description. I saw them but was not able to make contact until too late. I contacted those above me and am told to find out what plans they have, but now…' The woman shrugged her shoulders. 'Now what do I say?'

La Penne was intrigued, Allied Intelligence had obviously penetrated into Italy in far greater numbers than he had thought, and the woman was obviously Italian though her accent had strong flavours of another land.

The question of which land could be answered on another day as a far greater thought entered his head. 'You have a radio! This is how you maintain contact!'

The woman's smile vanished, and iron shutters closed over her eyes. 'How I maintain contact is none of your business, Captain.'

La Penne waved an apologetic hand. 'Of course, of course, but I can at least show you what path they have taken.'

He led the woman over to his table and unfurled a tattered nautical map. 'The fishing boat has no fuel and sails only with the wind, so its progress will be slow. They keep the shore in sight, so as to appear simple fisherfolk and avoid suspicion. By tonight they will be here, the day after they will arrive off this headland and so on.'

'A long journey,' said the woman '…and those poor children, they will be so cramped, so frightened.

A journey of perhaps ten days is no laughing matter,' agreed La Penne, '…but they will be safe enough. They have enough water and supplies and if there is a storm then they are close enough to make a run for the shore.'

His anger had gone now, and he shrugged rueful shoulders.

'It seemed best at the time, and the princess was most insistent. As for the Sergeant he is I think a hard man to turn from a task and not a man I would wish for an enemy.'

The woman did not acknowledge his words, but instead gazed with fixed eyes on the chart as if committing it to memory. 'Two days from now, Captain, where do you think they will be?'

La Penne thought hard, a lifetimes experience of wind, tide and sea meshing together to form a guess which was more than mere fortune telling and jabbed a long forefinger down onto the paper.

'There!'

'You are sure?'

He gave the woman a look which showed surprise that an amateur would call into question the opinion of a professional and this time it was the turn of the woman to offer an apology.

'I'm sorry captain, I didn't mean to doubt you, but this is important.'

La Penne told of tides, winds and currents, he told of a boatman's skill and how all would combine to place a tiny boat at a certain point on a huge sea.

All this he told and more until the woman nodded that she was convinced.

'Thank you, Captain I will pass your thoughts on in my report...and Captain?'

'Yes?'

'I was wrong, you are not a fool.'

And with that the woman left, with La Penne never knowing her name or where she went, but days later, three slate-grey aircraft roared over his kingdom and one of them dropped a hastily opened parachute from which dangled a box that held a carefully wrapped radio and an even more carefully wrapped bottle of wine.

There was order in La Penne's kingdom, order, discipline and control, and now there was an outside world that knew he ruled.

And that thought was sweeter than any wine.

Sergeant Yves Massu was a brave man, a resourceful man, a man skilled in all the deadly arts, but like all men he had a weakness and Massu's weakness was water. Streams he would ford, rivers he would cross, ponds he would laugh at; give him a mountain to cross or a man to kill and the task was as good as done, but the sight of a wave brought weakness to his legs and sent his stomach into rebellion.

A brave man was Sergeant Yves Massu, but the waves had defeated him, and he had no more to give. His mouth was over wet, his legs shook, and his stomach insisted on sending empty contents up into a mouth filled with aching teeth.

But worse, far worse than this was the fact that the priest, a man he despised as weak and untrustworthy, was unaffected by the waves. Indeed Father Domenico seemed to positively thrive on the ocean, taking energy from the very waves which sapped Massu's soul. He smiled and laughed and the more he looked at Sergeant Massu the more he smiled.

And that was another reason to hate the man. A sluggish thought ran through his head that perhaps a bullet would remove the man's good humour followed by a second bullet which would remove the water born agony that he felt.

He rejected the thought though not with any great energy or any great conviction.

He had a mission and had given a promise to the woman with windblown hair who sat in the stern of this accursed boat. The woman had renounced a royal title in the cause of healing her adopted land and had endured hardship and risked everything she held dear to further that quest and two bullets, no matter how well-deserved would not give her the aid he had sworn to give.

An errant wave lifted the boat and then dropped it with a twist and a lurch that nobody but Massu's stomach noticed. It forced a livid groan from his throat and caused him to wish himself in the midst of the most desperate battle rather than here.

He closed his eyes in pain and despair and such was his agony that he never heard Marie rise up from her children and place caring arms around his limp shoulders.

'My poor Yves. You knew this would happen, yet you accepted this pain in my cause. I will not forget this my brave sergeant.'

Massu only dimly heard the words and tried to force a smile onto a paperwhite face and failed. Another larger wave forced him to take a dry heaving stomach to the boats stern and face the fact that this would be an endless journey.

The images flickered through the tendrils made from burning tobacco and showed the latest war news.

A massive Allied landing had been made on Normandy beaches, while smaller but still important attacks had been made on France's Mediterranean shores.

The Normandy beaches had been bloody, and even edited the cameramen had captured every pain filled yard in a way that was both sad to see yet difficult to turn away from.

The images left France and began showing the last moves of the Greek campaign.

Stirring martial music accompanied the voice of announcer as he explained that a Greek armoured column had captured Germans accused of murdering fleeing villagers and darkly hinted that a rope awaited the prisoners.

Georges Mandel paid little attention to the sounds coming from the speakers or the dark and light images, instead he gazed intently at the man who sat with body thrust forward eagerly drinking in the pictures flowing from the screen.

How much does he know, Mandel wondered. How much did Churchill know about his half agreement with the Asturians, his talks with the Labour party, the hundred plots and counter plots that ran and counter ran through his fingers? *How much?* The man had given nothing away, no eyebrow had been raised, no hint had passed his lips and yet he must know something.

He looked again; Churchill was still intent on watching the screen with eyes that glowed with a remnant of their old brilliance. The war had been hard on him, the Greek adventure and the Normandy landings just a series of stops along a painful path that had mired him in desperate measures to keep past glories alive.

Churchill felt his eyes and turned, a slight smile birthing on a tired face as he met Mandel's gaze.

How much does he think I know, Churchill wondered, *and how much do I really know, and what do I do with the knowledge I have, and almost as important how much do I care?*

He turned back to the news reel, watching with grim satisfaction Greek flags being hung on the Parthenon and an angry German general signing a surrender document.

The Greek campaign had seen German forces split in two by an armoured fist that had driven east until the Ionian had been linked to the Aegean, but an empire stretched thin had been hard pressed and many Germans had fled north into the fratricidal pit that was the Balkans, lands made even more poisonous by the Turkish invasion of Bulgaria which had not only bogged down into positional warfare but had raised the already high Soviet paranoia to almost unmanageable heights.

Greece had been freed and if only he could stop the Greeks themselves from killing each other then he would count the campaign a success.

All were problems that must be faced on other days, but for now he must face Mandel.

The man had been friend, confidante and envoy, and at times opponent but whatever guise he wore there was always a restriction, always a hesitation.

Georges Mandel worked for France.

He had never made any secret that he worked for France and France only. Every thought, every action had that single master in mind. Polite, even charming, rarely angry, willing to work with others and supremely patient, but always, always, there was France, a new France that would rise and set course with Mandel at the helm.

There was much he knew about the man, but this one fact stood out above the others. And the question was, how to handle the man, for tonight Mandel left to land on the shores of France.

A French army had landed on the shores of France, a small army, an army protected by half-repaired ships, an army using machines borrowed or begged, but an army that was wholly French.

Mandel had pushed for this, growing from the seed bed of blank refusal a tiny plant of grudging acceptance.

The symbolism was more than powerful, and Churchill had no doubt that Mandel would nurture the plant until it became a sturdy legend and would follow it until the legend and name Mandel became one and indivisible.

But tonight, he wondered which Mandel he faced. Did he face Mandel the friend or did he face Mandel the French patriot?

There were ways to find out and a way which had but a small price, so her drew the slumbering cigar back into fiery life and gifted the man with his best smile.

'So, this is goodbye, Georges? The morning tide awaits.'

'It is more the morning flight, Winston, but the principle remains the same I imagine.'

A broad and very genuine smile lit the up Mandel's face like a great roaring beacon. 'Brave Frenchmen have begun the liberation of France and my place is with them. To land on the soil of my homeland, to kiss the sacred earth is a pleasure long denied and will be all the sweeter for having been withheld so long.'

Churchill's smile faded a little at Mandel's obvious pleasure. He had planned a similar visit to the Normandy beaches but the King had forbidden the excursion, pointing out that his First Minister was far too valuable a person to risk life and limb on a battlefield all too fluid. Churchill's vision of directing fire on hapless, fleeing Germans had vanished by royal decree and he was a little envious of the Frenchman who had no such over-riding power.

But now was the time to salve his curiosity, tease the Frenchman while perhaps finding out just how strong were his alliances with the Asturians and the Labour Party.

He gave a little more wattage to his smile and a little more flame to his cigar.

'By the way Georges I meant to mention that your disappearing princess, along with her family and two men have been seen in Genoa of all places. Quite how she has managed to get there and what is her state of mind are alas mysteries, but apparently she was able to find loyal friends and is taking a sea voyage south.'

Mandel's face expressed only polite interest at his words so he decided to lay out a little more line to see if the bait would become more enticing. 'I am sure you are receiving similar reports from the excellent intelligence net that your friend Comandante O'Neil has spread.'

There was a flicker from the man's mouth and the thinnest ghost of an arched eyebrow from Mandel, and Winston was sure that both were deliberate saying nothing but speaking plainly to those that could read them.

'France needs all the friends she can get, Winston, and I assure you that each and every one of them is not only valued, but cherished and will never be forgotten.'

The words were spoken with feeling, but their meaning was elusive. Was Mandel talking about France or was there a more personal aspect to his words?

There was no admission of guilt in the words either, so a little more line was laid out.

'It may be that her destination is Rome, and if this is so perhaps she can be a unifying force in the fractured muddle which is Italian politics and after that, who knows? It may be that she can help bring some cohesion to Europe itself.' A wry chuckle was allowed to escape Churchill's lips. 'Would that not be the supreme irony, Georges? That a member of a monarchal house brings unity to Europe where a century of Socialist efforts has failed to unite and have continued to fail.'

Mandel smiled at the words. This was game long played. To steer a twisting course between loyalties and ambitions took skill and above all patience. Churchill revealed some understanding, but kept to himself his full knowledge.

'The woman has been described as the only man in the house of Savoy,' he replied. 'Nothing she does would surprise me, though naturally I believe that a Europe united by Socialist ideals to be the preferred option.'

'With you at its head, Georges?'

Mandel gave a very French shrug. 'Who can tell.'

Churchill gave an expressive grunt, seemingly tired of the conversation. 'Then in honour of your principles I offer you a last gift, a parting gift if you will.'

Mandel lifted up his eyes expecting another attempt at discovery, but instead watched as Churchill's eyes glowed with humour.

'I have this morning given orders which will see His Majesty's forces presently blockading the Italian peninsula seek out your errant princess and take her and her party to whatever destination they desire with every good wish for their success. There, Georges, is that not a gift much to be desired, from one friend to another?'

The words were spoken with feeling, but their meaning was elusive. Was Churchill talking about France or was there a more personal aspect to his words? Was he aiding France or was he giving the gift directly to a man who had been both friend and adversary?

Whatever happened now it would always be remembered that it was the strong arm of the Royal Navy which had aided as well as Mandel and his Asturian allies.

Churchill had given himself a new card and had both helped and hindered, and though he had failed to breech Mandel's defenses he had assisted, though with self interest in mind.

Mandel looked up into the glowing eyes, saw the joke and began to laugh. 'From one friend to another, Winston. And a cherished friend at that.' He rose and filled two glasses with a large portion of the fine brandy. 'A toast, Winston. To friendship and to princesses everywhere. May all their wishes come true.'

A full moon had risen and then begun to fall, freckling the waves with shining bars of light that lived and died, each short life completed even as a new one was born.

A more active, less sick Massu would have been fascinated by the display of celestial fireworks that formed a living bridge between sky and sea and cast a silvery gleam upon the boat that had imprisoned him.

But Massu had no energy to admire nature's artwork. Every ounce of waning power was concentrated on staying alive and on hoping that his body could gain some substance from the meals that lay for scant minutes in a stomach that was in a permanent state of rebellion.

In his misery he never saw the silver bars flee before a long black shape that lifted itself out of the water in a flurry of white water and only raised up a weary head when alarmed cries penetrated dulled ears.

He reached for his pistol, more out of instinct than any belief that such a puny weapon could threaten the monster and then placed it back in its holster as a distorted voice thundered across the waves.

'In the boat there! Identify yourself!'

He heard Captain Marino call out in reply and the distorted voice give orders in return, and soon an inflatable boat was bumping up against their sides and Massu was standing on the still wet decks of His Majesty's submarine *Strongbow* which much to his relief seemed to be a positive haven of stability after the rolling hell that was the fishing boat.

He took the proffered hand and much to his embarrassment found that the sea had turned his grip into a weak copy of what it once was, but he received a smile which ignored the weakness and spoke words of welcome.

A dull crump made him turn back to the fishing boat to see it turn on its side only to be eaten by hungry waves. A few kilograms of explosive had shattered keel and split planks and he felt a perverse sense of relief that though his future was hidden from him, he could at least be certain that it would not include fishing boats.

A few moments later he found himself in a tiny cabin that smelt of too many men cramped into too small a space for too long, but Marie seemed unaffected by the air, while Father Domenico wore the sort of expression that martyrs have ever carried.

He ignored the priest but concentrated on Marie who was deep in conversation with a young man with a serious face and the shoulder tabs of a lieutenant. The conversation was in English, a language that he had failed to master, never liking its discordant sounds, but Marie was obviously fluent and spoke in warm tones that melted the somber look from the man's face.

'This is Lieutenant Troup,' she explained. 'He commands this boat and was on his way to fight in the Pacific when he was told to look for us.'

'And what now?' asked Massu. 'Are we prisoners? Are we to be taken to England?'

Marie looked at him, realising again how like her father the man was; steadfast, loyal and brave, all these qualities he shared with her revered father and all these qualities her husband lacked.

Her husband and his father were problems for another day, but for now she must remove the gloom from the face of a man she had come to admire and a man who was still useful to her.

She reached out and took his hand and placed it in hers.

'Poor Captain Marino is a captive, for such are the fortunes of war, but for us a different fate awaits.'

A laughing gleam sparkled in her eyes as she spoke.

The good lieutenant has spoken of his orders and they are good orders, Yves, very good.

'We are going south, Yves, south to Rome.'

Some of the men wore black shirts, Massu noted, but whether this was a final display of political allegiance or to disguise the blood that was to come he could not tell.

It did not matter; black or white the fate would be the same; the men were about to die, and fashion would be of little aid.

They were marched in close file to posts that were deep sunk in the earth and each man was securely tied so that movement was impossible.

It was a bizarrely unsuitable day to die. The Italian sun was warm, the pines which surrounded them scented the air with resin fragrance and provided cooling shelter to the birds that greeted the morning with their song.

A wholly unsuitable day to die and yet death was coming.

Some took it well. Mussolini thrust out his chest and remained silent, while Count Ciano even now thought words would save him and babbled out offers and entreaties that fell on deaf ears. And the sun shone, and the birds sang in the pine trees and the soldiers ignored the songs and seemed not to hear the pitiful wailing that came from Italy's former foreign minister. They placed themselves in front of the posts and awaited further orders.

Massu had no power here, no influence to change a single second, his attendance a courtesy and no more. And even if power was given him he would not apply mercy, for his hatred for Fascists ran deep.

A man in a deep black legal gown walked up and read out a long list of high crimes, spoke again the words which pronounced death and then turned on his heels, his task completed.

And still the sun shone and still the birds sang while Massu watched.

The priest, the same priest who had accompanied Massu in his Italian journey gave a last benediction. Like the lawyer he too was dressed in funeral black and like the lawyer he walked away, carefully distancing himself from the carnage to come.

Orders were given that saw the first rank of soldiers kneel while the second rank remained erect.

The sun dimmed a little and the birds ceased their song and looked down to the figures below, while Ciano's pleading rose to a shrill roar.

A single word rang out and the double row of rifles rang out in a last and final benison.

And brought an end to an episode which began on a sandy beach long weeks ago.

The interiors of Royal Navy submarines were never designed with comfort in mind; they were designed to give the maximum lethality in the very minimum of space. Any spare comfort had been given to the Princess and her children while Massu and the priest had been given bunks that were still warm from the bodies of previous grudging owners.

The priest used his bunk with obvious distaste but Massu treated his as the luxury it was and slept the sleep of the truly exhausted and woke to find the journey of H.M.S Strongbow better than half completed.

He was effectively alone on the submarine as Marie and the priest spent their hours deep in conversation, leaving him to converse with Captain Marino who had accepted his captivity with surprising goodwill.

'The war will not last forever,' he had said, smiling, 'And I have been introduced to a beautiful woman and that is never a bad thing.' He had paused then and looked thoughtful. 'And yet the beauty is no more than camouflage. I think that underneath she is steel and bronze.'

Massu had seen that hardness himself and yet he had seen a softer side as well and could only hope that the two would combine to aid the princess in her mission. And hope was all he could do, for if Marie had her mission then he had his, and though it had been long and difficult, it was surely over, for what use had the princess for a guide when her journey was all but done?

And so, Massu was left to the company of Marino while trying to entertain bored children with feats of magic learnt in camp grounds now long gone, while the Strongbow voyaged on with a compass that pointed a steady south, while Marie's conversations with the priest grew ever longer.

Massu hated the priest, hated the Church, and trusted neither one, but the priest had now come into his own and ignored Massu with an air of superiority which bought forth frustrated visions of hands wrapped around his neck.

But Massu was a soldier and the first lesson every soldier learns is patience and Massu prayed to a god he no longer believed in to one day deliver the priest into his hands if only for a brief moment.

But that day would be far in the future and all Massu could do was count the days until his feet felt dry land again.

There was not an eye that was still, for a surfaced H.M.S Strongbow was approaching the coast in bright afternoon sunshine and although it was true that the Mediterranean was an Allied lake this was still an enemy coast and every man wished himself a long life and one not cut short by lack of caution. So, the deck gun was manned and pointing at the small boat which had thrust its nose out to sea and sailed under a white flag of truce.

The caution was well judged, but unneeded as the boat was armed with nothing more deadly than smiles, which grew ever more broad as it hooked onto the wet sides of the Strongbow.

There were last farewells and salutes and Massu's final glimpse of the Strongbow was as it returned to its native depths in a wash of white water and bursting foam.

The boat headed towards the sand-edged land and a seaplane base which had once guarded Italy's shores but now was little more than a wreck, and Massu saw just how terrible the proper application of sea power could be. A collection of smashed aircraft had been piled in one corner, while burnt hangers stood with jagged rooftops open to the winds.

Still some semblance of order had been restored and a welcoming party with more gold braid than he had ever seen had been assembled.

And Marie vanished, lost in the gold braid and the procession of black cars that drove slowly over a hastily repaired road and towards Rome.

Massu was, if not ignored, then treated as an afterthought. A black car was far above his station and a battered sedan took him to a cheap hotel where a huge bundle of debased currency was placed at his disposal.

And then he was truly ignored.

He stood in the middle of his room and laughed. He had travelled from Spain, impersonated railway engineers and SS officers, guided his charges over a mountain range, protected them as they travelled through a Northern Italy ruled by Germans, suffered agony on a small boat and was now here in a Rome abandoned by its former ally and prey to whatever future fate had prepared.

His situation was beyond humour and his laugh echoed off the sparse walls of his room until his lungs ached from overuse.

If a soldiers first lesson was patience, then his second was that soldiers were disposable items and his laughter held no shades of disappointment, only amused realisation.

A suit and a collection of clothes had been laid on his bed and these and a cold shower transformed him from soldier into a new guise.

Tourist.

He still walked like a soldier and still carried a concealed pistol, for such transformations can be but partial. But now he walked the streets of a Rome, a city that was older than old and was seeing a decline the nature of which she had seen many times before.

As a tourist he sat in the sunshine drinking weak and overpriced coffee while reading newspapers made of recycled paper and printed with ink as weak as the coffee.

He read of the Pope's address to the people of Italy which was thundered from every pulpit and the arrest of Count Ciano who now joined his Father-in-Law, Mussolini, in jail. He wondered just how much of this was the work of Marie who had renounced her titles until the will of the people had been heard. Her own Father-in-Law and her husband had fled to Northern Italy where the Germans had installed them as the puppet heads of a government that did their bidding.

So now Italy was split in two, or perhaps three as the Communist party of Italy had declared itself the inheritor of Mussolini's power and declared a communist republic.

But Rome did not care and Massu did not care. He sat in the sunshine or walked admiring the grandeur of past ages.

He was a tourist, with cash and the willingness to spend it and so Rome loved him.

The days gathered together and turned themselves into weeks, the newspapers were read and read and still Massu played the tourist until one day he received a letter signed with a simple *Marie*. The letter was an invitation and gave a time and a place that he had visited often.

The Villa Borghese gardens were in the centre of the city and were famous for both their classical layout and the sculptured pine trees which were placed in artistic clumps throughout the gardens.

He smiled at seeing the signature, at least he had been remembered, at least he had not been forgotten.

He re-read the letter which gave no clue as to its purpose and shrugged. Of course he would attend.

It was only later that he realised he had been invited to witness a mass execution.

The birds remained silent while the sun regained its grandeur, receiving into its light the echoing sounds of the rifles and the pitiful groans of a single man.

The bullets had struck home and shirts black or white were now stained with blood and strained against ropes that still held tight. But one man still lived.

Massu could not tell if every bullet had reached the man, but one thing was certain; Mussolini still lived. He twitched and moaned and then opened eyes that showed utter fear until an officer walked forward, pulled his pistol out, pressed it against the man's chest and pulled the trigger.

Then it was over, truly over and the birds began to sing once more. First one and then two until whole flocks whistled and called as if trying to blot out with music the savagery of man that they saw below.

Massu though saw no reason to sing or even to comment. Death was no stranger to him. He had seen it in many forms, brought it to others for that matter, but he was no fool; what he had just seen was not the mere disposal of criminals. This was a political act carried out in a very public manner. Whoever had ordered this was making a statement that there could be no turning back from.

He saw Marie detach herself from a gaggle of generals and walk towards him with Father Domenico trailing not far behind.

'I ordered this; I ordered the shootings! Are you shocked?'

She gave Massu no greeting, but held her head upright with eyes glowing as if daring him to show disapproval and yet wishing that he would in some way sanction her act.

And then her hard shell broke and the head bowed in shame.

'I had to, Yves, I had to. There was no other choice!' She burst into tears and much to Massu's surprise flung herself into his arms.

Yves Massu was an undoubtably skilled man at the art of war; equally adept with gun, knife, or hand but, like all men, a crying woman reduced him to near panic. He looked around in alarm, seeing a nearby bench seat. Gently he led her, sat her down and dried her tears with a handkerchief which was a little less then clean, hoping that he would not have to stem any further flows and waiting for further words which soon came, though with many a hesitation and gasp for air.

'I had to, Yves. I had no choice.'

Massu sensed Father Domenico hovering near and turned to glare at the man. Marie had chosen to speak to him and him alone, so he needed no interference. The priest froze and held out his arms in surrender, allowing Massu to turn back to Marie.

'Tell me.'

He tried to keep his voice neutral, to become the friend and not the guide or the guardian.

Marie took a deep breath and began her tale.

'The Allies found us; do you remember. Yves? They found us and took us almost to Rome's door and surely that was a sign that they bore me no ill-will, but it was not absolute support. The Communists had rejected me, which left me with a much-divided Monarchy Party and the Christian Democrats who have the support of the church, the Liberals who had lost much ground to the Fascists and the Socialists who were driven underground by Mussolini.'

She gave a brief and fragile smile. 'There are others, Italian politics are much fractured. We have more factions than a dog has fleas, but they are the main ones. I gave my children into the care of the Vatican and that brought me the support of the Christian Democrats and the rump of the Monarchists. I declared my opposition to Communism and vowed my crown will not be worn and so the Socialists reluctantly walk with me, for though they hate the Democrats and despise the monarchy, still they hate the Communists more. These groups I then gather around me and we tell the Army that few questions will be asked if they will give us our support. They in turn talk to the judges.

'I talk to the people and I tell them that I walk amongst them once more, but I need their help and their prayers. Now I have an alliance from which a government can be made though in truth it is a house made with ill-fitting bricks. But I need more than prayers, for the Fascists under Count Ciano still rule, though feebly and he sends men to arrest me, but it is too late, and the Army moves against him. He is arrested and his ruling council also, and now I am left with little choice for many voices are raised against the Fascists who did not recognise a turning tide until it was too late.

'I am told that Fascist leaders must die, and die soon. For with the leaders of the Fascists gone, the Monarchists and the Liberals can divide the Right Wing between them, and the Democrats and the Socialists can send forth new shoots, free of interference. But Yves, I am the one who binds each to the other and it is my signature that must be used to sign the death warrants. Mine must be first and though each must sign in turn their guilt must be less.

'In return for my signature, I have been promised that a new armed force will be formed and will fight against the Fascists. This in turn will force the Communists to either fight at my side or fight amongst themselves between those who wish to ally and those who do not, but either way their power will be curbed.'

She gave a great sigh and her shoulders drooped.

'All this, Yves, I did, all this. Power was now mine and the price was so small, merely the lives of those who once sat at my table and drank my wine.'

She shuddered at a recent bad memory.

'And I signed, Yves. Every death warrant bore my name. Did I do wrong, Yves?'

Massu's head was beginning to spin at this tale of plot and counter plot although he suspected that he was hearing just the bare bones of many weeks' work. But the woman had asked a question and deserved an answer born out of honesty and a soldier's life.

'To kill Fascists is never wrong, Marie. The Fascists came to France and I resisted, the Fascists came to Spain and I fought, and Marie if you are wrong then so am I and a hundred thousand others. We are not wrong, Marie and neither are you.'

He did not know if this was the answer she wished, but the merest butterfly of a smile began to hover at the edges of her mouth.

'Do you remember, Yves? Do you remember how all this started? How you sat without permission on one of my best chairs and scolded me and told me that my father would be ashamed at my actions, how my father would rise up and act? Do you remember, Yves?'

The butterfly flapped sad wings and pointed to slumped figures tied to posts. 'This was the result of our journey, all this blood spilt today and the blood that is yet to be spilt, all of it was the result of us meeting in the mountains so long ago.

My father once told me that to rule was easy but to lead was hard. I was not born to rule perhaps but I was born to lead and lead I shall, Yves and I thank you for guiding me along my path.'

She reached out and touched his cheek, giving him a smile that was inviting, loving and predatory all at the same time.

'Perhaps you would like to guide me further? I still need your guidance.'

The offer was a subtle one, and if Massu was honest with himself, immensely tempting for Marie was a startlingly beautiful woman, but he was what he was, and the struggle was a brief one. For once his confidence deserted him and his refusal held more stammer than diplomacy.

He watched the emotions cross Marie's face like brief rainbows; a little anger at his refusal and flatteringly some disappointment, but at last the rainbows faded and once more the butterfly smiled.

She leaned into him and whispered in his ear. 'How like my father you are. To him duty was everything, the rest nothing. Go home, Yves, go home to your family and take my thanks with you…and my love.'

The butterfly lost fragile wings, strapped on a set made of tempered steel, rose to her feet and crossed to the group of generals staring at him with curious eyes, leaving the priest with a strange expression on his face that was a mixture of dread and something which resembled regret.

'Priest.' Massu's greeting was a harsh one but it did change the expression on Father Domenico's face.

'May I sit down?'

He received only a gesture which conveyed no particular desire, but indicated that if he burst into flames there would be little in the way of regrets from the Asturian Sergeant.

It wasn't much of an invitation, but a stronger one was not on offer so he sat next to the Sergeant and looked again into the face of a man who hated him and all he stood for but who had been so very necessary to this day. Father Domenico had placed himself on the first rungs of promotion and that event was due in no small part to the Sergeant's skill and yet the man bore him much ill will. For a moment The Devil whispered again in his ear and urged him to return hate for hate, but the conversation was an old one and he had already confessed that sin and taken penance and absolution had been given by God. Still there was a final confession to make.

'Forgive me, Sergeant for I have sinned.'

He beat down the tiny flame of pride that flickered at seeing the brief shock that flashed across the Sergeants face but took no satisfaction in the victory for it would be sinful to do so. Instead he plunged on.

'I have sinned, Sergeant and sinned against you. I have hated you, envied your skills and your strength and though I have confessed my sins before God, yet I feel that God wishes me to confess my sins before you also.'

There was mute incomprehension on Massu's face and he realised that unlike him the Sergeant felt no sins residing in his soul. Massu had cruelly hurt people, killed with swift and sharp instinct and yet he did it out of sworn duty to protect others. Massu's soul held little in the way of blemishes and his incomprehension was truth and not mockery so he decided to take a different path.

'If I may, Sergeant I will tell you a tale of a family who once lived very far from here. The soil there was thin and the people thinner yet, and the family struggled, for God had blessed them with many sons. Despite their poverty the sons grew strong; they ran and leapt and climbed and wrestled with strong muscles and keen eyes.

'But there was a last son, born when his mother was grey-haired, and his father was no longer a youth. This son had little in the way of muscle and his eyes were weak. His brothers disdained his efforts, for what help could poor eyes and a frail body give on the farm?

'But where his muscles were weak, his mind was strong, over strong for such thin soil and over strong for brothers who were set in their ways.

'What was to be done with such a boy who lived in perpetual war with uncaring and over muscled brothers?

'There was only one path to take and the road to the seminary was opened to the boy who took it with the curses of his brothers in his ears echoed by the silent curses he held in his breast. Ambition flared in that breast, fed by the curses and the boy became a priest and that ambition brought him to the Vatican.'

There was a particularly wistful tone in the priest's voice now, which Massu carefully noted.

'I am that boy, Sergeant, and my first confession to you is that I hated you because you reminded me of my brothers. Always sure of yourself, always confident that there was no task you could not overcome.'

A little of the strain had left the priest's face now but the confession was not over.

'Your obvious hate towards me and my church made it easy to remember my hate towards my brothers and so return your hate. My hate made me as blind as the Cyclops of old and I could not see your true soul. Nor could I see our blessed Lord's words about forgiveness. I am also guilty of the sin of envy. For I saw how the Princess leant upon you, how she admired you and how her children bonded with you as the father figure which all children covet.

'This, I told myself was my place to hold, and that you were no more than an upstart and a usurper. I longed for you to stumble but you never did. You held fast to your vows and I lost sight of mine. I have asked God for his forgiveness and now I ask for yours.'

Massu had sat silent during the priest's words and even now wondered if they were a trick. He had long since learnt that all priests were liars, and foul liars at that, who spoke untruths in support of Fascists and other killers of innocents.

Yet there was a way to test the priest and still protect Marie, who had set sail into rough waters.

He allowed his mouth to form a cruel smile that as yet held no certain indication of forgiveness.

'I will forgive, priest, if you make one promise to me and your god right here under these pines. Promise me that you will always protect Marie. You are cunning, priest, a creature of the shadows and see what others do not. Use those skills to aid her, vow that this will always be so, and my forgiveness will be yours. Make your vow, and make it now!'

Father Domenico was caught. The forgiveness he needed was on offer, but the price was higher than he thought. He had carried the Vatican's desires and it was he who had put the thought in her head that she should follow her revered father and build a coalition government out of the ruins of a nation.

It was also true that Italy needed a figure to rally around and the princess was loved enough to fill that role. He had steered her in that direction, the better to curb the Godless Communists who were the enemy of both Church and civilization itself.

But the woman was then to be cast aside for though she was a true daughter of the Church she had too much self-will to fit in with the long-term plans of those who ruled the Vatican.

The fate of the princess was fixed and Massu, for all his physical prowess was a political innocent, and did not know what he was asking.

And yet the demand began to turn the dark wheels of his mind, for if it was true that princesses could be discarded, then priests, no matter how aspiring were equally at risk in the flows and ebbs of Vatican politics.

So far, he had been a dutiful soldier, obeying orders, using gentle persuasion to push the woman along a path she was all too eager to follow. But when her career was over there was a danger that he too would revert back to obscurity and the glittering future he saw for himself would remain a thing of frustrated dreams.

But what if Massu was right? What if he went far beyond conveying the wishes of his masters? What if he advised the princess how to avoid her fate? A priest connected to a power beyond the Vatican would rise just as fast or perhaps even faster.

Still the risks were so very great and how long could he hide his change of course and was the princess to be trusted?

The black wheels spun faster and faster while Massu waited, until with a jarring crash the wheels stopped and he came to a decision, praying that it was a right one,caref ully placing a grateful smile on his face.

'Thank you, Sergeant, I agree. I vow here before you and Almighty God to give the Princess all the protection I can. She will have my aid and advice.' He lost the smile and replaced it with a very slight grin as another thought struck him. 'And I will do my best to curb her worst urges.'

Massu looked at the priest, trying to disguise his surprise. Had the priest guessed at the offer Marie had made him, or was this a hint at what passed between penitent and confessor?

The priest's face gave no clue other than the slight grin, but the grin did not matter. What mattered and mattered very much was that he had performed a last service for Marie, and he had not misjudged the priest.

A good soldier knows his enemies…and Massu was a very good soldier.

The priest's ambition was already well known but his tale had revealed another weakness to be exploited. The priest craved approval from a man who so resembled lost siblings and by giving conditional acceptance he would bind the priest to his vows in greater strength. He put out his hand, engulfing the priest's smaller fingers in his own and still keeping his eyes locked onto Father Domenico.

'Then we are in agreement, priest. See that you keep your promise, or I will return and God or no God I will make you beg for death.'

The words were spoken in a level tone with not a hint of anger, but they were a promise that was as certain and as deadly as Hellfire and Domenico tried to hide the shiver that ran up his spine.

He forced himself to gaze into the sergeant's eyes, willing the man to believe, but the eyes stared back promising only remorseless pursuit if he failed.

He would not fail, and the Sergeant would have no reason to return. His ambition would weld itself to the ambition of the princess in an unbeatable alloy…for the greater glory of God of course and Italy would be renewed.

Once more he repeated his vows and told himself that there was a softening of the hard eyes.

He made his farewells before Massu could make any further demands, knowing that his decision had been guided by the hand of God and that ambition in the service of the Almighty was no sin at all.

Massu watched as the priest walked over to Marie and very gently pulled her away from the group of generals to whisper in her ear. He was sure he had judged correctly, and the priest would out of self-interest protect Marie until she was strong enough to discard him. For Captain Marino was right, she had inherited her father's steel and time would only sharpen it further.

She glanced over towards him, silently asking if what the priest was telling her was true. He gave a brief, confirming nod and then turned on his heel, leaving behind the stately pines and the tuneful birdsong.

There was nothing left for him in Italy now.

It was time to return home.

HOME

Father Domenico watched as Massu turned and was lost in the crowd. He gave a last shudder that held only a little fear but much gratitude. Perhaps the renegade Frenchman had attempted to trap him, and if that was so then it was surely out of hate, for despite the handshake there was no love for the Church in the man's heart. Yet despite that perhaps he had done God's work after all, for his words had watered a seed which had lain half hidden in his soul. God had seen into his soul and sent Sergeant Massu to force the seed to send out green and tender shoots.

He doubted if Massu saw himself as a gardener but he owed the man a debt and so he would pray for Massu's soul; for if Massu had his duties then his duty was to send Massu's soul heavenwards.

The Sergeant had refused the mercy of the Church, refused to make confession and perhaps that was just as well, for even if he convinced the Sergeant to take some form of confession it would be incomplete because sins that are not felt cannot be truly professed. On the Day of Judgement Massu would stand before Almighty God and say 'I did what was right' and believe it with absolute conviction. A merciful God would probably understand and wave the Sergeant through to stand at his side. But there was always the chance that he would not, and so the more prayers that Massu could have in his credit the better chance he would have.

For he had sinned against the Sergeant and owed him a debt.

And so, he would pray for the sergeant, always.

And that would be his own penance, always.

Massu's return was far swifter than his journey out, for men and machines were pouring into Europe to bring down the walls built by an evil usurper. And even though he was a mere speck of dust in the crowded tumult of war, swift wheels and swifter wings sped his heels until one day he stood framed in the sunlight that poured through the open doorway of a modest home.

There is no need to tell of the words spoken between him and his family at this moment, nor to detail the tears of joy. The words and the tears have been repeated often enough by men and women throughout the ages, but later, later when the day was yet young though night still held sway, she turned to him in the darkness and asked of those he had met on his journey.

There was silence from him at first as he wondered how much he could tell, and then he thought that her rifle stock was engraved with many kill marks and that as a warrior she deserved the truth.

And so, he told.

Told of a mad old man who held the souls of a slaughtered village in his hands.

Told of the empty fields that once held the French Basques; of the brave giant and his sparrow of a wife; of the railway man who hid courage behind a sour face and of the prostitute who took the spirit of a murdered daughter and turned it into a bloody sword of vengeance. He told of the evil uniform he had been given and how it turned a childish prank into blood and guilt. He listed those he killed and those he spared and then spoke of a princess fled to a mountain refuge and how she had taken the memory of a soldier father and walked through danger to rescue her adopted land and of the priest who promised prayers that he valued not at all.

All this and more he told, while the night clock ticked and the night sky turned.

And then as the world began to stir, he ran out of words and lay silent while she spoke.

'You have wandered far, husband; wandered far and had many adventures but husband, that time is past.

'There is a time for wandering and a time to stay.'

Massu could not see her face in the darkness but her words echoed his own thoughts, and as the clock gave ringing support to the rim of the new day he was certain she was right.

Massu's journey was over.

His odyssey was ended.

FICTION FROM APS BOOKS
(www.andrewsparke.com)

Davey J Ashfield: *Footsteps On The Teign*
Davey J Ashfield *Contracting With The Devil*
Davey J Ashfield: *A Turkey And One More Easter Egg*
Fenella Bass: *Hornbeams*
Fenella Bass: *Shadows*
HR Beasley: *Nothing Left To Hide*
Lee Benson: *So You Want To Own An Art Gallery*
Lee Benson: *Where's Your Art gallery Now?*
Lee Benson: *Now You're The Artist…Deal With It*
Lee Benson: *No Naked Walls*
TF Byrne *Damage Limitation*
Nargis Darby: *A Different Shade Of Love*
J.W.Darcy: *Ladybird Ladybird*
Jean Harvey: *Pandemic*
Michel Henri: *Mister Penny Whistle*
Michel Henri: *The Death Of The Duchess Of Grasmere*
Michel Henri: *Abducted By Faerie*
Hugh Lupus *An Extra Knot (Parts I-VIII)*
Ian Meacheam: *An Inspector Called*
Ian Meacheam: *Time And The Consequences*
Tony Rowland: *Traitor Lodger German Spy*
Andrew Sparke: *Abuse Cocaine & Soft Furnishings*
Andrew Sparke: *Copper Trance & Motorways*
Phil Thompson: *Momentary Lapses In Concentration*
Paul C. Walsh: *A Place Between The Mountains*
Paul C. Walsh: *Hallowed Turf*
Michael White: *Life Unfinished*
AJ Woolfenden: *Mystique: A Bitten Past*
Various Authors: *Unshriven*

Printed in Great Britain
by Amazon

64385227R00129